ALMOST READY

A SMALL TOWN ROMANCE

THE BACK TO SILVER RIDGE SERIES

CLAIRE CAIN

Cover Photography by Briquelle Kayanne Photography

Cover Models: The Bivens

Cover design by Emma Robinson

Ebook ISBN: 978-1-954005-38-9

Print ISBN: 978-1-954005-39-6

*To the ones who love us for more than our petals—roots,
leaves, thorns and all.*

CONTENT WARNING

Dear reader,

Almost Ready is a closed door romance centered around a heroine with an abusive ex. While the toxic relationship isn't depicted in detail, the heroine does encounter this person again in the book. Though much of her healing has taken place prior to the story's beginning, she continues that journey during this book.

I mention this content in case this topic is one you'd prefer to avoid. I want you to walk away with only happy, lovely feelings, and hope you'll feel safe proceeding with this information in mind.

My very best to you,
Claire

CHAPTER ONE

Dahlia

In the back of my mind, I'd always expected this to happen. That dread I'd smashed down and sewn shut had a way of rearing its head, but I'd kept my focus on the life I'd made here and convinced myself, with every day that passed, that I could keep ignoring it. Maybe I'd hoped it wouldn't go down like this, but you don't escape a situation like I had and not worry about it coming back around to haunt you.

So very naïve of me, or maybe just plain stupid, to feel so blindsided by Devon showing up weeks ago. He'd materialized in the back of the room at the Christmas Auction for the Arts Jane Saint had organized this past holiday season, smirking as he topped several bidders for my basket—from it, he'd get a one-on-one session to learn some flower arranging techniques as well as a beautiful bouquet I'd put together, and the money would go to the arts council. But instead of claiming the prize, he'd made certain I saw he was the winning bidder, then disappeared. This effectively left me anxious, paranoid, and waiting for him to show his face and... I didn't know. He couldn't want anything from me after so long, and yet he'd come here. He'd bid on my basket and made sure he won.

Days later, when I hadn't heard a word from him, I'd asked the organizer if he had actually even paid. He had.

But no word to me. And how just like him to play that kind of game.

What absolute nonsense that my heart raced as he now stood outside and carefully perused the window displays right where I could see him from behind the register. I'd had nightmares to this effect for a solid year after moving here— I'd see him ghosting around a corner or slipping inside a building, then I'd wait, which left me weighted by sticky dread for days after. He'd never shown up—I'd finally realize I'd dreamed or imagined the whole thing, and, my life striking a semblance of normal in between, I'd brace for when the next dream hit. They'd come less often—it'd been at least nine months since the last one when I saw him at the auction. The fact he'd waited three years since I left, that he still wasn't done with me, shouldn't have surprised me. So now, on a random Tuesday in late January, there he stood.

I exhaled slowly, then pulled in a breath and inhaled the scent of the earthy cut stems in front of me. I grounded myself with a touch to the soft petals of a wilting rose I'd pulled from an older arrangement someone had forgotten to pick up. This place, this work, was mine.

"I am lovable. I am enough," I whispered under my breath.

The affirmations I'd clung to in those first months of

therapy after leaving him served to hearten me, and yet in some ways, the fact I needed them now, that just seeing the man could unhinge me so, plunged my heart to the pit of my stomach and threatened to smash it.

My phone buzzed with an incoming text.

"Did you get our present? Aren't you thrilled?" The message had popped up in the family chat between my parents, my two sisters, and me.

I read the words slowly once, twice. *Aren't you thrilled?*

My heart sank down, down, and my pulse spiked. I crouched as though getting something behind the desk, briefly wondering if I could escape into the back and just... ignore him. Just avoid him indefinitely. My heart rate pounded, absolutely racing, and I willed myself not to pass out, carefully drawing breath through my nose. I knew the feeling—the crush of adrenaline paired with the woozy sensation I got sometimes. Utterly awful, but at least it'd been a while, and better still, at least I knew how to stop it with focusing on slowing my breaths.

My mind ran over and over the message. My mother had sent it. A present.

She meant Devon.

Less than ten words and they'd crushed me. They'd taken the paper I'd worked hard to smooth back out, wrinkled though it may have been, and they'd crumpled it into a ball again.

"I am enough. I am enough." I chanted the words, running through all the things I knew to be true. *I have a life here. I have a business. I have friends who care about me. I have people who believe me. I am safe.*

Those last two proved the hardest to lean into, but I made myself; I promised myself. And it wasn't like he'd waltz in here and immediately start berating me. Whatever game he was playing now had everything to do with his arrogance and feeding his awful ego and very little to do with me.

Please let it have very little to do with me. A fool's hope, of course, because why else would he be here, in Silverton, in my flower shop—a business he'd laughed at years ago when I'd told him my dream of opening my own store.

It took a while, but I got up, busied myself checking the fridges where bunches of single flowers in groups sat in large black buckets of water so people could come create their own arrangements. On the other side of the register stood a similar fridge with premade arrangements.

I let my fingers coast along the rippled edge of a rose petal, keeping the touch light enough so it wouldn't cause a wrinkle or wilt. Normally, just being in my shop grounded me and chased away whatever anxiety gnawed at me, but not lately.

Not since he'd shown up in town weeks ago, and especially not now. Would he be coming in, or did he plan to just linger in my line of sight so I had no choice but to be aware of him?

I would never fail to be aware of him again—not after he'd started showing his true colors and I'd realized his "constructive criticism" was in fact emotional abuse. The memories flickering through my head made anger zip up my spine to fortify my determination not to cower despite the roiling stomach and unease twisting in my limbs.

He wouldn't have come back just to taunt me. Instinctively, I knew he wasn't going to tease me this time. He must know I wouldn't fall into that trap again. He'd be in soon—and that thought must've summoned him, because the bell on the door jingled. My heart jumped to my throat and my pulse took off as he stepped through the door.

Breathe, Dahlia. Breathe.

Not for the first time, I wondered what, if anything, would've been different if my family had believed me. If they'd actually heard me when I told them he wasn't a good man—that this person they were so desperate for me to marry was actually an abuser.

I'd spent too many hours on that train of thought, and now he'd come here. None of that wishing had made any difference. But I wasn't the same woman he'd tricked into falling for him before he started tearing her down. I wasn't weak. I wasn't alone. I had people who cared about me.

Without giving my mind a second to dig in its heels and stop the progress, I plastered on a smile and looked up. If I stopped and let myself prepare, I wouldn't have made it this far.

"There she is, my Dolly."

My teeth ground together and irritation spiraled through me. Of *course* he'd call me that. It'd started as a nickname, or so I thought, but it'd ended up feeling like a job description. I'd become something he owned, an object, and not a person with dignity who deserved respect.

I wouldn't be rising to that bait, though, even if the name sickened me. "Hi."

"Aren't you going to welcome me in? We haven't talked in years, and all I get is a half-hearted hi?"

I stayed behind the desk, thankful for the separation between our bodies.

By this point, the existence of my molars was pure magic and a testament to my superior dental hygiene regimen, because otherwise, they'd be ground down to dust or maybe turned to diamonds.

"Welcome in," I gritted out, a numbness covering me as I turned and slipped my phone into my pocket. *Welcome to the place I made, to my success, to the story I wrote in spite of all your naysaying and efforts to convince me I couldn't do anything without you.* The thoughts danced through my mind as I watched his slow progress toward me.

He wound his way around the shop, fingering a wreath here, touching a palm frond there, clearly not as anxious to get this over with as I was. I almost expected the buds and leaves to wilt away and crumble to dust under his vile touch.

"Nice place you have here. I checked out your website, figured it'd be great, but it's nice to see it in person. Didn't have a chance last visit."

Wasn't that a nice way of putting it? He didn't have a chance to talk to the woman he'd gaslit and emotionally abused? How quaint. Especially considering this little cat-and-mouse feel was exactly his style. Make it a game so my concerns and feelings were even less valuable.

Too restless to stay still, I launched out from behind the counter and to the other side of the shop, straightening a bow to avoid watching his movements. He'd always been good-looking, and he had this demeanor about him like he was just a handsome, nice guy—if that nice guy also moonlit as a male model with a perfect smile. It was the best camouflage for a rotten heart I'd ever seen.

"Really, Doll. You've done well for yourself."

I might've felt some measure of triumph at my body's lack of response to that praise because *that,* more than anything thus far today, proved my progress since I'd left him. And I'd made a heck of a lot of progress I held onto with a death grip.

But I didn't give him the satisfaction of a response because I worried he might see the truth—the fear. That would be all he needed to become even more confident.

And just that thought sent a pulse of rage through me. *How dare he.* But I wouldn't start ranting at him, because that wasn't what I did, and I suspected he'd take great satisfaction in that, which I refused to give him.

He'd looked at the website. Of course he had. He'd probably found some way to twist it into all of this work and planning being thanks to him. He'd probably erased the memories of how he'd belittled me from wanting to do something as inconsequential as "playing with flowers all day."

It wasn't like I'd changed my name, but I'd left the state. I hadn't told him where I was going, but my family certainly knew, and they'd obviously told him before. Why he'd waited three years to come harass me, I didn't know, but I willed all of this to end quickly.

"So... why are you here?"

He gave me a smirky little grin. In another life, it would've been charming.

In this life? I saw it for what it was—one more lie.

"I'm just glad to be with you, Dolly." He grinned, all charisma and tugging on heartstrings of our past he thought I'd fall prey to.

He'd always seemed smart, but he hadn't gotten the message. If only my three-year absence from his life were enough to send it clearly.

"I'm not sure—"

I swallowed my words when he reached out and covered my hand where it held the bright green stem of a snow-colored ranunculus shooting from a vase I'd taken from the fridge. My pulse pounded at my temple and neck, and my breath caught, trapped in my chest.

"I'm sorry it's been so long, Doll. I'm sorry we've been apart."

He sounded so... earnest. Intimate. Full of yearning and regret.

I pulled away. "I left. We broke up. I don't understand what you're doing here."

He frowned, seemingly perplexed. "I'm here because I love you and I always have. We got off track. I hoped this would be enough time. I want us to be together."

Oh, how he could play that card, and so well, too. I swallowed hard at the sight of those pleading brown eyes and the memories tunneling back at me. All the times he'd insulted me, then entreated me to understand what he meant, gaslighting me so effectively it took me years before I realized that wasn't the way people talked to their loved ones.

I didn't say you needed to lose weight. I only said you might be prettier if you tightened up a bit.

I don't know why you think I was insulting you. All I meant was that if you applied yourself, you could do more than fiddle with flowers. Do something meaningful. Really make a difference in the world.

You're being emotional, Dolly. If you'd listen, you'd realize I'm not trying to disrespect you. I'm simply saying that woman is beautiful, and any man who's with her is lucky to have someone who makes such an effort. Not everyone does that, you know.

All the times he'd held my arm too tight, but just above the line of a T-shirt sleeve. When he'd shake me, shove me, sneer at me...

My spine steeled with the influx of memories, and I said the only words that might deter him. "I'm with someone now, Devon. We're done."

My heart rate jumped yet again, the poor muscle

churning in my chest at the lie. But he wouldn't know that—he had no way to know.

His eyes narrowed and he inspected me like he knew it wasn't true. I swallowed reflexively, hating the way it might show weakness.

"Yeah? Who is he? How'd you meet?"

"Just here in town. We hit it off and it's been great."

He stepped closer. My pulse skyrocketed, fear slicing through me.

"Oh, Dolly, that sounds made up. You're not all that easy to get along with, you know that. Is this real, or someone from your little books?"

The tilt of his head had that same pitying cant to it, the same way he always started, but his eyes betrayed that hardness. The one that had sent a primal fear through me and warned me that if I hadn't left, his words would've turned into something far worse than forceful grips and shoves.

I could hardly force a response out, my body threatening to lock down on me as he took another step toward me. I backed up, unwilling to stay close enough for him to touch me again, and my heart hammered. Outside, people passed, walking here and there despite the January chill. And then it clicked. I needed to sell this.

He needed to believe I was with someone else and then he'd leave.

I cleared my throat. "I don't need to pretend. I—I love him and he loves me. Plus he's my—my—we're engaged."

Devon's laugh practically barked out of him, contempt made audible. "I doubt that."

Panic surged. That was one of his hallmark phrases. But instead of shriveling up into a little ball of defeat, the answer hit me as a man strode into view out the window.

Without any forethought, I made the decision. "There he is now."

My eyes locked with John's through the pane, and his brow furrowed as he slowed his gait.

Before he could roll his eyes and keep wandering, I burst out the door and grabbed him, hauling him down to me with arms around his neck and pressing a kiss to his cheek. "Play along and I will owe you. Please."

He didn't speak but let me tow him behind me inside.

"I'm so glad you're here. Perfect timing," I said, my words laced with a plea for him to just go with this.

Devon narrowed his gaze on us as John and I entered the space, which was suddenly much smaller than usual. John's sharp eyes read the scene, or tried to. I couldn't imagine what he saw beyond me, a woman who usually seemed to loathe him, accosting him with a kiss and hug and pleas for his cooperation.

"I—me, too. Glad this worked out," John said, voice steady and expression reserved.

Devon snorted. "That's convenient. This is him?"

I nodded, my chest tight and everything in me begging John to get it and not freak out.

As though he read my mind, John smiled that carefree grin I'd seen him give others and never me, and held my hand a bit tighter. "Yep, I'm him."

And because I knew this would all break down far too fast because no part of me had thought this through, I smiled at him. "Yes. This is John Wallace, my fiancé."

CHAPTER TWO

John

The fire usually blazing in Dahlia Price's eyes was notably absent. Disconcertingly so. I could see pleading, yes, but not that simmering intelligence that usually made me restless and fidgety. And said pleading... definitely a sign all was not right if I ever saw one.

I'd been friendly enough to Dahlia since she'd arrived in Silverton a few years back—well, okay. Fine. I'd potentially failed to be all that nice by occasionally being a grade-A jerk to the woman, but I had no qualms blaming her for it. Or, at least, I mostly had no qualms.

Fine. I had a small handful of qualms—baby qualms, really—but we were long past the point of no return. Her arrival to Silverton three years ago had come at exactly the wrong moment for me and, based on how much everyone universally loved her, the wrong time for her, too. Because she was awful to me and I'd responded... not well.

But enough about ancient history. We'd established a tentative rapport, something akin to cooperative, regretful enemies with a side of sarcastic banter. After all, she worked with Aidan, my cousin and best friend, frequently. And she also happened to be friends with Aidan's fiancée, most of my female friends, and... basically everyone else in town.

How?

I'd wondered about it now a few times. I mean, aside from her stunning physical appearance, her incredible talent with floral arranging and general business acumen, and her overall willingness to serve the community she'd up and joined *out of nowhere*, what was to like? Weren't people seeing the sharp edges? The glares? The superior disdain?

Actually, no. They weren't. Because those were resoundingly and exclusively reserved for me.

And maybe I should be ashamed of myself for it, but I loved seeing that fire in her eyes. Usually, some unknown force compelled me to try to get that flame lit. Just now? My brain flatlined for a minute there, right until she reached out and insinuated herself closer to me, angling herself into my body—and away from the guy.

Dahlia never chose to be near me even when she had to. But the second I'd glanced through the glass panes of the shop's front door and seen the expression on her face and her arms wrapped around herself, alarm had spiked through me. That wasn't Dahlia, and paired with her uncharacteristic behavior lately, I knew something was off.

Oh, and since I'm a genius sleuth, her grabbing my hand, kissing my cheek, and begging me to play along tipped me off, too.

Also, becoming her fiancé. We'd tackle that one later—more pressing matters to attend to. Like, the guy.

I slipped an arm around her waist and pulled her to me,

summoning words out of thin air. "That's right. I'm the lucky guy. And you are?"

Dudebro we were performing for, or so I'd gathered, stiffened like I'd offended him.

"Who am *I*? You don't know who I am?"

I glanced at Dahlia. Was he famous or something? He was handsome enough I guessed he could be, and he seemed well-dressed. I'd never had a particularly good eye for brands or fabrics so had no idea whether he wore something notably fancy or not. We certainly had our fair share of celebrities and other highbrow folk around, but I loved a good entertainment mag and still didn't know the guy from Adam beyond the fact that the tension between him and Dahlia was not good. Very different from the dynamic she and I usually had, aka a loosely hostile acquaintanceship, but in a nice way. We'd never actually hurt each other, and we, by some unspoken agreement, knew that.

This guy's entitled response and the way he seemed to be sneering at Dahlia made my hackles rise even more as he said, "I can't believe Dolly didn't tell you about me. You two didn't discuss your relationship histories?"

Dolly? I'd heard people shorten her named to "Dahl," which made sense, but Dolly was nothing shy of infantilizing. The tone made me cringe internally, too. It held this creepy, alarming edge to it, like she was *his* plaything, his *dolly*. I might be a beer brewer now, but my decade or so in family law had given me ample practice at observing people. This guy had hidden depths, but they were probably made up of some kind of primordial ooze that would spawn something demonic any moment now.

I snapped and pointed at him. "Oh, that's right. She did mention you in passing. But Dahlia and I are about moving forward together, not getting hung up on the baggage in our past. Right, love?" The nickname slipped out as I glanced down at her.

She radiated stress, her body all stiff against mine, but she held the edge of my shirt in her fist as if scared I'd move away. The hounds of Hell couldn't drag me away from her right now, if this was how she felt near this guy. If *I* was her safety net.

Not to put myself down, but if Dahlia needed *me*, then she was scraping the bottom of the barrel. We weren't friends, we didn't voluntarily spend time together, and if we're all being honest, we didn't like each other.

Well. She didn't like me. And I did my best in all circumstances to arrest the tendency to want to snarl at her. Something about this woman brought out the worst version of me, and it only drove me into more conversations where I became a jerk. But that was neither here nor there at the moment—point was, if she was *clinging* to me, this guy must be grade A bad news. Cue demonic ooze spewing any minute now.

Dahlia piped up. "That's right. So. Devon, did you want to place an order? I'm happy to take the information, or—"

Devon waved her off. "Don't worry about it. I've got a late flight, and it's time for me to go."

"Oh, shoot, sorry you've gotta run off, bud." Don't ask me why, but for some reason, I couldn't resist antagonizing him a bit. I would've indulged in razzing the guy a bit more, but based on the way Dahlia's muscles had somehow tightened even further, it was time to stop poking the bear.

His jaw flexed. "I'm sure we'll talk soon, Dolly." His eyes flicked to me, and then he turned and marched past us out the door.

Instead of slumping with relief or ranting about how

rude he was, Dahlia released me like a hot rock and steadied herself on the countertop with her opposite hand.

Ah, there she is. Disgusted by my mere presence, of course. Exactly as life inevitably happened around her.

I shoved my hands into my pockets because every impulse in me said *Hug that woman! Comfort her! Make her feel better! Fix this!* But she clearly didn't want to be touched or even be near me. And I didn't want to be near her, either, but the human side of me said she *needed* comforting. Oh, well.

"Well, that was interesting," I said instead.

She didn't answer. No cutting look or glare, no sarcastic retort.

Huh? My mind scrambled, more than a little thrown by her unusual... *everything*. And rather than addressing that, I went for the normal dynamic we shared, hoping it'd snap her back into herself and lighten the mood.

"So he calls you Dolly? Is that like, an old nickname or—"

"Don't ever call me that."

Her words sliced through the air as she whipped around, and when I saw her face, my chest tightened.

"Sorry. I won't, of course," I said, wishing I'd kept my stupid mouth shut. I shouldn't have needled at something like that, not in a moment like *this*. Not when I'd heard the way he'd used the name, like it'd make her feel small instead of with affection. But because I was me, and she was clearly going through something awful with me as witness, I backed up. "Are you okay?"

She took a controlled breath, her gaze focused a few feet in front of her. After a beat, she nodded. "Yes. I'm fine. Thank you for your help."

Her shoulders were straight as a hanger, and just as stiff,

but her eyes were moving now, her body shifting to grab a broom leaning against a corner behind the register, and she began sweeping. *Okay.* Apparently, she was not going to be explaining what just happened or what was going through her mind.

On a normal day, I would've pushed her for information. But on a normal day, she wouldn't have pulled me by the hand into her shop, greeted me with kiss and a, "I'm glad you're here," and she certainly wouldn't have called me her fiancé.

Basically everything about this day had been sideways, and though I worried leaving her was the wrong move and I desperately wanted to understand what the crap was going on, this wasn't the time to push her. I'd tried a nudge and it'd backfired spectacularly, so now was not the time.

And frankly, maybe there wouldn't ever be a time with her. She could pour out her concerns to one of her friends, and I'd give her an extra-wide berth for a bit. Still, that endlessly annoying part of me that demanded I help if I could piped up. "Is there anything I can—"

"No. Please. You've... you've done more than enough." Her gaze found mine. "Thank you."

My stomach bottomed out at the sight of those wide brown eyes. They'd always been stunning, a kind of stab at my ribs when my gaze connected with them during whatever spat we were having, but I'd never seen them like this. Pleading and guarded at the same time, and not edged with irritation or disgust.

My throat worked, surprise and genuine concern snaking through me. "Of course. Whatever you need. Can I stay and help—"

"Really, John. Thank you. H-have a good day." She turned away, busying herself with the clean-up.

And though it went against every instinct in me, I nodded, returned the sentiment, and left. I couldn't help but stop at the front door and look back at her. Her shoulders had sunk a bit, not quite so rigid, but her lips were still pressed into a firm line.

"Lock this door behind me," I said, my voice a little more demanding than I'd meant it to be.

And if everything else I'd experienced thus far hadn't signaled that this guy showing up had thrown her for a loop, her simple nod clinched it. She would've snapped back with something smart and probably a little funny. I would've walked away shaking my head, half-annoyed and half-charmed and holding new determination to avoid her for a while.

But today, I left feeling certain of only one thing: Dahlia Price needed my help. While I planned to respect her need for space, I wasn't about to let her deal with whatever that just was on her own. A good fiancé would never do such a thing, would he?

CHAPTER THREE

Dahlia

I doggedly focused on the arrangement in front of me, ignoring the buzz of my phone for the nth time this evening. I had Sunday orders to finish up and also needed to pick up my dinner soon. At some point, I had to respond to my friends and assure them I was doing okay.

I'd managed to convince them all I had plans over Christmas—that my family was celebrating another time since they knew what a crazy period Christmas was for me. After turning down all invitations to join them and for their help, I'd managed to hole up in my apartment and avoid everyone under the guise of looking forward to quality time with quiet and books. I'd needed the comfort of the familiar and the space to process—I couldn't have faced my friends without them noticing, and I wasn't ready to try to figure out what was happening with Devon, let alone try to explain it to someone else.

Well, mostly.

And since Devon's reappearance over two weeks ago, I'd gone farther under the radar. I worked. I went home. I didn't have a raging social life normally, but I usually saw a friend for lunch once or twice a week, or maybe grabbed dinner out with someone. No dating, obviously, but something to give me a little social outlet and connection between our girls' nights and book club meetings. Dating, after Devon? Not my thing. Seemed far-fetched to say I'd committed myself to being a lifelong spinster in this day and age, but that's essentially what I'd done. I had flowers, I had friends, I had books, and I had contentment—didn't need anything else, much less a man.

The holiday break had given me a natural reprieve, as people were busy with family stuff, and though it caused me some guilt about lying, it had been for everyone's good. No one wanted to be around me when I'd gone inside myself. Then, the natural crush of business surrounding Valentine's Day had given me good reason to stay buried in my work.

Inevitably, John Wallace had caught my eye no fewer than three times in as many weeks since I'd claimed him as my fiancé.

That thought, as it had every time I'd had it, sent a little whoosh of messy feelings in me. Shame for having done it, relief that it'd been him, this oddly hopeful twinge about the whole thing, and then... *ugh.* Too many things swirling around at once to tease out, but all very clearly feelings I didn't want to dwell on or deal with.

Helpfully, I didn't normally see the man, especially this time of year, but he'd almost managed to corner me in the market yesterday. Fortunately, I'd slipped out when he turned to say something to Luca, his cousin's son but basically his nephew. Thank goodness for that kid because John had to give me the inch and I took the mile and fled.

But John knew where to find me easily enough, and he hadn't come knocking. Granted, Silver Ridge Brewery had been insanely busy over the holidays, so maybe he was taking some time off and relaxing at his house. The brewery booked out for all manner of private parties and hosted a New Year's Eve party that was reportedly amazing. They also hosted a Valentine's beer and food pairing that'd become hugely popular. Good for them. Good for him. And kudos if he'd taken some time off. Sure, we neared March and one of my busiest seasons had just come and gone with Valentine's Day, but I liked it when people gave themselves time to recover after working a ton.

Not me. Also, not a topic I needed to be thinking about.

Based on his giving me space thus far, I figured we were going to ignore the gigantic lie I'd told and move back into our quippy enmity with all the grace two non-friends could muster for each other. Back to normal and all that, everything I craved, and he seemed to know and respect that. Frankly, I'd never liked him more.

Well, maybe *like* was the wrong word, but I'd certainly appreciated him going along with things and then backing off. He had every right to press me for what the heck had happened weeks ago, but so far, he'd let me be, save the market escape. We didn't have an elephant in the room with us—wait, what room? We didn't even have a room to deal with, much less something inside it that needed confronting. Definitely how I liked it.

But the time had come to confront my sisters. I'd see them soon enough and needed to get a handle on this whole Devon situation before they showed for my oldest sister Rose's wedding. Since doing that while arranging a bouquet would be far more calming than pacing my apartment upstairs, I dialed and breathed through the spike of anxiety that hit when my younger sister answered.

"Dahlia, *finally*."

"Finally?"

I could hear the eye roll in the silence.

"Yes. *Finally*. I've been waiting for you to call me, and other than a little merry Christmas text, there's been nothing."

Slipping a stem into the vase, I sighed. "Yeah. Well, I didn't have much to say."

After a beat, she spoke. "I should've reached out. It was really messed up of them to act like him showing up was a fun surprise for you. Honestly, I didn't want to ruin your holidays out there. You seem to have friends, and you're doing so well, I didn't want..."

I could hear her audible swallow, and my stomach clenched. "Didn't want what, Azalea? Please. If you need to tell me something, just say it."

"They want you back with Devon. I guess he got tagged by some group who wants to put him as frontrunner for state senate and he needs a wife. They're convinced it should be you. They've got it in their heads the wedding will be a perfect reunion."

I sucked in a breath, my heart immediately thrumming with dread.

"Why would they think that? Why don't they—" I clenched my teeth together to keep from crying, to stay the flood of anger and frustration and betrayal from drowning me. This was nothing new, but it still stung. Every time I felt their doubt, it made me ache. And here they were, announcing their disbelief, advertising how little they thought of me and how much they thought of him.

"It's stupid. I tried to tell them you'd moved on. I tried to talk to him, but he barely acknowledges me."

"I'm sure you stopped existing to him once you saw through his BS. I just wish I had, too."

She loosed a sigh. "Me, too. I'm really sorry. But it's still a ways away. I'll work on them and maybe you can convince them to stop. But obviously, he's Conrad's best man, so..."

I slumped onto the stool a few feet behind the worktable. Of course I knew my sister's fiancé and my former fiancé were best friends. That'd been a big part of the perfect picture for my parents—they'd loved the idea of their two girls getting married to two of our area's most eligible bachelors.

"I'll work on them," she tried again.

But we both knew how well that would work. As the youngest, and admittedly the afterthought of the family, our parents rarely listened to Azalea. She'd shown no interest in their matchmaking during college, refused to let go of the idea of her first love who'd left town when she was a teen. After they saw she wouldn't be making them any connections, they'd let go of any ruse to seem like she was important to them. I'd always envied that about her—both her stubbornness in ignoring their efforts and how that insistence on doing her own thing led to them discounting her almost entirely.

Honestly, I didn't know whether her position or mine was worse. Having social climbers for parents, especially in this day and age, when that wasn't the only way to survive in a society, was exhausting and provided ample fodder for therapists. When I'd started with mine after leaving town and leaving Devon, I'd begged Azalea to see someone. Goodness knew we both needed help sorting through our messed-up lives.

"You work on them, and I'll—" Somehow, the thought hit only then. I had a way to convince them to give up this Devon thing. We had given each other a wide berth, but maybe I could still beg for his help? "Wait. I can't believe I didn't think of this, but when he was here, I told him I was engaged. And I think he might've bought it because this guy came in and totally played along. So I could tell them..."

She chuckled. "You're gonna get a fake fiancé like in one of your books?"

I grinned into the space, appreciating that she knew how much I loved romances. "I am. It's perfect, too. Most of the plans will take place without them needing to see or meet him since everyone's coming in last minute, and I can probably... I don't know, I'll figure something out for the wedding itself."

"Okay, but wait, who is this person?" She gasped. "Is it the hot guy who just moved there?"

I blushed and laughed at myself, thankful for the lightness entering my system for the first time in months. I had told her about Bruce Camden last summer, one of the last times we actually did a video call and *saw* each other while we talked. In the way that seemingly everyone did, I had a little bit of a crush on Bruce. He was just handsome and nice and this actual American hero with a troubled past making a brighter future for his sister-turned-ward. *I mean seriously.* Someone write me that book.

But I'd never considered Bruce as actual dating material. That might've been because I didn't consider *anyone* dating material, but who was counting? If I couldn't summon the desire to ask the most eligible bachelor who'd make the Duke of Hastings look like an uncharismatic dud out, I clearly wasn't ready to date. It'd been three solid years since I'd left my life in Colorado behind, but the healing process had been slow. Steady, but slow.

"No, it's not Bruce. He's a good friend, though. It's my, uh, friend John." We absolutely wouldn't have called ourselves friends, but I probably owed him the gesture of extending friendship since he'd been there for me in an awful moment and, as far as I could tell, hadn't said a word about it to anyone. Never mind the mess of feelings and how calling him friend didn't sit right, but pretending we weren't friends didn't either.

I owed him. Already. Actually, some flowers were the least I could do—should've done. Definitely not roses—didn't want nor need him to get the wrong idea. A woman doesn't give a ridiculously handsome man roses platonically—that'd just be asking for things to get even messier than they already were. But hydrangeas would've been perfect, blue ones, too. In Japanese society, these meant 'Thank you for understanding.' Good luck finding any in winter, though.

"Wait, John like the guy you always complain about?"

I glared at the phone where the seconds of our call ticked away and saw the time. *Ugh.* I needed to close up and go pick up my order at Guac before they closed. I also needed to rewind my life and not be such a jerk to a man who had stood up for me in an extremely vulnerable moment. "What? No. I don't complain about him. And whatever, it's fine. He happened to walk by and played along. Maybe he'd do it again."

Maybe I could think of some way to bribe him if he wouldn't... Or ask nicely? Could I do that, with our track record?

Or maybe this required begging. John was, at his heart, a good man. I knew this like I knew my friends would love me even after they found out about this, even if I didn't have the personal history with John to prove it. Aidan did. Quinn did. So many people did, and I could trust their trust in him. So if I had to beg, I would. And maybe that innate goodness would extend itself to me, just this once.

"If not, maybe hot, sexy, fine Bruce would."

I chuckled, lighter feelings entering my chest for the second time in ages. "Maybe I need to introduce *you* to Bruce when you get to town."

"Eh, probably not. If his name isn't Robert David Waverly, then I'm not interested."

I snorted at her dreamy tone. She'd been in love with her high school crush, and as far as any of us knew, it'd been rather unrequited right up until the night he left for college. "I like how you sound sixteen when you say that. You haven't even talked to the man in over a decade."

"Hush. I don't need a lecture. I've had my great love and... and that's that."

That was a problem for another day, so I told her I loved her, and we hung up. I finished up the last of the arrangements and hurried across the street to get my food before locking myself into my apartment and turning on *Pride and Prejudice*, the 2005 version. Was there anything better than that glorious Mr. Darcy hand flex to give a girl butterflies and distract her from the looming dread?

I said nay, and watched it until far too late, ignoring what I'd promised myself I'd do the very next day.

CHAPTER FOUR

John

Nancy Wallace, my beloved mother, gave me her sweetest smile—the one that stretched her mouth a little too wide and made her cheeks crease. The warning lights flashed through my mind, and I braced for it. *Incoming!*

"So, youngest son and dearest treasure of my life—"

I coughed a laugh but covered it with my hand to avoid her censure.

"Will you please do this small thing for me?" She batted her eyes, the picture of innocence and maternal love.

Did I want to do this *small* thing? No. No, I did not. But would I?

Like the rising sun or the changing leaves, inevitably, I caved. "Okay. Sure. I'll be an adult body at the high school Spring Fling dance."

I hadn't wanted to be at a high school dance in high school, and nothing about that statement had changed.

My mom beamed. And I had to admit, sucker that I was, I did like making her happy. Normally, that job didn't fall solely to me, but my brother, Mike, had taken one for the team with Christmas on a few tasks, including decorating for a winter dance and... well, I supposed it was my turn.

"Perfect. And of course, you'll bring a date. Otherwise, it'll—"

"Mom, no. I'm not planning to bring someone to—"

"John Marcus Wallace, you will bring a date. And if it has to be a blind one, your beloved mother will set you up. Jenny even said she has a friend who—"

"Okay, no. I do not need my sister-in-law or my mother to set me up." I scowled at her, and she scowled right back.

"Don't sass me, son. I love you and I'm worried about you." Her brows pinched on her forehead.

Unease trickled down my spine as her words landed. "There's nothing to worry about. I'm good."

She stared at me, assessing every inch of my face. Sometimes when she did this, I felt decades younger, far closer to thirteen than thirty-six. Her concern didn't ease, and that need to fix the problem surged through me and compelled me to speak. "Listen, I'll find someone. I've just been busy— you know the holidays are always crazy for us."

She held me pinned with her stare but then broke with a grin. "Of course I know that, and of course you will. You used to go out all the time. I'm shocked you're not—well. Anyway..." She hauled her giant purse over her shoulder, blessedly refraining from openly bemoaning my lack of wife. "Thank you for volunteering, and I'll see you for family dinner soon, right?"

I nodded. "Of course. Love you, Mom."

Her pleased smile did nothing to loosen the tightness in my chest, but I accepted her "Love you, too!" as she exited. She blew a kiss to Liam, who sat in his office, and I was half-tempted to go complain to him about my fate. But he'd been up in the night with a sick kid, and my crap was trivial.

That was the thing. My stuff, the things floating around in my head, always seemed small compared to the problems my dearest friends and family faced. So why focus on that, especially when doing so only put me in a mood?

Focusing on the brewery should've helped. I loved beer —yes, to drink it, but I loved everything about it. I loved that the basic recipe of water, hops, barley, and time did incredible things, and with a little bit of imagination and variation, a whole world of possibility opened up in those few ingredients. I loved the process of it, the way it took time to let certain kinds mature, the way everyone had different flavors they liked.

Just being here helped. And yet today, I felt only a looming sense of dread about the chaperone gig and the likelihood that any time now, I'd have to let my parents down and admit I had no plans for dating seriously, nor had I been during the last few years. But just like I'd done since my ex, I'd probably just avoid that conversation altogether and pretend everything was fine. And somehow, find someone to take so that at least for this little event, I'd be off the hook and my mom wouldn't have that pained look in her eye when she saw me standing alone.

Alone, but not unhappy. No plans to date, but not exactly *not* dating, just not putting myself out there. Focusing on other things that mattered, like work and family. Good things. That's how I'd have summed up my future, and it suited me fine. Usually. Today... I sighed.

Nothing felt the same now. Not since that random afternoon when I got pulled over into a flower shop.

One long stretch of the afternoon trying to avoid thinking about all the women I didn't want to ask to be my date to the chaperone gig later, the woman who'd frustratingly never been far from my thoughts lately entered the heavy wooden door of the brewery and sent my pulse climbing. *What's she doing here?*

The question sounded off even in my head, and yet it pounded through me with a low-level thud in my chest. I *knew* why she was here, and yet some mechanism in me needed to stay naïve until she truly came to my door.

I watched Dahlia from behind the glass of my office window as she wound her way around the space, taking in the black-and-white photography of Silver Ridge Peak in its most glorious snow-capped or sun-lit moments, the large tanks in the brewhouse visible from the pub floor, and finally, her little wave to Liam in his office. My door was closed, but I could see her pretty smile and figured they must've been exchanging friendly greetings before she turned to me.

I swallowed reflexively, mentally scrambling for how I could manage this. Never in my life had I exercised more self-control than since the day she'd hauled me into her shop and called me her fiancé. Weeks had passed and we hadn't exchanged more than a cordial hello aside from one day in the market when she basically ran away from me to avoid talking.

I'd gotten the message then—she didn't want to explain herself. I'd started to wonder if maybe she *couldn't*. We'd never had a cooperative dynamic—she'd always shoved me away like I disgusted her and I'd taken it, accepting her lack of feeling for me and returning it without much close inspection. Could I really blame her reaction when I'd snapped back in response to her blunt words that first time we met, making no effort to smooth things between us since? I'd played into that edge between us, creasing the page and running a nail through it so neither of us ever forgot: we weren't friends. Every interaction we had reinforced that.

Until recently.

But our antagonism didn't mean I wanted her hurt or in danger. That just wasn't part of all of this. We bickered and avoided each other, embraced the reality that we had to coexist in the small town and gave each other as much room as we could when attending the same events. But I didn't want to do anything to hurt her, and if pushing her to tell me what had happened that day would, then I'd wait forever.

If she'd shown up today to explain herself, I'd certainly take it. I just didn't want to be overeager. Nothing repelled Dahlia like my friendliness if our first hundred interactions were anything to go by, and I'd finally accepted that years ago and embraced it.

She knocked lightly on my door, and we made eye contact through the pane. I straightened in my seat and waved her in, willing my heart to slow. Why was it rattling around in my ribs so wildly anyway? It had to be the novelty of having her here in my space. *Yeah, that's it.* She peeked in tentatively at first, then entered fully, leaving the door ajar.

"Do you have a minute?" she asked, hands clasping the strap of her purse where it crossed over her chest, almost like a shield.

She wore jeans and snow boots and a long puffy coat over top, and she'd likely walked from her shop, so she'd needed it. Temps flirted in the teens today, with snow predicted to start this afternoon. Winter would last at least another month in Silverton and Silver Ridge Resort would eke every possible ski day out of the spring, too. And obviously, I was not looking at her face because that just confused the issue, and *how about that weather?*

The spike of nervous idiocy bouncing around in my head had ratcheted up to level one thousand when she spoke.

"Sure. Have a seat."

Totally calm. No big deal that she'd come to my work, to my office, to talk to me. I shut out the shot of adrenaline her proximity infused into my blood, that handy fight or flight igniting as always, and attempted to observe her more clinically.

She glanced around, taking in the space with a little pop of her eyebrows at the succulents in a small pot on the corner of my desk and the large planter in the corner. Both had been gifts, but they clearly called to that green-loving soul of hers.

"How can I help you?" I asked, reverting to a weird version of my customer service self to kick things off. I'd been making calls to suppliers for Chris, our brewmaster, trying to source ingredients for a new IPA. Normally, he had someone to do this, but I'd volunteered because they were swamped dealing with some equipment issues. Normally, my job stayed more in the managerial range of keeping the business itself running, and lately, developing the plans for the pub that would open in the summer, we hoped.

One of Dahlia's brows rose now. "Uh, well. I wanted to talk. About... the thing."

She looked mildly uncomfortable but not borderline destroyed like she had before. That set me at ease and had a small chuckle rising in my throat at the title she'd given it.

"Okay. So what about the thing?"

She adjusted in her seat, sitting perfectly straight. "First, I wanted to say thank you. I appreciate you going with it and just... not calling me on the crap in front of him."

"You already thanked me, Dahlia, and you don't need to again." Did she really think she needed to keep saying thank you? Other than throwing me for a bit of a loop, she'd done nothing but take five minutes of my time—time well spent if it'd done what it needed to do.

She blinked, then again, and swallowed.

"Right. Okay. Well, so, I'm afraid—" She cleared her throat, more nerves on display now than I'd ever seen before save that one instance. "He's coming back. And long story that I do not wish to explain to you right now short, I could really use a date to my sister's wedding. It's their destination wedding at Silver Ridge Resort at the end of April and I'd, uh, I'd like you to go with me."

It took a minute for the words to penetrate. In that time, I kept waiting to hear something about the ex, but she'd bypassed all of that and gone straight for her ask. Unlike my mother's volunteer position, for some reason, a yes sat on the tip of my tongue, but that wary part of my mind jostled ahead and spoke first. "Why me?"

Her lips pressed together just slightly. "He's already seen you. He'll—it needs to be you."

"Not Bruce? Someone you actually want to date?" A pinch of something alarmingly like jealousy niggled at me, but why would it? Bruce was the obvious choice, and sure, I'd walked by the shop in the moment, but if she was comfortable lying, why not tell a better lie? Why not have someone like him instead of... someone like me?

She's said he'd be at the wedding—her *ex?* That seemed callous of her family, to say the least, but it definitely explained why she wouldn't change the plan to Bruce.

Her lashes fluttered. "I don't, uh, it hadn't occurred to ask him."

I hated the snake of envy that slithered through my gut. I wanted her to say, "Of course I wouldn't ask him when I want it to be you!" Not that I actually wanted her or that it made logical sense, but the thought swam strong. But hadn't that been my life? The second choice, the last resort, the afterthought. *And wow, is this a bitter pity party, or what?*

I didn't want to be with Dahlia in a real or imagined relationship, so all of those thoughts were a complete waste of time. *Why am I even thinking about that?*

"I'm sure he'd say yes."

Thing was, he would, too. He was just that good of a guy. Plus, I wouldn't be shocked if he had a little hero complex going on after years of being, well, an actual hero. And then, helping Dahlia would be a pleasure for anyone. Even for me since this whole situation hit all my little *helper* buttons.

"Is that you saying no?"

I blinked, surprised she didn't go for the obvious option, but quickly assured her.

"No. I mean, of course not. I'll do it. I just, uh..." I scrambled, suddenly insanely nervous at the prospect of whatever this would turn into. We'd spent the last three years bickering and trading jabs. I'd been in the right place at the right time to help her out, but thus far, this was the most companionable conversation we'd ever had. How would this make any sense?

Then it clicked. I actually *did* have a reason to do this, and it came right back to that meddling English teacher who called herself my mother. "I might need something in exchange."

She stiffened and gripped her purse tighter. "Okay. Like?"

"I just got roped into volunteering at the high school's Spring Fling dance. I need a date."

Her turn to blink back at me before speaking. "You can't get a date for that?"

"I could..."

"So why don't you?"

This was where, historically, things would devolve into barbs, but I didn't want it to go there. Not today. I wanted to stay in this nicer, softer place we'd made, if such a thing were possible, and I really didn't feel like outlining the reasons I'd grown tired of meaningless dates and hookups years ago and had made zero effort to find a partner since. "I sort of am, right now."

She huffed. "I mean a real date. You're a—a reasonably attractive man. Nice to most people. Everyone knows you. How do you—why aren't you going with someone you actually like?"

Now wasn't that loaded?

Instead of saying something insane like, *Well, Dahlia, first my almost-fiancée gave me a complex and then my cousin's wife died and showed me how awful actually loving someone can turn out*, I kept my wits about me and turned it around on her.

"I could ask the same of you. Why not just date an actual person and get engaged and get married? You're a beautiful woman with a successful business and terrible taste in books, and—"

"You did *not* just bring my taste in books into this conversation."

I shrugged one shoulder. "I'm just saying that Mr. Rochester is creepy, not romantic. But aside from that grave error in character, you're decent."

Her eyes narrowed a touch, but her mouth twitched with a hidden smile. "Decent."

I shrugged the other shoulder. "You could probably date just about anyone you wanted."

A beat passed while we sat there, eyes locked, and something twisted inside me. I didn't know what it was, exactly, but it wasn't all bad. *Weird.*

When she spoke, the feeling between us had shifted to less sweet and taut and something far more tense and edged with the usual frustration I got from her whenever I spoke.

"I don't want to date. I didn't want to before and I don't now, and my reasons are my own. Are you willing to do this for me? If so, I'll do the chaperone thing and whatever else. We'll figure out the details this weekend before your thing, and I'll... detail out more of what mine will entail in the meantime."

She didn't want to date? Neither did I. We might actually be onto something. Our interests were enough alike, so why not put them to good use?

I stood. "Sounds good."

"Okay. Good. And... until then, we tell no one. Nothing. I don't want this getting out."

I would've poked holes in that, pointing out how having the community behind us would make more sense, but maybe she didn't care about that. If her ex was only in town for the wedding and then leaving again, he wouldn't be likely to care whether anyone else seemed to think we were together.

"Fine." I held out a hand and waited.

And then, she slipped her small hand into mine. I swallowed hard, the sensation of her skin on mine, our palms brushing as we shook, sending a flash of heat through me with the simple touch. We'd touched hands and put our arms around each other the other day, but all of that had been shrouded in a buzz of confusion and disbelief, and I hadn't been able to fully register it.

She pulled back, staring at the place where our hands had touched, then turned and left.

The door swung shut, and I sank back into my chair, mind reeling with our interaction. It would either be the worst thing or the best thing I'd ever done… if I could figure out what the hell was happening.

CHAPTER FIVE

Dahlia

ook club was my absolute favorite part of any month,
and yet tonight, only low-level dread and exhaustion
accompanied me up to Jane Saint's door. I rang the bell,
fully aware I'd arrived fifteen minutes into the allotted
thirty-minute social time, and sucked in a breath to
mentally prepare as Bruce pulled open the door.

"Ah, there she is," he said, killer bright smile likely
melting the panties off everyone in a one-mile radius.
Everyone but me, who'd never really owned the ability to be
charmed by handsome, book-loving Bruce, the literal hero of
my dreams minus the shocking lack of chemistry between
us. *Pity.* I mean, of course he always charmed me, but there
was nothing budding. No sense of possibility, of awakening,
or something on the verge of blooming with just a little
water and sunlight. And that seemed like a pity for someone
else—a woman who wanted a man. Not me. I wouldn't be

dating Bruce in real life even if we did have zings between us. Bruce was a man and I was a woman burned once, and that there already put a stop to it, period.

"Here she is," I said, a sad excuse for a greeting.

His eyes narrowed on me in an instant. "What's wrong? Are you okay?"

I chuckled and pushed past him. "I know old observational superpowers die hard and all, but I'm fine, my friend. I don't need saving. I appreciate your concern. I'm just tired." *The irony*.

Jane and Darcy, who'd announced their Vegas Valentine's Day wedding to us last month in a blaze of deliciously rushed later-in-life romance, and Kieran, the half-Irish brooder, were already seated and chatting with Quinn, who was telling some kind of story, gesturing with large motions and her back to me. Sarah was in the kitchen plating something that smelled amazing.

"Hello, friend," she said in greeting, then frowned at the man hovering over my shoulder. "Bruce, give her some space."

He exhaled loudly, an embarrassed kind of sound that made me look back at him.

"Sorry. I'm paranoid lately. We've got a lot going on at work and Kiley's got this kid texting her..." He grumbled something unintelligible under his breath.

Sarah grinned. "Bruce is making it sound like a bad thing, but this boy is apparently a straight-A student and adorable and very respectful."

Bruce's face looked the closest thing to sulking as I'd ever seen. "He better be."

I stifled a chuckle. That's what I needed to flip the switch from nerves and dread to embracing why I'd come. I liked these people. They were my friends, and other than the girls who didn't come—Calla and Sadie—they were my closest friends in Silverton.

Well, and Aidan. And maybe now John? *Ugh, don't think about that mess right now.*

"I love that Kiley's chatting with someone, but I can imagine that's a little scary as the big brother." I gave him a small smile, absolutely adoring the way this man loved his sister. Honestly kind of heartbreaking, really.

Bruce ran a hand through his hair. "It's scary as a brother, and it's downright terrifying as her parent-not-parent. I don't know what the hell I'm doing, and I'm trying to resist that old nonsense of me sitting on the porch and cleaning a shotgun. Plus, I wouldn't clean a shotgun. I'd clean a—"

"Pretty sure we don't need the weapons details. And I think you can trust Kiley. At least until she proves you can't, right?" Sarah's kind words, her generous spirit, shone through as it always did. And so did the part of her also being married to a former special ops soldier who thus had no interest in a litany of the weapons he'd clean on the porch instead.

I patted his hand, marveling how the contact felt so congenial and absolutely nothing like the handshake I'd shared with John days ago. He'd been amenable to my stumbling proposition to be my fake fiancé—kind as usual, with a side of snark I couldn't help but appreciate since it signaled things weren't completely different between us and I needed some semblance of normalcy. But then... then we touched. His hands weren't super calloused, but they were a little rough and warm and big enough that mine felt small in his.

It must've been the nerves and the piles of worry I'd been carrying around like buckets of cement, because with that one simple touch, those weights dropped away and a little fire lit in my belly. A spark more than anything, but it was there and undeniable, and I had no place to go with it but out. Away. My mind screamed *leave this building!* And I obeyed. But that flame didn't die until I'd buried it under work hours later. *Don't think about that right now either. Focus on right here, right now.*

"I think it's great that you're resisting that urge. She doesn't need you scaring him or making him feel like you'll murder him and hide the body if he hurts her. If he knows who you are, he knows you *could* do that. What she needs is for you to show you believe her, you support her, and you will be there whether this guy works out or not." I almost marveled at my own ability to verbalize all the things I hadn't been given—obviously, I'd thought about that.

Bruce and Sarah both nodded, and he thanked me before going to help Darcy with something. Sarah finished her plating duties and rinsed her fingers before hauling me into a hug.

"I've missed you," she said, squeezing me a little harder before releasing me.

Infuriatingly, the combination of waxing eloquent about what teens need from parents followed by Sarah's affection had made a knot rise in my throat. "I missed you, too."

Her soft smile held a hint of concern. "Are you okay? I don't mean to pry, but you've been quiet. If that's busyness and life happening, great. But if there's something else going on, I want you to know you can tell me."

I bit down on the emotion threatening to spill over and out onto the countertop and sniffed. "It's probably time for us all to catch up. But I am doing okay."

"Well, can you come be okay over here so we can talk about this book? I need someone to explain to me why I was forced to read it and why anyone likes this nonsense." Quinn scowled at me but winked, then held up her copy of the romance we'd chosen for the month of February. I'd talked them into a romance and wasn't about to apologize for it.

"Quinn Darling, you can't enjoy a book unless there's murder, is that what you're saying?" Jane grinned at her from where she sat snuggled with her husband.

The rocks in my throat dissolved, and I leaned into the scene, into the night. I couldn't help but relax as the conversation about our book of the month bubbled around the room, each participant sharing their perspective with enthusiasm. Even Kieran, who sometimes stayed so quiet one would forget he was there if he didn't look like a hot Irish pirate under cover, had opinions on the matter.

By the end of the evening, my heart had been patched up by friends and books and good food. The salve of a good romance smoothed over my stitches, reminding me once again that it was never foolish to hope, even if life had taught me otherwise.

But once I got home and checked my phone, much of that hope drained away when I saw John's text asking when we could meet. The messages I was getting were either family notes telling me to be glad they'd foisted my abusive ex on me, or the man I'd coerced into playing my fake fiancé trying to make sense of this whole mess I'd gotten him into. Not love letters or sexy texts or whispers in the dark with someone I loved.

Maybe someday I'd have something like all the books I'd read. I'd find a partner who wanted me, who put me first, and who didn't try to mold me into something I wasn't, to see how far I could bend before I broke. But my reaction to all of this mess with Devon and my family had pruned away the leaves and revealed a rotten branch in me—I hadn't dealt with my past like I'd thought, and knowing that meant I wasn't anywhere near thinking about a future with someone. If I even wanted one with some man somewhere.

For now, I'd deal with the reality that my only romantic experience had been a nightmare, and I was still cleaning up the mess.

With a giant sigh he'd fortunately never see, I messaged John that I could meet him at the shop tomorrow or Saturday morning at eight, his choice. I'd roped him into acting as my fiancé, and at some point, I'd have to tell him more about the situation so he wouldn't be completely blindsided by my family's dislike of him. And other than Azalea, they would dislike him because he wasn't Devon.

But for now, I could do whatever he needed me to do for this dance, and then I wouldn't be so far in his debt. It was a small show of gratitude for a person who'd been unwaveringly supportive and kind, so much so it hardly made sense, but I'd do my best.

CHAPTER SIX

John

Dahlia's voice drifted through the shop to greet me as the door shut behind me. "I'm in the back!"

Apparently, that meant I should join her there? Her shop didn't normally open until ten, so it made sense she wouldn't need to greet customers until later. But on that note, why was she here so early on a Saturday?

The counter and fridges on either side were crammed with more arrangements than I'd ever seen. I didn't ever come in the door, but I often peeked through the window displays to check it out and sometimes get a glimpse of her. Not in a creepy way, obviously, just in a... keep your eye on your enemy type deal.

Or, you know, because I liked catching sight of her when she didn't see me and start scowling, because though I might dislike her as a person, she was still rather beautiful. And if I was going to be honest, I might admit that I'd wondered what would've happened if we hadn't gotten off on the wrong foot.

I moved through the shop admiring the décor, the little knickknacks and garden items and whatever else all this was and how it all fit together to make something a little like a fantasy garden before I stepped through the doorway into her workroom.

Dahlia had her hair piled on her head, a thick headband holding all but a few dark tendrils out of her eyes, her dark gaze focused on sliding a stem into a tall vase at just the right angle. "Thanks for coming back here. I'm slammed, and if I don't stop for the next six hours, I'll only have like a hundred arrangements left to do tomorrow."

"That... seems like a ton of work." I'd known she had a good work ethic—anyone who owned a small business had to. Plus, she'd gone from new business in town to one of the most sought-after florists in the area, according to more than one article in the local paper. I simply hadn't considered this part of her life—or any of it, in truth.

She didn't look at me for another minute while she fiddled with that rose, then tsked when she did. "Yeah. Exactly my point."

"Oh, right. Coffee?" I held up the tray in one hand, hoping maybe it'd cover for my ignorance.

Her mouth opened, then shut abruptly. "You brought coffee?"

I probably should've been offended that she was so completely shocked by the gesture, but I had to remember she didn't actually know me, just like I clearly didn't know her. "I thought it might be nice to have a warm beverage while we talk, yes."

She blinked, still stunned, apparently, and the dumbfounded response had me shifting on my feet. "And pastries, of course." I held up the waxy paper bag containing some of Rise and Shine's delights of the day.

Her gaze shifted to the bag right as her stomach growled. She pressed her hands over the apron neatly wrapped around her waist and huffed. "Guess maybe that's my sign. And... thank you. I appreciate it."

She gestured to a space on the other side of the table that was slightly less overflowing with flower trimmings and vases, so I sat the tray and bag down while she moved to a sink behind her to wash her hands.

"Don't you have an assistant? Employees? Someone to help with all this?" So many flowers crammed into this room that it made the space feel particularly small. Had she not had the back door propped open, the scent would've been stifling, but instead, it gave a woodsy, crispy tinge to the air.

"Of course I do," she said, a familiar tone entering her voice.

I hadn't had my coffee yet, so clearly not up for a verbal battle so early. I'd hoped maybe we'd avoid it altogether, but that had been my wishful little soul running away with me again. "Sorry, I didn't mean that to sound like criticism. More that it seems a shame you have to be here so early and have so much work ahead of you. Do you even get a weekend?"

She took the paper cup from the drink tray and held it, cupping its warmth close to her chest, and studied the lid before speaking. "I take Mondays off a lot of weeks, and I'm usually closed Sunday except for deliveries, which I hire out. So yes, normally I do."

"Normally?"

"Yeah. Typical weeks, I don't work through my days off, and often I don't come in at all on Sundays unless there's something specific happening. I have two part-time employees and a few people I hire for certain events if they're big enough. But the weeks leading up to big weddings are usually insane, so I try to just... embrace the madness." She shrugged, then took a sip.

The depth of my ignorance slid into place. It was the weekend. The weekend before two huge weddings at Silver Ridge Lodge. I only knew this because Liam had mentioned that his wife Wells' place, The Silverton Inn, was completely packed this weekend and next, all for the weddings. We also had a bachelor party tonight at the brewery—thankfully, our taproom manager managed all that.

The high school dance would take place Wednesday night, but I'd asked her to meet on what had to be one of her busiest weeks not even a full month after Valentine's Day, which I already knew was one of her busiest times of the year *and* I'd asked her to attend the dance that same week.

"Dahlia, I'm an idiot, I—"

"How did you know my order?"

I glanced at her to find her eyeing me with a mixture of suspicion and what I could only call something like awe.

"Uh, I asked Garrett if he knew. He said he did, so I had him make it. He also said you like to get ice waters there, so that's for you." I nodded to the venti iced water still in the holder and grabbed my own coffee so I'd stop talking.

"That was really thoughtful, thank you."

I huffed, embarrassed at my obliviousness. "I wish I could say it's because I knew you were slammed, but I'll admit I'm completely ignorant to the demands on a flower shop. The brewery has a beer pairing event this weekend, but I didn't even think about how crazy it is. I'm sorry."

She blinked at me again like I'd said something not just surprising but downright mystifying. Then, after a moment, she responded. "It's fine. I don't expect you to keep track of my schedule."

Eyes locked with hers, I had no idea how to proceed. I mostly wanted to say something ridiculous like, "I would happily keep track of your schedule," but that would sound weird and made no sense, so instead, I held up the bag of pastries.

She took it, peeking in, and her smile flashed before she could stop it. "If Sadie wasn't about to get married, I'd probably propose to her myself." She fished out a pain au chocolat and took a bite, groaning in ecstasy and eyes falling closed as she chewed.

I knew this about Dahlia. A scrap I'd collected along the road of our well-established sniping. She loved sweets. *Loved* them. And when she liked something she ate, she couldn't hold back.

Still, even knowing it was coming, I couldn't help but clear my throat and look away. Watching Dahlia Price enjoy a pastry had never seemed like something that could cause me harm, but right now, I recognized the danger of letting myself enjoy her experience. One more sign this whole situation had changed the rotation of the earth or something else fundamental.

Unwilling to interrogate the thought any further for now, I wandered to the back door and peered out at the small patio.

"This is a cool little spot." My words sounded a little rougher than they should've.

"Mmm, yeah. I paved it last summer."

"*You* paved it?"

"Yeah, I added the stones and stuff. I was thinking about using the space for something, so I wanted it to have the same feel as my shop, but I've had so many weddings I haven't been able to plan anything. Now, I mostly use it for overflow when I have huge orders." She dabbed her plush lips with a napkin.

That explained the ten-by-ten white tent that looked almost like a little greenhouse. In either case, the creative use of space made me... well, I liked it.

"Sounds like a good problem to have, ultimately, but I understand having ideas you want to accomplish but not being able to make them happen." I had a laundry list of things I'd like to do at the brewery, including hire a full-time chef and use the space we'd always tagged for a pub as a full restaurant, but we just hadn't made it happen yet.

"You guys have been open for quite a while, right? Like, five years?"

She probably didn't mean for it to sound like a reprimand, but I took it that way, the old wound opening like it'd never fully healed. *Maybe it hasn't.*

My ex had always been unimpressed. And not that I needed someone to be *impressed* by me, particularly, but nothing I did was good enough, interesting enough, exciting enough. Her parting words had been something along the lines of, *"John, you're a sweet guy. I just don't want to live my life with someone who's so... milquetoast."*

I'd had to look up the word after the fact to make sure I understood the criticism, though the thin spread of her lips, the regret tinged with a dab of disgust, had told me well enough. According to my friends at the dictionary website, I was ordinary, feeble, and bland. *Ouch.*

Silly me, but I'd thought the life I was building—working toward leaving the family law offices and pursuing opening a brewery with my best friend—was pretty exciting. Turned out that *she* thought exciting meant someone who had a whole lot more money and lived in a city a lot larger than Silverton.

Would've been nice if she'd mentioned that sometime *before* I'd proposed, but at least she'd been honest and hadn't just said yes in the moment.

Dahlia didn't know about that baggage, nor would she. "Yep, five and a half, actually. It's been a slow build, but we've both had to extricate ourselves from other work and— well, I'm happy with how things have gone so far, even if there's more to do."

Dahlia finished her pastry, and though I could feel her eyes on me, I avoided looking at her.

Eventually, she crumpled up the bag and tossed it into her trash can. "So this dance. I'm assuming your mom put you up to this?"

Already primed to take offense, my usual defensive response jumped to my lips before I could stop it. "I'm doing her a favor, yes."

Her brows jumped. "I didn't mean anything by that. I just want to understand what we're doing."

After a cleansing breath and reminding myself not to react to everything she said like I normally did, I calmed down and explained. "Yeah. She had a bunch of teachers back out due to some tournament this week and needed volunteers. I'm already vetted to help and we can get you all set easily enough. Since it's off-site and after hours, it's less of a process. But basically, we stand around and make sure no one sneaks booze into the punch bowl or starts any trouble. They're a good group so it'll be fine."

She nodded. "Sounds good. I think I can handle that."

"You sure you can get away? It's terrible timing, I realize. I can figure something else out if you don't think it'll work." The overstuffed workroom demonstrated the reality of her schedule, and now that I knew this was such a busy time, I didn't want her feeling forced into this just because she needed me to help her out at her sister's wedding. "I'll still do the wedding."

Her cheeks turned a deep red color and she stood straighter. "I'll make it work. It's the least I can do."

"That's not really true, though, is it? You could just do nothing and I'd still help you out."

Her jaw flexed like my comment irritated her. Maybe I was being annoying, but I also needed her to understand that showing up to chaperone a high school dance two days before her double wedding weekend wasn't exactly *the least* she could do.

"Seriously, just tell me if you can't. I'll still—"

"John. I'll be there. Text me the details and I'll see you Wednesday."

And then, she turned and started messing with an arrangement, and I took the hint. I left without another word because, what would I say?

We'd go to this thing and I'd have a break from my mom's not-so-subtle suggestions she set me up with a friend's daughter. Dahlia would feel less beholden to me for the whole fake fiancé thing since she would be showing up for me.

And I'd ignore the twisting anticipation and anxious energy that jumped through me and, I suspected, wouldn't abate until the chaperone gig had finished.

CHAPTER SEVEN

Dahlia

After checking my makeup one last time, I exited the car and promptly jumped out of my skin when John said, "I wasn't sure you were ever going to get out."

Hand on my heart, I slammed my car door. "You cannot just appear out of thin air. You almost gave me a heart attack." I hated the instant snappish tone with him, but I was jumpy as all get out and he'd popped up out of nowhere.

He smirked, then held a hand in front of him like I should go first. "My apologies, m'lady."

I huffed but proceeded down the sidewalk, grateful whoever was handling the snow had shoveled and salted recently so my heels weren't completely submerged in slush. Also, better this than him walking ahead of me. Because he had on a dark wool jacket with a scarf, and it looked... kind of dashing. The same word had popped into my head last summer when I'd seen him in his tux at Night in Bloom. And this moment when he saw me in my dress...

His eyes had widened and then slipped down over me—the dress on me—with a hooded gaze that felt heavy in a delicious, desirable way. And then he hadn't been able to speak—I'd seen his full lips open when prompted, but he was just taking me in and I'd never *ever* felt so beautiful. Of course, that had been all thanks to the dress, but something had to be said for this man seeing me in that dress.

A fluke. A one-off I'd shoved to the back of my mind because I didn't have the pace for it then, and *best we not think about that right now.* But the memory, once it got its hook in me, maintained its grasp like it sometimes did. I'd thought about his eyes on me, how he'd seemed to stumble over his words long enough that Maddie had jumped in and complimented me, as had Aidan, too many times. It didn't make sense until I remembered that as a man who constantly seemed to bemoan my presence, I liked the idea that I could make him a little speechless. It wasn't so much the feelings that moment summoned in me as much as that surprising effect I seemed to have on him—*of course* I'd enjoyed that.

Never mind that seeing him in his tux had made me a little fluttery. *Never mind that!* Tonight, he wouldn't be wearing a suit, but the fact that he wore this long wool coat instead of his normal puffy winter jacket made me... twisty. In lieu of trying to explain that, I marched ahead, determined to get inside the car dealership as fast as I could.

And *yeah.* This dance was taking place at a car dealership in an emptied out showroom. Real weird, but I'd learned not to question the mysteries of small towns and their dance venues. Apparently, they couldn't afford to rent

Silver Ridge Lodge's large ballroom and the smaller places were booked, and everything else was, too.

John shuffled ahead and pulled the door open for me. I hustled past him and slipped inside as he entered. I noticed a coat rack, and though I didn't want to say goodbye to my layer of warmth, the heat was cranking in here, and I'd want to ditch it soon enough.

"Let me help," he said, grabbing one shoulder of my jacket as I turned and slipped out of it, then sliding it onto a hanger as he shrugged out of his.

We placed our hangers on the rack at the same time, and our eyes caught. Had I ever stood this close to him? Beyond the day I'd claimed him as my fiancé in front of Devon, I wasn't sure we'd ever been this close and it... it made me oddly fuzzy. My heart beat a little fast and my breath came up a bit shorter than it should, and his face was so simply, obviously handsome I couldn't think.

"Nice dress."

Apparently, I hadn't been breathing, but his comment made me suck in a breath. "Thank you. Nice... shirt."

I didn't give myself much time to admire it because, for some reason, it looked really nice. Had he always had such... sculpted... everything? I didn't go to Grit, Warrick's gym, but after spending a little more time than I should've on admiring the very nice fit of his very nice shirt on his very nice body, I wouldn't have been surprised to learn he did. I hadn't wanted to touch or be touched by anyone in a long, *long* time, but something about the blue of his shirt made me want to slide a hand down the front placket and feel the contrast of the buttons under my palm and the curve of his pecs against my thumb and pinkie finger, and *what the heck is happening to me?*

With an exhale, I blinked away that completely inappropriate and unexpected fantasy and focused on what he'd said.

My dress was a simple little black dress that was frequently featured in my work life. I had black and gray suits, too, and depending on the event, I adjusted. Sometimes, I got to set up far enough in advance I didn't have to dress up, but I liked to be professional, especially when people were paying a premium for my work.

Had the dress comment been sarcastic? It wasn't all that nice of a dress—fairly nondescript, actually. If I'd been wearing the glorious confection Maddie had loaned me for Night in Bloom, I would've believed him. I'd never felt so much like a princess as I had that night, the dual pleasure of wearing the most beautiful, perfect thing I'd ever seen and basking in the hard work of *months* of planning and effort coming together in one night... *sigh*.

"Thank you. I appreciate you being here." His thanks seemed genuine enough.

But should that surprise me? No. At this point, it shouldn't. "Well, I appreciate you being my fiancé."

A sharp inhale drew our attention, and dread sluiced through me. "Hey, Cara."

Quinn's daughter stood there, all dressed up and looking crazy mature at just fifteen. But she knew me. And she knew John. And she'd just heard me say...

"You guys are engaged?"

"Uh..." I panicked, my pulse surging loud in an instant. If I said yes, she'd tell Quinn. She'd assume Quinn knew.

But if I didn't, it might get back to Devon. I didn't know who he knew in this town, but I wouldn't put it past him, based on the way he'd just dropped in out of nowhere twice in the span of a few weeks, to have someone local who he wanted keeping tabs on me.

"Cara, yeah, uh—" John looked at me and must've read my expression, God bless the man. "Yes. We're engaged. It's really new and we haven't—"

"What!?? My baby's engaged!!!?"

Oh, no, no, no. Mrs. Wallace came busting in, hands reaching to cup John's cheeks from ten feet away. High school kids filed by and attempted to hang jackets on either side of us since we stood blocking half the rack.

"Mom, uh—"

"How did you not tell me? When did this happen? Who is this delightful creature?"

"Mom, you know Dahlia," he said, her hands pressing against his face distorting his words a little.

Something about that flipped the switch in my brain and made me giggle, then say, "Mrs. Wallace, you know me."

She beamed. "Well, of course I do, Dahlia Price, but I certainly didn't know you were going to be my daughter-in-law!"

I cringed at the volume, exuberance, and overwhelming enthusiasm of the woman as she hauled me into her besequinned arms and squeezed, rocking me side to side. Over her shoulder, I could see John's wide eyes, face pale, slowly registering the full reality of what'd just happened.

Not only had he agreed to pretend to be my fiancé to my sister's wedding, he'd now told our friend's daughter and, more profoundly, his own mother, that we were engaged.

My heart thudded in my chest as John's mom squeezed me once more before releasing me, then held me by the shoulders to look at me like I'd done the best, most wonderful thing by becoming engaged to her son.

"You are just beautiful. I've always said that, haven't I,

John?" She gave him no time to respond before shaking her head. "Oh, my, you'll make a gorgeous bride. Do you have a date set? Are you doing your own flowers? When will we meet your parents?"

My throat locked up, the barrage of questions hammering home just how serious this was. Not that making my abusive ex think I was engaged had ever been a lighthearted matter, but this involved more than just my family now. I didn't mind lying to my parents or my eldest sister, and Azalea already knew it was all fake to get Devon off my back.

But... Mrs. Wallace was about the sweetest woman I'd ever met. I'd heard stories about how special she was, what a difference she had made for Sarah all throughout high school when her parents were so awful, after she got pregnant and then later, when she lost the baby. I knew this woman to be nothing short of an angel, and we'd just lied to her.

How had I not thought of how much all this seemingly innocent endeavor implied?

"I—I—"

John swooped in, his arm sliding around my waist. "Mom, it's really new. We haven't figured out the details, and right now, we've got a job to do, right?"

"Oh, shoot. I guess you're right. Can we please have you both to dinner this weekend to hear more?"

My eyes grew wide, and I was about to accept, but John's hold on me tightened just slightly.

"No, we can't. This is one of Dahlia's busiest weeks of the year. She's going to be exhausted come Sunday. Maybe the next weekend. I promise, we won't leave any detail out when the time comes."

Relief swept through me, followed closely by another

wave of dread because he'd only bought us a week. But still better than nothing—better than trying to figure out how to let her down in a matter of days instead of over a week. *Ugh.*

"All right. I'll accept. I'm inviting Jenny and Michael, too, and the kids, so just..." Her eyes twinkled at me. "Brace yourself to become a Wallace."

CHAPTER EIGHT

John

Dahlia and I went through the motions of laughing and smiling at high schooler awkwardness and antics.

Not only were we not talking, we weren't looking at each other, acting more awkward than any of the teen couples here. *Granted, none of these kids just lied to their mother and friend's daughter about being engaged.*

If anyone had been paying attention, the fact we were both stiff-shouldered and mentally spiraling through the ramifications of what we'd done an hour ago, they would've known something was off.

Fortunately, my mom was the emcee tonight since the young hip English teacher had gotten sick, so she was busy enough that we had a little breathing room. And maybe she was heeding my plea for her to give us some space.

That said, every time I caught her eye, she beamed back

at me. And she wasn't a fool, so I couldn't pretend she didn't have questions. She had a hundred and one, and I'd be facing them well before Dahlia and I showed up for dinner next weekend.

"So, uh, I'm going to go take a break for a minute," Dahlia said, speaking to the shiny linoleum floor between us.

"Why don't you both go? I'll man the punch bowl for a few." My mom had appeared out of nowhere and winked like we'd take a break and, what, go whip up a grandkid?

"Oh, thank you," Dahlia said, a pretty smile on her face that didn't meet her eyes.

Her gaze met mine, and my idiot stomach flip-flopped before I started moving.

"Yeah, thanks. We'll be back in a minute." Because my mom would definitely be watching every step of our movements, I took Dahlia's hand. My heart kicked as our palms pressed together and our fingers linked, which had to be adrenaline spiking yet again.

Once out of the main room and around the corner, I led her to a little alcove where a drinking fountain sat unused by the punch-drinking crowd in the showroom and turned to face her.

She stared back, apparently waiting for me to start. *Fair enough.* I'd been the one to double down on the lie.

"Okay so... that happened."

A laugh slipped out. "Yes, it sure did." She swallowed. "I didn't mean for you to be so involved."

I raised a brow. "You didn't mean for me to be so involved in me playing your fiancé?"

Her eyes darted around and she stepped closer. "I didn't mean for you to have to lie to your family. I only planned on lying to mine. If I'd thought through things a bit more, you wouldn't have had to do that, and I'm sorry I put you in this position." She tucked her lips together and shook her head.

My pulse inched up even as I wondered about that—about how comfortable she was planning to lie to her family. It made something shift in me, all my previous impressions take a slight tilt to one side as I contemplated that she had certainly been lying to everyone in Silverton, too. Maybe her closer friends knew about her past, but something about her lying to Cara, one of her best friends' daughters, told me she hadn't.

And maybe all of that clicked in the moment, and that's why I hadn't told my mom the truth. The simplest explanation, and therefore, the most likely. And at least she was sorry. Not that I wanted her regretful and walking on eggshells, but I appreciated her saying something.

"Well, too late to go back now," I said belatedly.

"Really? Seems like you could easily explain this to your mom and avoid having to lie to your parents or anyone else. I can tell Quinn and Cara privately and—"

"And when Devon's back? Will he buy it if we're never together, living separately and functioning like we always have?"

Her chest deflated with an exhale. "I don't know. I honestly don't know what he'll do. I hate that it matters."

The hard edge in her voice when she said the word *hate* made my gut clench. She hated the guy and whatever he'd done to her. Not for the first time, it hit me that she had been genuinely harmed by this man. She wouldn't be willing to lie like this otherwise. Even if I didn't know her perfectly, I knew her that well at least.

"I'm sorry. And I'm not expecting you to tell me everything, but if we're really going to pretend we're engaged, that's going to... affect things."

Her jaw flexed—not an angry look, just nervous. On edge. "What things?"

"How we talk to each other. How we *are* around each other. I don't know if we have to change much in the meantime, because it's not like my parents are on the lookout, but once we have dinner with them, the town will know. And if we're not acting like we're in love, we'll get called on it."

She frowned. "We don't have to be in love to be engaged."

I sighed. "Well, anyone who knows me knows I wouldn't get engaged without being in love and making sure the woman I'm engaged to is in love with me."

She stared at me, a hard expression, and then blinked. "Except in this case."

"Obviously. But this is… extenuating circumstances."

Her eyes narrowed. "Why are you doing this? I don't want to sound ungrateful, but this just got a lot messier than one date to a wedding. What's in it for you? And please, don't try to pretend there's nothing, because I'm not an idiot."

Irritation zipped through me. "Of course you're not. I wouldn't pretend you were."

She glanced at the ground, maybe a show of repentance or… who knew.

She sighed and pressed a hand to her forehead almost like she was taking her own temperature. "I'm sorry. I'm not handling this well, and I don't mean to be like this. I—I don't understand you, but I am grateful. And I am trying."

Her voice shook at the end, and my heart squeezed in my chest.

This whole situation was messed up, and I wasn't quite sure how to reassure her or even how to tell her what was in it for me. Part of it was to help her—that's just what I did. I helped people with an almost compulsive degree of fidelity. She hadn't been a person on my list to help like that, but I couldn't ignore that's how I functioned. She'd roped me into a scenario that for some reason meant I could help her more than anyone else, and whatever our history, I wasn't about to bail on that.

But there was another reason I could tell her that might help. "I know you're trying. I am, too. And as for what's in it for me, you saw my mom when she heard the word *fiancée*. And maybe it makes me pathetic, but our family has had a hard few years. She's always worried about me finding someone, and I don't mind giving her a little happiness for a while, thinking I'm settling down."

She could've laughed or scoffed, but she did neither. She didn't seem to pity me either. Instead, she nodded, a softer expression taking over. "And what happens after the wedding? What happens when you tell her the truth?"

I swallowed reflexively. "I'm not sure I will. I might just say we grew apart—maybe the wedding brought up things we hadn't talked through, and we decided to part amicably."

She did scoff a bit then, but it ended on more of a laugh than something angry or edgy. "Yes, we tend to be very amicable."

I sighed, maybe a tad dramatically to play it up. "We're going to need to."

"I can handle that. We'll just need to—"

"Practice. Exactly."

She squinted, her pretty lips tipping into a barely there curve. "Yeah. Like I was saying, we'll need to practice."

I nodded and resisted the urge to sigh again. She really was insanely stubborn. She seemed all sweet and flowery with others. She loved romance novels, and I'd always thought she was a little head-in-the-clouds about things except for arguing with me, but clearly, that was not the case.

"Well, let's do our best to get through tonight without biting each other's heads off and we'll go from there. We'll smile at each other, we'll be helpful to the kids, and we'll leave before my mom corners us to talk. I'll make excuses so you can bolt a few minutes before it's officially over since you do have a ton of work to do, and she won't be able to argue with that."

For the next hour, that's what we did. When anyone's attention fell on us, we smiled at each other and through clenched teeth said things like, "your smile looks weird," or "I can't imagine anyone buying this if we're really supposed to be in love," until I put a stop to that. No use continuing if this was how we were going to proceed. So, I asked her about her favorite recent orders. She raised a brow at first but then told me in a few spare but willing sentences and then asked about what plans we had at the brewery. I kept my response short for fear of boring her and asked what she was reading. Her eyes lit at that, and I realized I should've started there, though I'd thought flowers would've been the trick. She got caught up in expounding on some book by an author named Josie Wade and only stopped when someone interrupted to ask where the bathrooms were.

Sadly, that flipped a switch for her, like she felt she'd gone too far in being friendly, or maybe she'd just lost her fizz. I could understand that as the night wore on, and we watched teens alternately grind against each other to fast songs and sway awkwardly to the ballads. By the end of the night, I was exhausted, and Dahlia had grown more and more quiet.

My mom sidled up next to me while discreetly folding

up decorations during the last dance. "So what do you get a florist to celebrate her double wedding weekend?"

I blinked back at her with a blank look.

She looked horrified. "Don't tell me you haven't thought about this, John Marcus. This woman is your fiancée—which we *will* be discussing in the very near future—and you aren't going to get her something to celebrate accomplishing a huge task like providing the flowers to two huge weddings in one weekend, one of which will be featured in *Celebrity Magazine*?"

My eyes grew wide, but my mouth came through with "Of course I have something planned." How did I not register that Regina Corolla's wedding to Gregory Fontaine would be one that Dahlia had a hand in?

Holy crap. Because that was going to be a huge wedding. It was taking place at the newly expanded lodge on the top of the mountain. Though it wouldn't be a huge gathering, the pomp and circumstance of two of TV's biggest stars ending their years-long standoff with a dramatic live TV engagement on the Danita Carl's show. And no, I would not be sharing my intimate knowledge of the event with my new fake fiancée, but I did feel like a giant tool for not realizing she'd be hammered by the demands from two spoiled celebs. In truth, I had no sense of what she actually had to do—how last minute or far ahead she could work considering it was all fresh flowers. But what I did know was it would likely be a huge drain on her.

My mom only arched her brows and pursed her lips like she knew I'd just realized it... here's hoping she didn't.

"I'm not telling you. You're not my fiancée. And... it's a surprise for her. Maybe she'll tell you when we have dinner." Not that I wanted to remind her of that, but here we were.

She made a sound like *hmmph* and wandered off, hollering to another teacher and leaving me to dump the remaining snacks from the refreshment table. No one wanted to keep the tail end of the chip bowl.

But as I nested empty bowls and bagged up all the extra napkins and utensils, I thought of exactly what I'd get Dahlia. In fact, if we were a real couple, I'd get her the same thing. And wasn't that the idea? That I treat this like it was real?

If it made her happy, I'd take it—a thought I'd genuinely not ever had, and yet this mess had forced me to see things from a new angle. She could use something nice in her life, amidst the pressure to make everything this weekend a success and to navigate her sister's wedding with whatever kind of family dynamic required a fair amount of deceit.

Despite the low levels of dread and *this is gonna be a disaster* churning inside, I recognized that maybe this fake fiancé thing wouldn't be all bad.

CHAPTER NINE

Dahlia

Friday at four in the afternoon wasn't typically a time I found myself leaving my apartment unless the incentive involved guacamole and my friends. But today, I was walking toward Basta for dinner with my new fake fiancé.

Nerves swirled in my belly and my head ached. Maybe I'd been clenching my teeth, and I didn't have to guess at the tightness in my neck. Six days after a double wedding weekend and it didn't feel like I'd slowed down for weeks. Considering Valentine's Day and February were long gone and that whole month tended to be crazy and require recovery, plus then I launched into other projects, the two weddings, and dealing with low-quality anxiety-fueled sleep, I really hadn't had downtime. Add to that the impending doom of my sister's wedding, seeing Devon again, and now lying to John's family, my friends, and the entire town—a wonder I hadn't collapsed with nerves already.

Except we weren't in a Victorian era romance, so I couldn't just loosen my corset and apply a warm compress or go for a walk in the fresh air. Though I could admit, the chilly spring air and the sight of the mountain peaks towering over the town did help remind me there were things bigger than me.

I didn't have much of an appetite, but I hadn't had one for big meals for a while. I wasn't dainty about food—I liked to eat and had often been criticized for exactly that when I had been with Devon. The box sitting outside my shop door last Friday popped into my mind, and my stomach flipped.

I'd awoken early that morning knowing I had to finalize all of the arrangements for the events that night and prep everything I could for the wedding on Saturday. I'd been in the shop hours before I'd opened it at ten, but when I moved to the front door to flip the sign to *Open*, a pink box with a white bow had caught my eye. It sat on the welcome mat outside the shop in a clear plastic bag.

Reaching for it with trembling hands, I glanced around and didn't see anyone. I feared it might've been from Devon, but he wouldn't do something to bring me pleasure like this. Anything he did came with an edge to it—something to remind me who he was and who he thought I was.

Because I'd been working nonstop all week and my part-time help would be arriving soon, I hustled the bag into the work room and pulled out the beautiful box. It was cotton candy pink, the bow made of a satin, glossy white ribbon that was just as good as any bow I tied.

The scent hit me before I opened the box, sweetness and yeasty, beautiful promises made of sugar and fat and all the best things in the world. I slipped a finger under the edge of the white sticker with *Glazed* written in a puffy retro pink sealing the box at the front and gasped when I opened the lid.

Six pink and white donuts of all varieties shined back at me in sugary perfection. *Wow.* This had to be from Sadie or Sarah. Sadie had told me once that she didn't do donuts, but had she started?

Only after I'd taken a giant, ravenous bite of a gloriously pillowy yeast donut topped with smooth strawberry icing drizzled perfectly over the top did I notice the card slipped under the edge of the bow.

My pulse ticked up as I opened the card, then shot through the roof at the words. *Happy Double Wedding Weekend to you, fiancée. May your day be half as sweet as you are.* Then a heart and *John.*

I blinked rapidly, breathing through the confusion, until I cackled aloud, almost choking on my next bite of the delicious confection in my hand. That snarky little jerk! I knew for a fact he didn't think I was sweet.

But the gesture had been. His mother probably put him up to it, but still. If I hadn't been more cynical than gullible, I might've had tears spring to my eyes. I might've felt kind of... precious.

If this were real, I'd want to find him. Immediately. I'd march straight to the brewery or his house or wherever he was at eight in the morning, and I'd kiss him with frosting-sweet lips, then demand he share one with me—just one bite. And he would. And I'd tell him how he had no idea what it meant that he'd thought of me, that he'd do something like this, and that it would be something I really enjoyed, not something that served a purpose or somehow satisfied *him* more than me. All of Devon's gifts were ones that he wanted *for* me—an outfit, a skin treatment, a *light lunch* with leafy greens and grilled chicken topped with sadness as dressing.

Okay, maybe that was a bit much, but John's donuts had been... gosh, they'd just been so... much.

Shaking my head of the memory and the confusion over the gesture, I focused on the here and now. I was walking to Basta to meet John so we could nail down our story in order to effectively deceive his mother when we had dinner with his family on Sunday. I did not have the mental capacity to think ahead to how nervous I'd be for that event, and so instead, I'd been focusing on all the details we'd need to identify to prepare.

But then, I rounded the corner and nearly ran directly into John.

"Whoa, sorry. I didn't mean to startle you," he said, hands up. But just as soon as he held them up, one shot out and grabbed me before I stumbled backward off the curb.

Once I found my legs, I shrugged, studiously ignoring the little zaps of awareness his touch had triggered. "It's fine. My bad."

"No one's bad. Just an accident, right?"

His furrowed brow made it seem like it was odd for me to admit that I'd rammed into him after being so preoccupied as I walked.

"If I do something wrong, I'll admit it."

His brows jumped. "Uh, okay. Well. Hi, Dahlia, nice to see you."

My lips pressed together in a line. Maybe it was all the times I'd bickered with him before this, or maybe the general exhaustion I'd been feeling the last few weeks, but I couldn't get over my irritability. Not with thoughts of Devon and the wedding, the impending doom of seeing my parents in person and generally feeling so unsettled by everything in my life right now. And so, despite my logic begging me to stay polite, at least, what came out was, "Hi, John. Let's get this over with."

He chuckled, but it had a tinge of bitterness to it. "Ah, yes, the words every man wants to hear before a date."

I couldn't blame him. I *couldn't*. But I also couldn't stop my gut response before it barreled out of me. "I thought you said you don't date much?"

"Did I?"

"You did." Why was he being so obtuse? Why was *I* being such a jerk?

"I guess you do know everything about me, don't you?"

I reared back, finally admitting this had gotten weirdly out of hand and we hadn't even sat down. I'd lost all sense of self-control if I was being this rude to a man who'd brought me donuts and was doing everything he could to help me. My headache intensified at the same moment, and I shook my head. "Obviously not. Let's just get some food and do what we need to do."

He squinted slightly, almost like he could see the way my eye was starting to ache, then nodded and turned to grab the door. He held it open for me but, stubborn woman on a bender for being uncooperative that I was, I gestured for him to go ahead. He breathed through a beat that passed between us, then shook his head and preceded me inside against all his delicate gentlemanly sensibilities.

He really was a gentleman. A big part of me delighted in that—or would've. But the Dahlia that'd lived through what she had just couldn't take it at face value anymore.

One might wonder why a romance-novel-loving reader like myself had such a resistance to his polite manners. And normally, I found all of that kind of stuff really appealing. I'd been charmed by that stuff and had fallen for the trap once before and a thousand times after. Nice manners, seemingly thoughtful gestures—the stuff of my relationship with Devon when we started out. And whenever he'd be a jerk or insult me, then turn around and gaslight me, inevitably some sweet, thoughtful gesture would follow.

John wasn't Devon, but they had some similarities. Both were seemingly good men—well-liked in their communities and by their families. Both were more attractive than they needed to be—like seriously, did this one here really need to wield those stunning hazel eyes all the time? And both, upon meeting them, had sent my stomach tumbling.

The memory of my first time seeing John gripped my mind as we waited, silence between us, for the hostess to seat us. I'd just arrived in Silverton a few weeks before, signed my shop's lease, and would be opening soon. After joining the local chamber of commerce, I'd walked in, and *bam.* There he was. Close-cropped beard and sparkly hazel eyes, grinning at everyone he talked to, shaking hands and greeting people like he knew them all by name.

Warning! The word had been more a feeling, a primal reaction to learned realities than a cogent thought. I'd left Colorado and my life tethered to Devon four months prior. I'd been planning the move to Silverton for a long time, had been researching, and had finally left when I knew I could make a life somewhere new. Devon was moving up in our area as a bigwig manager at his family's powerful real-estate business, and he'd run for office someday—moving out of state had been one of many levels of protection against him since I knew he wouldn't follow me. He couldn't stand to move somewhere and not be *known.*

And John Wallace greeting me with his superstar nice guy smile, his unassuming plaid shirt and relaxed jeans, and that friendly hand reaching out to welcome me had sent alarm bells absolutely blaring.

"Hey, welcome to the Silverton Chamber. You're the new owner of Bloom, right?"

And because logic didn't always rule when you'd been hounded by an abusive ex and self-criticism for the same, I didn't simply say, "Yes" and move on. I jerked my hand back and said, "Not interested."

His brows shot up and his mouth dropped open, then snapped back shut before he crossed his arms and replied, "Duly noted."

I'd wondered what might've happened if I'd said something else. *Anything* else. Because I had set the tone for every interaction of ours until the last few weeks. Maybe that was why my brain felt battered and bruised and my limbs heavy as we moved inside of Basta and found a small table tucked away in a corner. In another life, it would've been romantic.

But in this life—the one where I, Dahlia Price, was the heroine? In this story, this table had a function, a purpose, and the man seated across from me did, too. There was no romance in a fake relationship and no good would come from letting any of his thoughtful gestures—real or imagined —confuse the issue.

CHAPTER TEN

John

I wasn't actually surprised by how terrible dinner with Dahlia had been. That said, it'd been shockingly bad. So... *cool*.

We hadn't managed much conversation, and I didn't know anything more about her than I had before the dinner we'd planned expressly to get to know each other better other than she was one of those women who didn't eat a lot on a date. That surprised me because any other time I'd observed her, she'd seemed unself-conscious about enjoying food, but Friday night, she'd taken a whopping eight bites of the pasta primavera she'd ordered and she'd stuck with water. No wine. No anything else.

There'd been something shrinking about her. Different than how she'd been with her ex that day in her shop, though. She'd had a few moments when she'd tried to buck up and engage in conversation—I'd seen her pull her shoulders back and slug down some water like it was something stiff to fortify her. I'd wondered if I made her *that* uncomfortable or if something else was wrong, but since we weren't communicating well, I hadn't asked. And maybe it made me awful, but I was relieved to leave Basta and walk her to her shop and then go about my merry way.

All except the merry part because I couldn't think of anything but Dahlia and how we hadn't gotten our story straight and how my mother would be asking for all the details here in a matter of hours when we showed up at my parents' house for dinner. I'd put my head down and plowed through a ton of admin work we'd fallen behind on with the start of the year, then worked on some menu pairings for an upcoming beer and food tasting with the Silver Ridge Resort. Their chef always approved them, but I liked dreaming up the combinations and then time dependent, we'd do a trial tasting to make sure it all worked together.

Focusing on that had given me a nice little rabbit hole to fall down most of the day yesterday. Then last night, I'd gone to hang with Aidan and Luca since Maddie was traveling this weekend. And today? Today, I'd scraped the bottom of the barrel and was running out of tasks.

"This used to be a regular thing, but I haven't seen you in on a Sunday in years."

Liam sauntered into my office with a baby strapped to his chest. One of my many honorary nieces and nephews—I had two actual nieces thanks to my brother, and then I'd been dubbed uncle by Liam and Wells' kids as well as my cousin Aidan's son. No doubt he and Maddie would get hitched any time now that they'd gotten engaged, and then they'd crank out a few, too—if Maddie wanted kids. I actually didn't know, but I hoped she did. Aidan was the best dad, and their kids would have great parents.

"Yeah, I try not to come in on Sundays anymore. I just..." I shrugged. None of the ends to that sentence proved worth saying out loud.

"You just?" He moved inside and took a seat across from me, cupping his baby's little feet in his hands as he sat. The inert legs and tuft of hair popping up of the top edge of the carrier told me she was asleep.

I sighed, then rolled my eyes at myself. I needed to tell someone about this mess, and Liam wouldn't blame me. He'd proven time and again he was a supportive friend—one of many reasons I'd gone into business with him.

"So, I got into a situation." Maybe not the best way to explain it, but it didn't exactly fit to say, "I got engaged."

Liam's brows raised. "What kind of situation?"

Shifting in my seat, I sighed again. "Uh, kind of a weird one, really."

"What's this?" Aidan materialized in the doorway to my office.

"What's what? What are you doing here? I come to my office for some quiet work time and now both of you are here to check up on me?" I'd meant for my tone to strike a jocular note, but instead, it came out as genuinely irritated. He'd asked if something was off last night, and I'd brushed it off as being tired. Unfortunately, my friends seemed to know me well enough not to buy my half-hearted lies, the jerks.

Liam glanced between us as Aidan held up his hands. "I called you earlier and then texted. I was already in the neighborhood, so I thought I'd swing by and see if you were in. Didn't mean to intrude."

"And for the record, I was not checking up on you. I left something in the office and saw you were here." Liam leaned back in the chair and dipped his chin to press a kiss on his baby's head.

I grunted. "Sorry. I don't know why I'm being an idiot."

They both stared at me. These two men who were my best friends, like brothers to me but in many ways even closer than my own brother, who'd gotten married young and had felt rather separate from me. Instead of dragging it out, I laid it out for them in a way I hadn't been ready to do last night.

"Fine. Actually, I do. I ran into Dahlia when she was in an awkward situation and she told an ex that I was her fiancé. I played along because I'm not actually a jerk and she seemed to need the help."

A mix of emotions I couldn't name swirled in my gut. Regret? Embarrassment? Something like concern, for sure, and maybe just a little bit of pleasure at being the one to help her when she needed it.

Crap. I was such an idiot.

"Okay... weird, but not all that bad. Dahlia's great, and even though you guys don't get along, you're both good people."

Liam's cheery response came out quickly and confirmed I needed to finish giving the details before they chimed in.

"Uh, right. But then she asked me if I could act as her fiancé for her sister's wedding in April. I said I could, but in return, since my mom had been hassling me about finding a date to chaperone the dance last week, I said I'd do it if she came as my date to the dance thing."

Both of them stayed quiet this time, sensing I had more. Needing to talk it through, I continued. "Then at the dance, one thing led to another, and my mom overheard that we were engaged. She flipped her lid in that special way only Nancy Wallace can and then invited us to family dinner."

Their gazes stayed on me, each of them blinking as though to help absorb the information. Aidan spoke first.

"So instead of telling your mom it was all for show or whatever, you perpetuated the lie that you guys are engaged?"

Yep. Definitely embarrassment lacing through my gut. "Basically."

Liam frowned. "And you did this because..."

Wasn't that the million-dollar question? "Honestly, the words were out of my mouth before I could think. I confirmed what she'd heard rather than told her the truth."

Aidan squinted at me. "She was excited, I guess?"

I nodded. "Yes. And last week, she'd mentioned *yet again* how much she hoped and prayed I'd find someone. I guess part of me just thought, 'What's the harm in letting her have this and giving myself a break from all that pressure?' Plus, it's better for Dahlia if everyone in town thinks we're engaged when her ex comes sniffing back around." I didn't even fully understand what that dynamic was, but clearly, it hadn't just been a bad breakup.

We all stayed quiet for a minute or two—an interminable span of time, really. Then Aidan left his post in the doorway and sat next to Liam. "This isn't like you."

I made a weird growly grunt of sound composed of pure frustration, and raked my hands through my hair. "I know."

He continued. "I don't mean that to sound as bad as it does. I just mean... I'm worried about you. I don't want you to get hurt, or for Gig and Doodle to have their hearts broken if they fall in love with Dahlia and then find out this was all a sham."

Gig and Doodle were the grandparent names my brother's kids had given my parents. Gig somehow translated into Grandma and Doodle was, inexplicably, Grandpa. Weird as all get out, but most people found it ridiculously endearing, including Liam, whose amused smirk undoubtedly came from Aidan's use of the names. Since his own son, Luca, called my parents Gig and Doodle, it made sense.

Liam added his two cents. "It's right in line with you wanting to help someone, though. I see how you'd want to help her out."

"Even though we fight whenever we're in a ten-foot radius?" My question emerged with a sharpness I wasn't proud of. Maybe all the self-recrimination had caught up with me.

Aidan and Liam shared a look.

My hackles rose. "What? What's that look for?"

"Honestly? I always assumed you kind of liked her."

Liam's comment shouldn't have hit me the way it did since people liked to joke about me and Dahlia, but knowing how we'd started—with her *"not interested"* and how uncomfortable things had been between us, it stuck in my ribs.

"Yeah well, maybe in another life. But in this one? We just don't get along. Except now, for reasons I don't even understand myself, I need to figure out how to at least cooperate enough to sell the story that we're engaged for a few weeks until her sister's wedding."

My phone buzzed and I flipped it over. Several missed texts and a missed call from Aidan earlier—whoops—and something from Dahlia. *"Sorry to cancel but I can't make it tonight."*

Frustration lit instantly. She'd agreed to this. *We'd* agreed to go all in and convince my parents and everyone else. And she was bailing?

I fired back. *"Really? I already put them off a week. You sure you can't swing it?"* I didn't want to sound completely selfish, but I also couldn't sit here and pretend it was fine that she was totally blowing this off.

Her response came immediately. *"I'm sorry, but no. I came down with something. Let me know if they can do next weekend."*

Alarm spiked and I blinked at my phone, mind racing. Was she really sick? If she was, did she need help? Soup? Meds?

"Everything okay?" Liam asked.

"Dahlia just bailed. She said she *came down with something.*"

"You don't think she did?" Aidan asked.

I shrugged. "I don't think she'd lie outright, but here I am, the guy who she's pretending is her fiancé. I'm realizing I have no idea whether she's an honest person or not."

Aidan frowned. "To be fair, you're also lying to your own parents, and that's atypical. I'm not sure you can judge her based on this. And in my experience, she's honest, reliable, hard-working, and fun."

I scowled at him. "Are you giving her a reference or something? Come on. Let me whine."

He and Liam both chuckled, and Liam spoke. "Well, sounds like you need to do your duties as a good fiancé and take her some soup."

I stared at him.

"He's right. You should. It's an olive branch, plus if it was anyone else, you'd be over there in a heartbeat," Aidan added.

Exhaling slowly, I shrugged for the hundredth time today. "Yeah, but she doesn't want me there."

Liam patted his little one's head, and Aidan gave me a

look that felt oddly like disappointment before he spoke in that gentle truth-telling tone I didn't often hear directed at me.

"You have nothing to lose then, right?"

CHAPTER ELEVEN

Dahlia

A sign of our maturing friendship, I no longer felt mild awe when I caught sight of Maddie—AKA Madeline Reynolds. One of America's shiniest tech stars—or she had been until she stepped down in order to live her life in a way that meant more to her. I respected the heck out of that choice, and though I'd never been a CEO millionaire tycoon type, I related to it. In fact, all of us in our little friend group did.

Calla had run from the music business and rewritten her place in the industry. Sadie had broken free of her old habits and patterns that'd kept her living a life isolated by her anxiety. Quinn had taken the reins on her life by, ironically, allowing someone else to help her a bit, and in the process had fallen head over stubborn-as-all-get-out feet. And Sarah? Ugh, I still got squishy feelings inside thinking about her and Wilder. But more than reuniting with her first love, Sarah had escaped a toxic situation that'd held her for years.

When I thought of it that way, it was a wonder I hadn't told them about Devon. These women would understand me. I knew it in the depths of my soul, and yet I'd been too scared and reluctant to tell them.

But approximately ten minutes ago, Quinn Darling had burst through my door and pinned me with a look that meant I wasn't escaping this time. Even my protests that I was sick held no sway, and sooner than I could've imagined, Sadie, Sarah, and now Maddie had arrived. Calla was out of town right now or no doubt she would've made the haul down the canyon for me, too.

"I ran into John downstairs. He gave me this to give you."

Maddie held up a canvas bag, which I took, still more than a little bewildered by the reality that they'd all descended on me so quickly.

Then her words clicked, and a funny feeling hit me between the ribs. "Wait, John Wallace?"

"Yeah, your fiancé, right?" Quinn's raised eyebrow told me the time had come.

But Sadie and Sarah, bless the sweet angels, both frowned at her, and Sarah spoke up. "Can we get this woman her medicine? Maybe some soup?"

"I'm really not that bad. I canceled my day earlier because I had a fever, but it's gone now." And I'd felt pretty terrible from the disaster dinner on Friday and onward, but thankfully, it seemed to be improving.

Curiosity for the bag's contents got the best of me and I did, in fact, want to avoid telling them the whole mess, so I set the bag on the counter and started pulling things out. A large carton of hot soup, a loaf of bread that had to be from

Sadie's bakery, an assortment of cold meds, an electrolyte powder, a book from one of my favorite authors, and a little bookmark with a cat hanging onto a branch and the script that read "Hang in there!" and a little note.

My heart flipped when I saw John's handwriting on the small envelope, though I ignored that. It was just the surprise of the thing. I'd expected him to be annoyed with me for canceling, or maybe to show up in person to see if I was really sick. But this? Not just the soup, but a book? Really? Like he knew me that well?

He obviously does...

Something warm and cozy and sweet melted in me.

"That's a pretty good little goodie bag. Your fiancé sure is thoughtful." This from Quinn, who still bore that impatience in her tone. I knew she'd ultimately be empathetic, or I would've been frustrated with her for pushing.

"It's, he's—" I didn't have words yet. And his note was just... what was his deal? It read:

I'm sorry you're under the weather. Hoping this helps. I would've sent dessert but was worried it might make it worse. Dessert on me when you're better. Let me know if there's anything you need. Your devoted fiancé,

John

I huffed. That little sign-off made it all feel a little sarcastic, and yet it was just so nice. So dang nice. And I knew based on everything I'd observed beyond my own interactions with the man that John was universally thought of as a generous, nice person. I had proof in my own life with this whole mess.

I could no longer pretend he was this distant person I fought with. He was now a man who knew enough to send me things that cut through all the hazy nonsense of our bickering, of our past, and got right to the heart of me. Even if there was no way he could know just how much all of these small gestures meant to me, he'd made the effort. And it wasn't an act... it was just him.

"Seriously, honey, I don't want to push you, but I want to make sure you're okay. Or is this all a joke? I don't want to sound like I don't think you deserve a wonderful man because of all the women I know, you do, but you and John haven't even been dating..."

Quinn trailed off, and something twisted in my belly. I hated that everyone would feel this way. That *I* still felt this way some of the time.

With a sigh, I busied myself with the soup, removing the lid and getting a bowl from the cabinet while I started explaining. "I have a messy history. An ex who was abusive."

Quinn swore, Sadie covered her mouth, Sarah sucked in an audible breath, and Maddie put a hand on my arm. Emotion hit my eyes and cinched my jaw tight, their show of upset and support all at once giving me an overwhelming sense of gratitude and yet anger at having to tell them this about my life.

"At first, it was emotional—just words. But he got physical a few times before I had a chance to make a clean exit."

I'd worked through the shame that reality brought on me. I reminded myself what my therapist had said a hundred times. I'd made a plan to get out and I had. And even if I hadn't, I hadn't been the one who'd hurt me. *He* had. I was away from him, and I was safe.

I was working on making sure he'd stay gone for good. And if I lost sight of that in the midst of all the craziness, that's what I'd come back to when it came to me and John.

"I'm sorry," Maddie said, low and sincere, and the others murmured their agreement.

"I got away from him, but only one of my sisters believed it was happening. He's this beloved son of our town, practically a public figure, and my parents always wanted me to marry him. We almost got married..." I cleared my throat, hating the grief that sliced through me as memories flitted in, of my parents convincing me time and again that Devon *hadn't meant to hurt me.*

"You told your family and they didn't believe you?" Quinn's voice hinted at barely lassoed fury.

"They didn't. No one but Azalea. And she was young enough at the time, no one listened to her. My older sister's boyfriend—now fiancé—is Devon's best friend. It was just a mess. Our lives were so enmeshed and I'd become reliant on him, which I realized later was definitely part of his plan. He'd criticized my job at a flower shop there, but also didn't want me to do anything else. He said once he was elected, I'd quit and do ladies' lunches and stuff like that, but until then I could continue my hobby."

It'd been something that I'd foolishly swallowed without question because I loved flowers, and even though the flower shop was minimum wage, he was taking care of me and so sure of our future. My therapist had helped me see that my passion for flowers hadn't been the problem—his desire to contain me, to own me, had been. All I needed was to look at what I'd built here with Bloom in order to remember that.

They all waited with anticipation, so I continued. "I started looking at building a life here. We'd gone on a trip to Park City, but we'd dropped into Silverton before it grew into such a bustling place and we'd skied the mountain. I'd loved it here, and once I saw the town was growing and I might be able to build the business, I moved."

Quinn marched to me and waited for me to slide the

bowl of soup into the microwave and press *start* before hauling me into a hug. Arms around me, she spoke. "I'm so sorry that happened. I'm sorry they didn't believe you. I'm sorry you had to leave. I'm so freaking glad you came here."

"Yes, so glad you're here," Sarah said, and Sadie and Maddie joined the chorus, too.

"Thanks. I am, too. I'm honestly happier than I've ever been. Or, I was..." Next to the actual stress of the situation, what worried me more than anything else was how upset I felt. Shouldn't I have better coping skills for this? Could I really say I'd healed and moved on when I felt like I was drowning now?

Quinn gave me some space before asking, "Until John? What's he done?"

If only they knew how much John had done, but in all the right ways. "No, no. John is... I'll get to that. Devon is who bid on me at the auction last November."

As if choreographed, their mouths all dropped open. Maddie summoned words first.

"You didn't say anything. Did he talk to you? Hurt you?"

With a careful exhale, I got through the rest. I told them how he'd made sure I knew it was him, but he hadn't showed up to get the basket or time with me. How I'd been looking over my shoulder for weeks, and then how he'd waltzed into Bloom a few months ago and acted like he hadn't been an abusive nightmare and I'd eagerly come crawling back at the sight of him.

"What did you do? I mean, you were alone, right?" Sadie's voice shook with upset.

"I told him I was taken, and then I saw John. He looked in the front window and I just went for it. I ran out to him and pulled him close and begged him to go along with me, and God bless the man, he did."

"He's a good guy," Quinn said, nodding sagely.

"The irony of it being *him* is kind of incredible," Maddie said, more aware than anyone how much John and I butted heads. Since she was engaged to John's cousin and best friend, she'd seen us at our worst.

"I have to give him so much credit. He didn't miss a beat. He had no idea who Devon was or why I was acting like he hung the moon, but he rolled through the whole exchange like we'd been dating for years. And he even left me in peace before I fell apart after." A slice of humiliation ran through me like it so often did when I thought of those moments after begging John to pretend and then breaking down after he'd left. And yet, *he'd* never made me feel that way—not even close, not even once.

"Oh, sweetie," Sarah said, pacing to me and hugging me. We took a moment, then composed ourselves before she asked, "How did it go from that to everyone in town thinking you're engaged?"

"I realized my family had basically sent Devon to me—my mother was so excited. So I made sure they knew I was engaged. I haven't actually talked to them but it's coming. And I realized I needed John to play fiancé for the wedding next month, so he asked if I'd be his date to the high school's dance because his mom has been desperate to set him up. I don't really know his deal other than he's willing to help and he just needed me to go with him, but then Cara overheard us..."

Quinn's eyes widened. "Oh, yeah. And she's not subtle."

I chuckled, some measure of humor seeping in despite the mess, but kept my eyes on my hands. "Yeah. She said,

'You're engaged?' and Mrs. Wallace was there, and instead of denying it, John leaned in. I still don't know why. We haven't really been able to talk, but I'm supposed to go to his house for dinner and... ultimately, we decided it was better for the whole Devon situation if everyone in town bought into the narrative."

Bracing myself, I looked up. Concern shone in each of their faces, and something else on Quinn's, but no judgment. No disappointment or disgust.

"I hate that you felt you had to lie to your family, but knowing all of that, I get it. I'd do the same thing, too. And now, you just tell us how we can run interference or help, and we'll do it. We're on your team, Dahlia, whatever comes your way. If that's being gaga over you and John and how adorable you guys are as fake fiancés, then sign me up."

Relief and something not unlike hope settled in my chest. *People believe me. I'm not alone.* How many times had I said the mantra in my head? I'd known it with a gut-deep certainty, but thus far, I'd only had Azalea and John. Now my friends—my chosen family—were with me. They always would've been, always had been, even though they hadn't known about this part of my past.

"We're on your team, Dahlia." I couldn't imagine sweeter words, especially in the midst of this messy game Devon insisted on playing. With these women with me, and with John's steadfast help, Devon better prepare himself for a shutout.

CHAPTER TWELVE

John

My smile dropped away immediately when I saw Dahlia's scowl as she marched toward me. I held open the door to my car and she slipped in, staring straight ahead. *Okay.*

Last we'd interacted, she'd thanked me for the soup and bread and book. She'd seemed genuinely grateful. When I'd talked to Aidan later, he'd said Maddie reported that she'd told their girl gang the whole story and that Dahlia seemed relieved *and* that she'd seemed to feel better by the time they all left that night.

Oh, and he'd mentioned that Maddie had made it clear that my little care package had been a *very* good surprise. I knew it was all fake, but I'd wanted her to feel cared for—to feel better. Knowing it'd worked out, that maybe that stupid bag of stuff had brought her a measure of comfort or pleasure proved... alluring.

That had been five days ago. We'd texted to work out the logistics, but neither of us could make time to see the other, though I suspected maybe that was due to neither one of us wanting to relive our failed date at Basta. In retrospect, it'd been clear she was starting to feel bad—I'd even thought she looked a bit off, but I wasn't about to bait her and start yet another fight, so I hadn't said anything. That made the whole thing feel a little better when I reflected on it.

But... date? Meeting? Whatever it was, it'd been rough. And now here we were, setting the tone for another delightful evening, albeit on the stage in front of my parents.

"So, how was your week?" I tried, because someone had to.

After a beat, she turned to me. "You know, it was terrible. Just freaking awful."

I blinked, eyes on the road, and resisted the urge to look at her. There'd been no sarcasm in her voice. "Is everything oka—"

"Don't even ask."

Frustration rocked through me, and despite my mental promise before I arrived, I snapped back. "Okay. My apologies for attempting to be civil."

"You know what, you are—"

Her words cut off and I glanced over. Her lips were pressed into a stark line, her arms crossed over her chest. If I wasn't totally mistaken, her chin wobbled.

Guilt and the awful reality that I'd not only let myself be provoked but likely hurt her feelings while I satisfied the stupid habit of lashing out at her instead of staying calm rang clear in my head. And having gone from zero to total jerk in less than five minutes, I'd had it. I turned onto the street that would eventually lead to my folks' house and pulled off on the shoulder.

She didn't say a word until I put the car in park and turned to face her. She craned her neck to look around and had to notice there were no houses or driveways right here. I saw the minute it clicked.

"Are you about to murder me and bury the body in these woods?"

Something about the look in her eye or the way she threw the question hit me just right. All the frustration and anxious energy burst out in a loud bark of a laugh. Her eyes widened like she thought I was insane, and sure, maybe I was.

"What is *wrong* with you?"

I appealed to the heavens for strength, for the right words, and my laughter faded. Nerves had me running a hand through my hair before I attempted to explain. "That's a good question. But first, no, I have no plans to murder you. I pulled off because we need a minute before we get to my folks' house and they're only another two minutes up the road."

She swallowed like it took effort but nodded. "Okay."

"Okay. So..." I said another silent prayer that I could, for once, communicate clearly without getting my boxer briefs in a twist. "I'm sorry. That's what I should've said earlier—that I'm sorry you had a bad week. And then, I should've asked if I could do anything to make it better."

She blinked, absorbing, but no response, so I pressed on. "If you don't want to go tonight, say the word and I'll take you home. This isn't something that should make a bad week worse, and I get it. I've been nervous for days. I'm not particularly excited for the night, but I can promise my parents are nice and my nieces are cute and my brother and sister-in-law are pretty great. Everyone's going to love you, but if you don't want to do this, say the word."

Her mouth dropped open, but she snapped it shut.

"Truly, Dahlia. I don't want to pressure you. I'll still do the wedding—this isn't a bargaining chip. We can put it off a week or indefinitely. I don't want—"

"No, it's fine. I—" She swallowed again and took a deep breath before continuing. "I didn't expect you to say that."

"That I'm sorry?"

She tipped her head to one side. "Well, that, yes. But giving me the option... I'm not entirely used to that in relationships, I guess. Or even in family dynamics. But I appreciate it, and I can do this."

The look of determination that took over made my heart squeeze for some reason. "You don't have to grit through it. Let's do it another time."

"No. No, really. I want to. And I'm sorry I'm so prickly."

I chuckled, the pressure in my chest deflating a bit. "Me, too. We've gotten into this messed up habit, and I suspect it's going to take some work to break it."

She gave me a chagrined smile. "Yeah, probably so."

Exhaling, I held out a hand. "So, what do you say? We team up and work together on this. We try to convince everyone we're engaged and not biting our tongues to keep from insulting each other. And after the wedding, we can go right back to sniping back and forth like it's our jobs."

She chuckled, a reluctant grin on her face as she shook her head. But she then took my hand and shook it.

Time slowed, paused, stopped.

Her small hand slid into mine and clasped it. Her dark eyes met mine, and muscle memory made me raise and lower our hands in a mimic of a handshake. Everything around us was quiet—of course it was. The low hum of the engine, the whisper of the chilly spring wind outside, the rustle of trees all muted against the thudding of my heart. It'd grown weighted, heavier, with the touch of her skin, the slide of her palm against mine.

I forgot to breathe, but she clearly hadn't experienced the same whirl of sensation that turned her brain into a useless blob based on the way she nodded and dropped my hand, almost like it'd grown hot in hers. Basically just like the last time we'd made a handshake agreement.

I would've kept her hand in mine. I wouldn't have let go for... for who knew how long. *What the hell just happened?*

The quiet moment between us died when she asked, "John? You okay?"

Adrenaline jolted me back to life. "Oh, yes. *Yeah.* So, we have like two minutes to get our story straight," I said, shifting to drive and merging back onto the road.

"Oh, shoot. Yeah. I guess your mom will want to know."

"Yes, she will." Nancy Wallace was not about to accept a skim version. She'd want the heavy cream recount, but churned into butter and slathered on warm toast.

Okay, so maybe I'd gotten hungry. That had to be why my brain had full-on shorted out at Dahlia's touch.

"It can be simple, right? Maybe we just went out to dinner and then after, you proposed?"

"Hmm."

A breathy chuckle made me glance at her as we parked.

"What does *hmm* mean? You'd do something more elaborate?" she asked.

I eyed the front door, half expecting my mom to burst forth and corral us into the house instead of waiting for us to enter of our own free will. "If I was getting engaged to you? Yes."

"What does that mean?"

I heard the edge in her voice. "Put down your sword, Price. I'm just saying, if I were your boyfriend planning to propose, I'd think about how *you* would want to be proposed to."

"And?"

"And if I had to guess, I'd say you're a romantic at heart. Granted, I don't actually know you all that well, but I do sort of know that. And in that case, I'd make sure you knew I'd put in some effort." Daring to meet her eyes, I raised a brow in challenge. "Make sense?"

She frowned. "I suppose it does. But that doesn't give us any details."

"I'll come up with something. Let's just avoid the subject and maybe she'll forget while she's busy getting to know you. When Mike brought Jenny home, she spent the entire night asking her questions about every part of her life."

Dahlia's eyes widened into saucers.

"Crap, no. Not in a—Jenny's a talker. It was fine. You'll be fine. I won't let her do that with you. I swear, we'll leave. Just give me that look and I'll know. We'll call Bruce and Wilder to come extract you from the torture."

A smile cracked that expression and her shoulders relaxed. "Okay. Sounds good."

Maybe I didn't love the idea that she'd appreciate my offer of having Bruce come get her, but it wasn't an empty offer. Though we were only loosely friends, I bet I could text him and he'd be over, no questions asked. Not that it'd be needed, but if she felt more comfortable knowing I meant it when I said she wasn't going to be subject to inter-rogation, then all the better.

"Oh, shoot. What about a ring?" How had I not even thought of that?

She was already waving it away like an engagement ring didn't matter for a fake engagement. "I'm a florist. I don't wear anything on my hands, not even a watch most of the time. So we can just say I don't normally wear one."

Could that be true? What would she do when she was actually married? "Uh, okay. But wouldn't I have given you one to propose?"

She sighed. "Of course. But if anyone really digs in on it, we can say I'm always coming straight from work and you're always pestering me about it, and it's fine. Let's just leave it at that for now."

Our culture seemed to focus a fair amount on the engagement ring—I certainly had in the past. But maybe she was right. Our situation was unusual already, so why not let this be another unique part of it? "Alright, let's get in there. She won't be able to contain herself much longer if we stay sitting out here."

We got out, and though I jogged around to her side, Dahlia beat me to the door and exited without my help. If she were really my girlfriend, I'd take her hand or link our arms. I'd touch her at every possible moment since I was both a tactile person and not an idiot. If Dahlia Price were mine, I'd want everyone to know *and* I'd want to revel in it—as long as she didn't mind.

Of course, that was the alternate universe where either of us wanted that. Yes, she made it impossible not to feel a little weak just looking at her, but that attitude... yikes. Plus, maybe it was foolish of me to hold onto our very first encounter and that *not interested* she flung at me, but having gone through a years-long relationship that ended in essentially the same way, I wasn't about to let myself get ideas about a woman who'd never liked me to begin with.

"Wait, just a sec," she said, her hand on my arm halting me.

I turned back to her to see her biting her lip. *Don't look at her lips right now, genius.* Hadn't I just said her whole pretty picture thing made me weak? I needed all my faculties about me if I was going to sell this to John Wallace's biggest fans, numbers one and two.

"Sorry, it's just, your hair kind of looks like... do you mind?"

"It looks... *oh.* Yeah. Sorry. Please, go ahead. Thanks," I babbled, realizing I'd messed with it earlier and it probably looked insane. I didn't use much product, but it had enough body to probably be sticking up.

Biting that lip again, she reached up. The gentle brush of her fingers that I could only barely feel hit me with a surprisingly strong grip, and I almost closed my eyes to savor the contact, but I resisted, instead watching as her gaze followed the movement of her fingers. It was dusky enough that I couldn't see the details of her irises, but I already knew they were killer. Probably for the best I didn't have the full visual just now.

And if the lightest touch from her was making me... *whatever this was,* I needed to find a date. As soon as the wedding was done, I'd force myself to get back out there. It'd be unseemly to say the least if I tried to see someone *now,* but after the wedding, it'd just look like I was rebounding fast. Even that would probably ease my parents' mind.

"There. Better. You look presentable now." She dropped her hands and gave me what looked like a shy smile.

"Thanks. See? That was a very fiancée-ish thing to do."

She nodded and nudged my side as we walked toward the door, each step heightening my awareness of her and what we were about to walk in on. Poor Dahlia really had no idea...

It could go just fine. The last few minutes in the car had been fine. But also?

It could be a total disaster.

CHAPTER THIRTEEN

Dahlia

The door swung open before we ever knocked or rang the bell, and Mrs. Wallace beamed at us. "John Marcus, why on earth have you been lingering outside and making my poor future daughter-in-law face the threat of hypothermia?"

John huffed. "It's like fifty-five, Mom, she wouldn't get hypothermia. Plus she—never mind." He shook his head, then held out a hand for me to precede him right as his mom stepped out of the doorway and made a grand gesture for me to enter.

"I'm so happy you're here. Are you recovered from your illness? Was it flu? Another virus? What about —"

"Darling, let's let them get inside before you start your interrogation." The man's voice made me turn to find a familiar older, slightly stouter version of John. He had a kind of charming silver beard, and the way he hugged his wife to his side with an adoring, knowing look made me feel a little melty. I'd seen them around town here and there, and they always held hands—always. If I wasn't misremembering, they were a best friends to lovers story with such a lovely happy ending.

Somewhere inside me, just like it'd been doing since John had stopped the car and halted my insane, angry-cat defensive responses to him, my heart whispered a warning to me.

"I'm sorry. I'm just so excited. But I also don't want to scare you away. You know? I'm going to go check the rolls."

She bustled away so quickly, I hardly had a chance to open my mouth, let alone say, "Thank you for having me. I'm glad to be here. I'm sorry for the delay."

"Think nothing of it, Dahlia. We're just glad you're here." John's dad smiled at me, and though I'd seen him around, he offered a hand. "I'm John."

I smiled, appreciating his natural warmth. "Nice to meet you, sir."

"Oh, no, none of that formality. And before you ask, no, my first-born son is Michael—Mike. We named him after this one's father, and I got to name our little boy after me." He hugged Nancy around the shoulders as she rejoined our small group, and she grinned up at him.

My cheeks pinked, but I nodded, accepting the information and demand for first names. I had only met one other set of parents—Devon's. That experience had gone okay, or so I'd thought, until he'd berated me all the way home for embarrassing him after the fact. I already knew John wouldn't do that, but the tone of the evening and the Wallaces themselves were also completely different, so even though I was on edge, these first minutes had let me relax just a touch.

I slipped my hand into the pocket on my left side, where I'd stuck the tiny notecard that'd been sitting on my doormat when I left earlier—a note from my sweet friends. Inside the three-inch squared bright green cardstock were the words, "You've got this. We love you." And wasn't that just what I needed? It hadn't changed what'd happened right before I'd left my apartment, but once I'd calmed down in the car, I'd pinched the little note and tried to channel their confidence. Part of *having this* was being myself, not the defensive, suspicious woman I'd been when I'd first gotten in the car.

"Can we help with dinner at all?" John asked, ushering me farther inside.

Of course he'd be asking. I should've thought of that. But John's presence, and even his parents', was calming, not accusatory or full of expectation. It was like they were just happy we'd come, and I couldn't help but relax a little more as that became clearer by the minute.

"I think your mom's got it under control. Laney's sick so Michael and Jenny won't be here." He made a sad face, then continued on his path to the dining room.

Their home was modest and well lived in, but it looked really homey and nice. Lots of wood and cozy rugs and throw blankets on the back of the couch. I wondered if this was the house John and his brother had grown up in.

"I'm sorry," John said so low, I almost didn't hear it.

Turning to look at him, his brow was furrowed, and he looked truly bothered. What was he sorry for? "Why?"

"I thought my brother would be here with his kids and it'd be a little more... circus and a little less *intimate dinner with your fiancé's parents.*"

Oh. Yeah. "Might've been nice, but hey. We're in it now.

Better make it count." I winked, for some reason wanting to reassure him I was fine.

And miraculously, I was. I'd been a raging beast as I walked out of my apartment, more angry with my family and myself than anything else. The note from my friends clutched tightly in my fingers, even their faith in me couldn't wash away the harsh reality of what'd come just before. I'd finally accepted my mother's phone call and aside from her questioning my choice of fiancé and demonstrating she'd clearly searched him online and found him lacking—which was an entirely separate issue—she'd pushed Devon in my face *again*.

"You know you belong together. He's approaching a very busy time in his political career and he'll need your support —he'll want you by his side. I thought maybe getting away and having this little adventure in Utah would be good for you, but it's time to come home to your family and enter the next phase."

"I'm not ever going back there. I have a life here now, a thriving business, and my fiancé and I are moving in together soon." I had no idea what John's house was like—I'd made it my mission to think about and know as little as possible about him over the years, but maybe I should check on that. Did he own the house? Have a weird roommate situation I should know about?

"Devon's your sister's future husband's best man, and I'll expect you to be cordial at the very least. We're doing the spa the weekend prior to the wedding, and I hope you know you'll be expected to—"

"I'll be fine. Please make sure he *knows that it's inappropriate to treat me like anything other than another guest at the wedding."*

Her astonished gasp made my hackles rise even further.

"You'll show him the respect he deserves, Dahlia. He's a future senator, if not more. I just hope you don't embarrass us."

I couldn't respond then, the rage and hurt and lingering disbelief clogging my throat for long enough that she sniffed and claimed she had to "jump off" before I found words. I'd hung up and gotten John's text that he was waiting outside...

Talking to my parents never went well, but this one had been a real gem. Part of me had wanted to believe that when they heard I was engaged, even if they weren't happy, they'd put to rest the Devon thing. They'd encourage him to bring a date and live his life without this weird fixation on me that'd apparently lingered far too long. But those comments about me moving home and respecting him, about his political future... I knew what that meant. In my gut, I knew that unless John and I played a very convincing game, they'd be shoving him at me again.

And worse, they'd be doing things to try to make me look good to him, just like they'd done years ago when they'd set us up. Our dating hadn't been completely unnatural, but it had been the product of their urging. And anytime I even remembered that, I grew sick to my stomach.

No amount of encouragement from my friends in our group text or even the quick phone call from Sarah, perhaps the most familiar with toxic parents, had calmed the twisting hurt in me. They'd done their best the last few days, but those efforts couldn't quell the tide of emotion that churned in me after that call.

Launching out of the door and into John's car, I'd felt small and helpless and so, so angry. And he'd gotten a face full of it with my snippy retorts.

The fact that he'd had the presence of mind to pull over and give us a minute, that he'd apologized and... that he'd given me the choice to go home with no questions asked... it'd disarmed me. I'd like to say *completely*, but I didn't know the last time I'd been disarmed completely around anyone but my girlfriends and maybe, *maybe* the book club.

In the kitchen, John Sr. took a large platter from the stove right as Nancy picked up a basket and smiled at me before saying, "John, will you get the salad dressing? Dahlia, honey, why don't you get the tongs there on the counter."

In another minute or two, we were seated at a set table in the dining room. A dove gray tablecloth, bright white plates with matching cloth napkins, and pretty silver goblets already filled with water adorned the table.

"This looks fancy, Mom," John said as he set his napkin in his lap.

Nancy grinned. "Doesn't it? I just got the new linens and I love them. It's a nice stop between winter and full-blown spring. But don't worry about spilling—it's supposedly stainproof. I doubt we'll test that theory too thoroughly since the girls aren't here, but we'll get there soon enough, I suppose." She winked at me.

"They're ten and six?" I asked, doing what I could to recall any details about John's nieces. I didn't know them from him, but I'd asked Maddie a few things so I didn't seem like a total idiot. Why hadn't we done a thorough recap of his family? Or mine, for that matter? What if his mom asked him about my family and he didn't even know I had sisters?

Wait, no. He knew I had sisters because this whole thing started when I asked him to keep up the ruse for my sister's wedding.

"Yes. Absolute little demons, but we love them," she said, laughing before reaching her hands to either side of her.

I watched as John Sr. took his wife's hand and set his palm up on the table not quite halfway between us.

"No pressure, Dahlia, but we usually say grace before we eat."

"Oh! Sure. Yeah." I took his hand and John's, a confusing mix swirling in my gut at how unlike my family everything about this had been. John Sr. said a few words in thanks for the food and the hands that had prepared it, and then they dug in. A few seconds of contact, but I still felt the slide of John's hand after we released.

I would've moved on, not fazed by the prayer so much as the warmth at this table, in this home, and how unmoored by it I felt. But then, something drew my attention down between my chair and John's.

Out of the corner of my eye, I saw it.

His hand—the one that'd held mine—flexed before it curled into a fist, though his gaze stayed on his food, a slight frown at his lips. A fluttering in my chest made me swallow, but before I could study his face and attempt to decipher the meaning of that movement, Nancy's question stole my attention.

"So, let's hear the engagement story. I want every. Single. Detail!"

CHAPTER FOURTEEN

John

Of course I knew she'd want details—I'd just hoped I'd have a few bites of dinner down the hatch and a little more time before I had to start getting creative.

Dahlia's posture had gone from excellent to downright streetlamp levels of straight, though she had a pleasant enough expression as she looked at me. "Do you want to tell it, honey?"

I nodded, accepting the challenge hidden in those words since I'd been the one to say keeping it simple wouldn't work. And if she knew me, she'd know it wouldn't, especially not in front of my parents.

"Of course, flower girl. I'd love to," I said with a wink, then slung an arm around the back of her chair for good measure. "One thing you need to know about Dahlia before I tell you this is that she is an avid reader and a true romantic."

Dahlia's lashes fluttered next to me, but I worked to keep the thrill of her closeness from distracting me.

The *aww* that came from my mother sounded genuine and full of pure delight. She clapped her hands but pressed her lips together to keep herself from interrupting me. She was a little like that Kristin Wiig character from SNL that just got *so excited* she burst through walls and couldn't keep secrets.

Everyone knew you didn't tell Nancy Wallace anything you didn't mind getting around. She wasn't a gossip, she was just *that* enthusiastic. And though it might sound overbearing or exhausting, it resulted in her reaching students who were isolated, alone, hurting, depressed… somehow, that warmth and excitement held a magic for her English students. I'd been told a hundred times how my mom had been *the* teacher to keep a person sane / safe / on track / etc. during their time at Silverton High.

But oh, did she have to work not to interrupt, and I could see it now. Too bad for her, this story was unfolding in front of her eyes, so while I scrambled internally for details, it'd be a slow process.

"Knowing her love of, well, love, I considered going straight forward—you know, classic on-one-knee-in-a-restaurant type deal." I played with Dahlia's ponytail that sat high on her head and was so cheery and beautiful with its dark curls and waves, I had to remind myself to only *just* touch. In reality, we hadn't discussed that either—what was her comfort level with me? I didn't want to force the issue and get a bad reaction in front of my folks, but we'd need to hash that out stat.

For her part, she didn't seem bothered, but she did glance at me and one brow rose slightly enough no one else would see it.

"Instead, I thought about her favorite books. I considered proposing in a rainstorm and insulting her family, but that would've been too easy."

My mom giggled and Dahlia stifled a laugh while I kept spinning my tale. "My ability to mimic Rochester's shot since I don't have a secret wife in my attic—"

"You don't have an attic at all, so that really nails that coffin shut," my dad added, familiar enough with the classics thanks to being married to his English teacher wife for coming up on forty years that he could follow my nonsense.

"And I didn't want to get friend-zoned like Laurie or have to wait forever like Behar..."

Dahlia turned to me then, with narrowed eyes. Questions lurked in those depths, and part of me itched for her to ask them, but those would wait. Still, her attention sent a shot of adrenaline into my veins, and I dipped my head and touched my forehead gently to hers in a show of *ain't it sweet we're engaged* tenderness. Her lashes fluttered, and I straightened to continue.

"I haven't read nearly enough of her more recently published romances to manage mimicking those either, but in the end, I decided it just needed to be something that showed her how lovely and imperfect and wonderful she is." I indulged in a light touch of my fingers to her soft hair again.

"John Marcus Wallace, you should not be telling a woman she's imperfect!" My mother's indignation rang clear, and my father shook his head like I should know better.

"I know you guys are about to celebrate forty years and know a lot more about this, but for me and Dahlia, that's what she needed to know."

She turned to me, a slight wrinkle in her brow as my dad asked, "What's that?"

I swallowed, nerves creeping in a touch before I said, "That she's not perfect. She's real. I don't need or want her to be perfect, because every part of her is beautiful to me—the good, bad, and messy. I want the whole of her, not just the prettiest parts. I want her petals and her roots, her leaves and her thorns. I want it all."

The room was silent but for the track of instrumental version of pop music playing low in the background. Nerves bubbled through my veins, making my head feel like it was floating. Did I really just say all of that?

Holy *Crap*. Talk about an overshare. And, obviously, not real. Not at all. I didn't even know the woman. I only knew the bits and pieces I'd put together over the years. Sure, I'd had an oddly antagonistic relationship with a person I'd found immeasurably attractive and intelligent and engaging and compelling but... I didn't feel like *that*.

At the same time, the little part of my heart that shrank from those bold words got muffled by the larger chambers beating harder now, reinforcing the thoughts and willing them into reality. Because whether it was me or someone else, Dahlia deserved to know she was imperfect and that was okay, and something told me that hadn't been the dynamic with Devon. *Everyone* should find a partner who loved them as they were, not as they had the potential to be. Starting a relationship with changing the other person as Plan A was purely toxic. *Ask me how I know*.

"Well said, son. Well said." Dad turned to Mom and dipped his face. "On that note, darling, you're quite imperfect."

Mom choked out a watery "Oh" and hugged him to her, whispering words I shut out as Dahlia turned to me.

The earlier confusion resembled a partly cloudy sky compared to the thunderstorm raging in her eyes now. "That was quite a show."

I swallowed hard, not sure how to respond.

She gazed at me as though lovesick, but whispered, "You're a good actor. I never realized."

My parents broke apart and began eating, complimenting my speech and Mom gabbing away about expectations and what all couples should consider before getting married. But I couldn't hear a word of it because in that instant I knew, with utter certainty, I needed Dahlia to be very clear about one thing.

"Not really, no." I wasn't that good of an actor. I could fake it, and I tended to rise to her baiting, no, but that wasn't acting. That was *reacting*. Just now? That speech?

That'd been real—something that should be said about her and that I'd want said about me. And that didn't make a lick of sense to explain to her right now—or ever, so relief rolled through when Dahlia turned back toward my parents without another word and the conversation moved on. Mercifully, they didn't actually ask about the how since I'd given them the... well, the *what*, I supposed.

That would've been great until I registered what they'd moved on to. When I tuned back in, my mom was saying, "It's just so much better this way. I can tell how much you mean to him, and I'm just so happy. All this time, I thought he's been by himself, but I understand why, after last time, he didn't want to be so *out* there about it."

Dread dripped from the top of my head over every inch of me, a slow slide down the side of my neck and into my shirt at the comparison between my fake engagement to Dahlia and my failed one to Tina. Dahlia didn't know about any of my past—nor had I ever planned to tell her.

Dahlia's expression appeared confused, though she attempted to mask it with a little grin. "I'm a pretty private person, too. I think he's tried to be respectful of that." And then, she reached over and squeezed my arm.

To anyone else, it might've seemed like a loving, familiar gesture, but when I met her eyes, I could've sworn she was telling me not to worry. Not to feel that slow trickle of shame and regret and embarrassment continue its methodical path to my gut.

I dipped my chin to acknowledge, hoping we could somehow move away from all that ancient history, and thankfully, my dad chimed in about something having to do with Mike. The conversation moved onto the grandkids and Mom's students and Dad's plans for retirement in another few years. I forced a smile for a few minutes until a story about my nieces loosened the knot in my chest, and by degrees, I forgot about the unfortunate reveal.

Forty minutes later, we were stuffed full of food and the constant, joyful banter between my parents. Dahlia had stayed quiet, but not alarmingly so. I'd never been in a situation like this, but I wondered whether what I'd usually read as coldness in her demeanor might have been more like introversion or even shyness.

"Looks like some rain coming down now. You kids should probably git before the roads muck up." My dad patted my shoulder and winked at Dahlia.

"Probably so. Thanks for dinner, Mom."

"Yes, thank you, Nancy. John. It was lovely."

My mom bustled over and hugged Dahlia tight. "You'll come to the anniversary dinner now as our future daughter-in-law. How perfect!"

My gaze shot to Dahlia and her eyes widened, but she

was smiling, thankfully. "Of course. What a gift to be a guest, too."

Of course. I'd forgotten that my sister-in-law had hired Dahlia to do the flowers for the event, but now here was one more obligation. We'd need to discuss it and I could figure a way out of it if she didn't want to do it, even if the thought of telling my parents about my broken engagement while we celebrated their historic marriage filled me with dread.

Mom leaned in and said something into Dahlia's ear that I couldn't hear, and frankly, I wasn't sure I wanted to know. All the requisite thanks and farewells dealt with, Dahlia and I ducked out into a drizzly evening. I jogged to open her door, then ran around and started the engine as quickly as I could.

"Your parents are great," she said after a moment.

I backed out, then nodded. "They are. A bit much sometimes, but mostly, I appreciate that about them."

She chuckled. "Yeah. I got that. I'd heard it from others, but after tonight, I have a better feel for what that actually means."

I grinned at the tone in her voice—not judgmental or critical. Kind of... affectionately amused, if I had to name it.

"So, the anniversary dinner."

"The Friday after the wedding. Might as well stick it out until then, if you're okay with it."

She sounded resigned but not in a bad way. More like she accepted that we'd gone this far—dinner with my family, selling the story to her entire family and the town overall, so we might as well roll with it.

"If you're good, I'm good."

We drove the next few minutes in silence. Compared to the jumpy, anxious version of my brain before dinner, I felt flattened. Deflated. I'd said some things that probably hadn't hit Dahlia like they did me, weirdly, and then my mom had told this woman I was barely friends with about my biggest, most personal failure. Granted, I'd worked through the idea that it was a failure in a lot of ways, but tonight, it pressed against a still-raw place in my heart I hadn't been prepared to shield. And now, we were going to ride this rather bumpy road together an extra week longer.

It'd be fine.

I pulled up in front of her shop, which was only a few feet from an entrance to the building where she could get to her apartment above Bloom and parked, eager to say good-night and go put this day to bed.

Unbuckling, I decided to leave the car running so it wouldn't get cold, but Dahlia stopped me. "You don't have to walk me. I'm fine."

Well, we were both obviously *totally fine.*

And the other thought that came through? *Of course she's fine.* Silly me for wanting to treat this like anything other than a clinical arrangement. "Okay."

She shoved open the door and got one foot out but then turned back. "Listen, I—I don't know exactly what your mom was talking about tonight with the 'last time' stuff, but I wanted to say that I... I don't know. I'm sorry that things didn't work out, if you wanted them to."

I opened my mouth to say something—anything—but she slipped out, shut the door, and bolted to her building's awning as though in a downpour and not a cool spring evening. I watched to make sure she got inside okay and waited another minute, just in case she ran into any issues. After a moment, I texted her. *"You get in okay?"*

"Yes. Thanks. I'll talk to you soon."

If I'd been looking for something else, she didn't offer it. And I didn't know what I wanted from her. Not really fair for me to sit here waiting for some mysterious thing I couldn't even name, especially after her heartfelt apology. It only made the pit in my stomach grow since I recognized I'd need to clear a few things up, namely that she wasn't fake engaged to some guy who was still in love with someone else. My feelings for Tina had faded completely, but it didn't mean her finding out about it didn't... well, suck.

But we'd met my parents and they'd loved her, just like everyone did, and I'd said... things. She probably wouldn't remember them after tonight since she'd clearly thought they were all for the sake of the story. She was probably already on to thinking about her favorite book or Bruce Camden's Crest commercial smile, or whatever new flowers she'd be getting in the shop. She would sleep soundly having done her part in this agreement, and we'd... talk soon.

And me? I'd remember all the good I did have in this world and not the one I thought I'd had and lost because I wasn't worth choosing. I'd remember that though I'd thought I loved Tina, I'd learned a lot about those feelings and how thin they were, especially as I'd watched Aidan grieve for Viv.

And more than anything, I'd remember I didn't have any of those same hang-ups or issues. I was helping out a good woman, and in the end, we'd go back to before and I'd be fine.

CHAPTER FIFTEEN

Dahlia

Bruce and Tristan clapped and our small group passed out high-fives and hugs to each other. Saint Security had started a trial self-defense class and Bruce had lightly suggested I consider joining at book club last month. I'd happily joined, but I still didn't know why he'd told me to.

The fact that half the group was made up of my friends had made it an easy yes, plus I liked the idea of knowing how to handle myself a bit better. Having my fake fiancé firmly in place and present at the wedding would ideally mean Devon wouldn't try anything, but if he did, he'd be in for a surprise.

"Thanks for being patient with us. We're going to work up a curriculum for a weekly class starting at the end of the month, so if you're interested, let us know and we'll keep you in the loop." Bruce smiled at all of us and winked at his sister, Kiley, who rolled her eyes and turned away, arms crossed.

I wrinkled my nose and gave Bruce a sympathetic look right as Quinn walked up and patted his shoulder.

"Fear not, friend. She'll come through it. I swear I thought I'd pull my hair out with that one—" she nodded toward Cara. "But once she emerged from the haze of teen rage, it's been mostly smooth sailing." She nudged him with an elbow.

"Thanks, Quinn. How encouraging."

His deadpan delivery made me chuckle.

Quinn gave him the cheesiest set of finger guns, clicked her tongue, and winked. "Keep me on your list, Camden. You know the husband attracts crazies."

Bruce shook his head. "Yeah, I do. That's why he hired the best for his security team."

She waved that away. "Right, but still. Keep me on it. And if you do another one in the summer, I bet Cara will do it, too. She's too busy during the school year."

He nodded, tapping something on his phone. Quinn hugged me, shoved something into my back pocket, which I'd bet was another little note of encouragement, and sauntered off with only a "See you Thursday!"

"That woman..." Bruce said, with another shake of his head.

"She's very much her own person. I love her and Julian together. I couldn't have picked it but..." I sighed.

"Billionaire romance?" he asked, looking out after her.

"Oh, yeah. Single mom. Billionaire." I made a chef's kiss. "Plus he's adorable with Cara."

Bruce chuckled and waved to a few people who'd gathered their bags and were exiting the large room they'd set up for the class. I'd had no idea this room existed in the mill, but here we were. Apparently, they'd rented out this place but were already planning a significant expansion of their main office building to incorporate training space like this.

"What about Wilder and Sarah?" he asked.

"Second chance romance perfection. Seriously. Also, we can throw a little broody hero in there, maybe wounded veteran feels…" I thought about that, but before I could really nail it down, Bruce's laugh caught my attention.

"Wait, am I a wounded veteran?"

The glint in his eye told me he found this whole conversation amusing. He'd poked fun at my love of romance in a lighthearted way, but he was merciless with my tendency to cast different people in the roles of my favorite tropes.

Bruce? Bruce was basically too good to be true. He wasn't grumpy like Wilder. I wasn't tracking any past lost loves, though I had to believe there must be a decent trail of broken hearts left behind. He had taken guardianship of his little sister in the last few years, and I wondered what the full story there was, but it'd never really been up for discussion.

That in mind, I responded. "Are you wounded, Bruce?"

The soft, sad smile he gave seemed so unlike him, I never would've believed I was seeing it, but it quickly widened. "You know me, Dahlia. I'm doing all right."

And with that, his attention shifted to Catherine, who worked at the diner. She was super shy but really sweet, and I knew it must've taken guts for her to approach him, so I waved a farewell and grabbed my bag.

"Ready?" Sadie asked, slinging her own bag up and over her shoulder.

"Let's deliver you to your man," I said, wiggling my brows enough to make her roll her eyes.

We wandered around the side of the building and

admired the bluebird sky. Several old mill buildings peppered this area. This one housed Sadie's bakery, her fiancé Warrick's gym, and then the little offshoot room he planned to use for cycling classes when he got more bikes. The other just across the way was the home of Silver Ridge Brewing.

"There's my love," Warrick said, jogging toward us and hoisting Sadie into the air with what looked like zero effort. He braced her legs and held her flush to him so she was looking down on him, cheeks pink and grin a mile wide. Warrick's delight at being near her rolled off him in waves as he asked, "Can you officially beat me up with your pinkie now?"

She grinned and cupped his cheeks, their eyes locked in the way that told me everyone in the world had faded away. *Le sigh.* They were so adorable, and I couldn't wait to get through my sister's wedding so I could focus completely on theirs. Their fake dating to really in love story just killed me. I'd always been a sucker for a fake relationship trope, and this shy-heroine-meets-her-match real-life love story was better than any I'd read. Plus, nothing was more appealing than a cinnamon roll hero in a big brutish NFL player body, and Warrick encapsulated that beautiful dichotomy to a T.

"You'll have to wait and find out," Sadie said in a soft voice, her lips a scant inch above his.

A crackle of heat I felt from feet away snapped, and Warrick moved. He hiked Sadie's legs around his hips and jogged in the direction of the gym door. *Okay, then.* I guess he wanted to test the theory.

"See you soon, Dahlia!" Sadie yelled through a laugh before they disappeared inside.

Standing alone—*ah, familiar*—I watched the place

where they'd gone in, a jumble of exhaustion, happiness for my friend, and longing rolling around clumsily in my gut.

Whenever anyone asked about dating or marriage for me, I waved it off like I had no interest. And most of me, after everything that'd happened with Devon, genuinely felt that way. I'd known with a clarity I'd rarely possessed that entering the dating pool, let alone attempting another relationship, was simply not going to make my list of priorities. I'd embraced that right along with my new home here in this burgeoning little town.

But lately, maybe thanks to the giddiness of Sarah's pregnancy and Sadie's impending nuptials, and Maddie's utter bliss with Aidan and their new engagement, I'd felt a little different.

I'd never just wanted to find *someone* and settle down. I'd wanted to find *the one*. And fool me had thought maybe Devon would be that person—or at least that with time, he could become that. When he first started showing his true colors, I'd convinced myself I was misunderstanding him. That *I* was doing something wrong. Basically, I bought his abuse hook, line, and sinker, and I'd almost married him.

Even before it became abuse, Devon had never been kind. He never seemed to know me or even really be at ease with me. He was a restless sort of person anyway, but in quiet moments, I never felt fully relaxed. I always wore makeup, always had my hair done, never let him see me in my rattiest sweats or anything less than composed.

"I want the whole of her, not just the prettiest parts. I want her petals and her roots, her leaves and her thorns. I want it all."

John's words cut a path through my thoughts and the ache set in. I'd felt it on and off in increasing measure since he'd said them days ago—over two weeks now, in fact. I hadn't spoken to him either, save for a text days ago asking if he needed to arrange a tux for the wedding. We had a few weeks to go until the big day...

How had *that* man been the one to say such a beautiful thing? And how had he said it in a way that felt real? I'd been genuinely shocked at his words and, more than anything, how convincing he'd been.

Maybe it made me pathetic to admit it, but those words had tumbled around inside my head until I'd had to write them down. I'd needed to see them, to ingest them in my favorite format and see if they hit me differently.

What I came away with was this longing. He'd written me the perfect lover's declaration, but it wasn't really for me. Maybe it'd been for the ex Nancy had mentioned, which might make sense. But the truth that hit me over and over again? I wanted those words to be for me. I wanted someone to feel that way about me.

I hadn't realized how much I'd wanted it until I'd been sitting at a table with my fake fiancé's parents and hearing him recite a speech he was supposedly giving me. But he'd said those words to his parents, not to me, and even though I'd felt them in my gut, in my soul, they'd been for show. For effect. And I'd do well to remember that.

And maybe more than remembering John was simply fulfilling his end of the deal—I had no business having feelings for him or anyone else. All the junk emotions coming at me since Devon had reappeared should be sign enough that even if part of me wanted to find *the one*, I had no business doing so right now.

But what I did have—what built my confidence in facing this whole mess with each passing day—was John. He was on my team. If he would put on a show like that for his own parents, then he was committed. Not that he'd ever given me reason to doubt, but that night had bonded us. The truth lay buried underneath thoughts and feelings I didn't dare look too closely at—that night had changed things. And for now, I embraced it as one more sign that I wasn't alone. Another affirmation with teeth.

"Hey, Dahlia, how are you?" Liam Morrison said as he approached, hand in hand with his wife, Wells.

"Doing well. Just finished up with a self-defense workshop Bruce and the Saint Security guys put on. How about you guys?"

"Heading for an early dinner while the grandparents have the kids. You want to join us?" He hugged Wells tighter against him.

"Oh, no. You guys have a date night. Enjoy the momentary freedom, right?"

They chuckled and went without protesting any more, thankfully, and for some reason, I stayed glued to the spot watching them go. Now that I'd left the inside of the mill building and all the other single people, I couldn't escape the loving couple parade that was Silverton. I didn't have anything against them. Usually, I reveled in these friends and good people finding each other and making their lives together. It satisfied me. That was one part of being a florist that drove me—I loved seeing people come together on their wedding day surrounded by my arrangements, loved the idea of my flowers gracing their holiday table or hospital bed after the birth of a child. Of course, there existed many other occasions for flowers, but I'd always loved love.

It just felt so far removed from me for so long. Especially once I'd realized I hadn't ever loved Devon, not really, and he certainly hadn't ever loved me, accessing that part of myself that wanted something like that was like a flower trying to get water from a stem that had been pruned away.

Until recently. Maybe it came through the threat from Devon, the betrayal of my family, the reality that I'd be seeing both Devon *and* my family soon for Rose's wedding, or more likely, pretending to be engaged to someone as close to an enemy as I had in this town. Whatever the case, the long-dormant roots buried deep were waking up, and I didn't know where to go with that other than to tell them to stay asleep because now was not the time.

"Hey."

As though I hadn't been chatting with people on and off all morning, I startled violently, gasped, and swirled around. It wasn't so much that he'd spoken as that *he* had spoken. While my mind had run around all the confusing, layered thoughts surrounding dinner and Devon and my family and those words, I hadn't expected to be presented with the man in person.

"Sorry. Guess I snuck up on you," he said, shoving his hands into his pockets and rocking back on his heels.

"My fault for being jumpy." I shrugged, staunchly ignoring the little flip in my stomach at the sight of him. He really did look annoyingly handsome. In the past, I'd just blurred out his face and hands and... general person, shooting whatever comebacks his direction while avoiding his sparkly hazel eyes and cut jaw.

All a bit excessive, really, and the more I got to know him, the more we interacted, the harder it became to continue avoiding eye contact. Nice, helpful business owner John, who was a loyal friend and adorable son... *too much.*

He studied me a moment, serious and a little more withdrawn than I was used to. In the past, before this whole fake fiancé mess, John came out guns blazing with me. He was bold—provocative, almost. Like he wanted to get a rise out of me.

And he'd gotten one every time. Even that very first encounter when he hadn't meant to and couldn't have seen it coming. But today? His whole demeanor seemed closed down, or shut off somehow.

"Any chance you want to get lunch?" he asked, still that unsure vibe coming off him.

I glanced at my watch. "Lunch?"

He frowned just a touch. "Late lunch? Early dinner? Four o'clock snackies? Whatever you want to call it. I'm hungry and grouchy, and I want to eat in your vicinity for some insane reason, fake fiancée."

A laugh tumbled out of my mouth, his grumpiness hitting me just right to break my worry. "Well, with that kind of invitation, I can't possibly say no."

He shook his head slowly, an unexpectedly serious expression on his handsome face. "You can always, *always* say no, Dahlia."

I swallowed, my throat tight. Why did the soft yet insistent voice he'd used make me feel like crying? Why would him saying that about something so inconsequential matter *at all* to me? It wasn't him, anyway, was it? It was just that novel idea that I could refuse him. Everything with Devon had been so entirely focused on him—pleasing him, which devolved into appeasing him, then in the end, whatever I could do to avoid his displeasure. I wasn't sure he'd ever given me an option—*any* option—and John was constantly, persistently reminding me I had them.

Clearing my throat, I waved it away with a flick of my hand. "Just so happens I'm hungry, too. But I need to get cleaned up. Can I meet you in an hour?"

"Sure. That's great. Guac?"

"See you there." I turned and beelined for my street, relief at the sight of my shop's sign hitting as I approached.

John had veered off toward Main Street, but I hadn't given him the chance to walk with me. I was too mixed up, too confused by his handsome, serious face and his offer to go to lunch-turned-dinner and those words he'd said the other night.

I needed to collect myself quickly or this dinner would end up being even more awkward than the last.

CHAPTER SIXTEEN

John

In order to see her coming, I'd chosen the side of the shiny red booth facing the door. Still early for Saturday dinner, but the restaurant was filling up quickly, so I'd decided to get seated a few minutes early just in case.

Plus, after the way I'd been stressing this meeting, I needed eyes on her the minute she walked in the door.

Not like this was an ambush. I'd asked her to join me, compelled to approach her when I saw her earlier just standing there gazing toward town in her yoga pants and sweatshirt. I hadn't allowed myself to take in the view of her like I wanted to, so dressed down and casual, but something in my chest had glowed hot all the same.

Right on time, Dahlia rushed inside and glanced around almost frantically before relaxing slightly when she saw me. Now dressed in jeans and a sweater, she beelined for the booth and slipped in, all in one smooth movement.

"Sorry I'm late."

I glanced at my watch—yep, right on time. "You're not late. You're right on time."

"I guess you were early."

Yikes, she seemed stressed. What had happened in the last hour? We'd had a pretty good interaction before. "I was, but only because I wrapped up all my errands and figured I'd grab a seat and have a beer rather than wander aimlessly."

Her lips pursed for a second. "Then I'm sorry for not being early."

"You have no reason to be sorry."

She blinked a few times, her head inching back a bit. "Okay."

My hands raised in a sign of surrender. "If that came out wrong, I didn't mean it to. I meant that you're right on time and have nothing to apologize for. I wouldn't expect you to be early even if I was. I don't want you to feel like you have to apologize."

She nodded, then took a long drink from the water in front of her. I'd told Brodie she was coming, and they'd already brought her water and small bowl of salsa. I could've sworn her hand shook just slightly before she set the glass down and exhaled long and slow.

"I don't really want to explain why I just freaked out, but I feel like I owe you an explanation." Her eyes flickered around the room as she craned her neck over her shoulder, then straightened and finally met my gaze.

"If you want to. I have some stuff I want to talk about, too."

"Okay. Do you want to go first?"

I couldn't tell if she wanted me to or not, but I wanted to break the tension. "How about we get margaritas and some guacamole, talk about the day, and then we get to the heavier stuff?"

"You don't have to do that for me. I'm fine just diving in."

I wondered whether we'd ever have a conversation that didn't have some edge of heads butting against each other. "I'm not doing it for you. I'm doing it for me. I want a margarita and I want chips, and I want to order so that I can drown my sorrows in piles of guacamole and cheese. That okay with you?"

She tucked her lips together, but I saw the smile. In fact, I could swear that was a pleased look on her face—not that I knew her face all that well, since I'd forbidden myself to look as much as I might've been tempted to over the years.

"Fine." She sighed. "I mean, that actually sounds great. I think I passed the point of hungry an hour or so ago, so you're not getting my best here."

"I don't need your best. I'll take you just like this," I said, and the waiter popped up right in time, asking whether we were ready to order.

"Perfect timing, yes. We're ready." I ordered and Dahlia did the same, then Brodie left with a promise to be back with our drinks as soon as possible.

"So what were you up to at the mill building today? Working out at Grit?" Warrick's gym was busy any time he was open, but especially on weekends when he ran extra sessions of his group workouts.

"No, I was with the Saint Security guys. They did a self-defense workshop. Bruce mentioned it last month at book club, and it's been on my mind. I figure I might as well know as much as I can."

That jabbed at the worry I'd been suppressing since the

day I'd seen her with her ex. "Are you worried? About...
that?"

I didn't want to name it—didn't want to say what I was
afraid she might have endured.

Brodie, bless him, brought us our drinks, two towering
baskets of chips, and a huge bowl of guac. We thanked him,
and she took a chip, plunged it into the guacamole, and ate
the whole thing in one ravenous bite.

Her aggression caught me off guard, and I coughed to
cover my delighted laugh. She chewed vigorously like she
needed fuel in her body before she responded to my last
question. Maybe she did.

That thought served to slice through the amusement
and drive home the severity of what we were talking about.
She held up a finger, and as she chewed, she scooped
another serving and ate it immediately after swallowing the
first.

It shouldn't have been charming. It really shouldn't
have. But something about the way she was attacking the
food and not holding back made me antsy in the best way.
My leg bounced with energy under the table, and I took my
own serving of the delicious appetizer and relaxed as I ate.
What a change from our failed date at Basta.

That night, I'd been on edge the minute I'd realized
she'd been on edge. And unlike the dinner with my parents,
I'd done nothing to defuse the situation. As much as that
charge between us burned hot—not the physical one that
made me almost ache to touch her, but the other one that
made us butt heads—I understood. She was facing down an
abuser, and from the little I'd gleaned, possibly emotionally
abusive parents as well. That was no small feat, even if she'd
worked through a lot of those feelings. That was part of why
I hated when I didn't keep my cool. Tonight, that wasn't the

case. I wasn't waiting for her to snip at me—if she did, we'd figure it out.

But more than anything, it was her. That chomping, crunching sound and the way she took a long drink of her margarita before she spoke. The way the air between us crackled when we held eye contact.

And now, the way she patted her lips with her napkin, drawing my attention there, before she took another quick sip.

A minute later, Dahlia was ready to talk.

"So, uh, I don't know if I'm exactly worried about him hurting me or if I just need to know I've done what I could. I used to think I was crazy for worrying about it, but then… then he did."

My gut clenched and I swallowed the sip of margarita I'd taken like it contained rocks—and not the kind made of ice. "I'm sorry."

She shook that off. "Not your fault. Not anyone's but his, in the end. But as the wedding approaches, I like the idea of being ready. And it feels good to be in a room full of other people taking that same challenge. Plus Bruce and Tristan are great teachers."

"I'm sure they are. I have no idea how often they needed those skills during their active duty time or with what they do now, but I'm sure you couldn't find anyone more qualified." If a thin wisp of jealousy slipped through me at the thought of her spending even more time with Bruce, I ignored it.

I had no claim on her or her time. Fiancé ruse aside, which Bruce probably knew about, wouldn't she be better off with someone who could literally defend her?

"Yeah, that's true. They're also patient, which I liked.

And I hadn't really gotten to know Tristan much, but he seems nice, if a little quiet."

She chomped another chip, so I did the same. After a pause, she continued. "So Devon and I got together years ago and at first, things were fine. He was a little... different than what I'd expected based on what I'd seen in public. We're from a fairly small city, and his family is well-known. My sister had always had a crush on his best friend, and he was a little old for her at the time, but my parents always had an interest in me and Devon getting together."

When I narrowed my eyes at that, she explained. "My parents are, at their roots, social climbers. My mom came from a really poor family and married well. My dad did well in his business, but they've always wanted more. And I guess they saw Devon's prestigious family as a connection they wanted. My younger sister wasn't an option, and Rose has always been completely head over feet for Conrad, so..." She shrugged a shoulder, took a sip of her drink, then smoothed her napkin down in her lap.

"Sounds like a lot of pressure on you," I said, not wanting to seem like I knew what any of this felt like but certain staying silent wasn't really the right thing.

"None of that really matters because if he'd been a decent guy, it wouldn't have been so bad. We would've gone our separate ways. But he started isolating me, gaslighting me, making me second-guess everything. One of his first little tricks was to make me feel like I was late by being on time instead of early. It sounds really dumb, but it didn't matter what I did, he wouldn't let me forget I was one minute late, or right on time when he'd supposedly asked me to be early."

I didn't know the man, but now I knew enough. I had all the information I needed to know I needed to have a talk with Bruce and Wilder and whoever else over at Saint security and let them know this man would be in town and we'd need their help. Maybe we could work something out—I could give them event space in trade for paying for security or something. Based on their clientele, they couldn't be cheap. But maybe....

"You okay?"

Her gentle question cut through the rampage of thoughts in my head. "Yes. I'm sorry. I should've said something. I was mostly thinking I don't know if it's a good idea for you to be around this guy at all."

She laughed a mirthless, forced sound. "Yeah. Well. No choice there unless I want to ruin my sister's wedding. But I won't be totally alone with him, right? I'll have you?"

The gravity of that statement, of even her smallest show of faith in me, wrapped around my heart and squeezed. When I spoke, it came out gruff with feeling. "Yes, Dahlia. You have me."

CHAPTER SEVENTEEN

Dahlia

The way he said those words felt heavy with meaning. I didn't like that I needed him, but I did, and though we'd nagged at each other and fought like juveniles instead of adults, I didn't doubt that I could trust him to do this for me.

He'd proven himself already—from the very beginning. And even though we were barely friends, just now budding into that new phase, I believed he wanted to help me. I was relieved he wanted to help me and had shown I could trust his word. At this point, I didn't have to keep relying on the fact that Aidan knew he was a good man, or Quinn did, or anyone else. I knew it for myself.

And it scared me and made me feel an odd sense of anticipation at the same time.

Good grief, that's confusing.

"Thank you," I said, then sighed for what felt like the

tenth time tonight. "Let's change the subject. You've heard my tale of woe. Now let's talk about you."

He coughed out a laugh, then picked up his drink and held it out to me. I took mine and touched the edge to it, then we both took long slugs of the tangy liquid. I hadn't planned on having a drink tonight, but it was Saturday, I'd had a good day, and though I wouldn't have chosen dinner with John, and certainly wouldn't have wanted to be talking about Devon, I was kind of enjoying myself. *Odd.*

"So. What my mom and dad hinted at the other night."

Ah. Yes. I hadn't thought about that nearly as much as I had his most perfect words, but I hadn't forgotten his mom's comment. "That you were engaged before?"

He tipped his head to one side, then straightened. "*Almost* engaged. I told everyone I knew how I was going to propose, a big public thing, and then she broke up with me right before."

I winced.

He widened his eyes. "Yeah. It was great. And then, she told me I was—well, never mind that. The point is, I guess they bought that I would be a little less out there with the whole dating and engagement thing thanks to that miserable failure so, cheers." He held up his margarita again, then took another long drink.

As though that wasn't absolute catnip, silly man. "Oh, come on. Don't shy away from the sad details. I just told you mine, now you tell me yours."

He eyed me, those hazel eyes indecipherable for a moment before a breathy, embarrassed chuckle slipped out. "Fine. Your opinion of me has already been formed, so I supposed there's no real shame in telling you what hers was."

The flush to his cheeks hinted at his embarrassment,

and my stomach flipped. What an odd moment to hit me like this, but his willingness to be vulnerable stabbed me right in the heart. *Goodness,* I liked this side of him.

"She said she couldn't stand the thought of a life with me because it'd be like being married to a cardboard box."

My eyes widened in shock. *Wow.* "That's... incredibly cruel."

"Oh, it got better. She said she was embarrassed of me—that I'd washed up as a lawyer and my little brewery was going to fail and she didn't want to be around to watch it happen. She said I was—" He cleared his throat, then continued, that blush deepening. "I was too soft, too *nice.*"

My mouth had dropped open, and every mean thing I'd ever said to him flashed through my mind. It'd all been circumstantial or silly, like calling him a bridge troll, but I regretted every word.

John was a nice guy. Aside from his consistent bickering with me, I wasn't sure I'd ever seen him disagree with *anyone* unless he was lightly harassing his nieces or Aidan's son as a joke. If John were a romance hero, especially now that I knew him, he'd be the nice guy. And wasn't this the classic *nice guys finish last* version of a story? A woman thinks he's *too* nice?

Maybe she'd never been ill-treated. I hoped not, for her sake, even if she was an idiot for being so horrible to John. If she'd never been treated poorly, she wouldn't realize what an utterly beautiful thing it was to have a man who was genuinely kind—not *soft*, but gentle, even, at times.

I could hardly stomach someone telling him off that way —and wasn't that ironic? Not that I would've celebrated actual cruelty against the man in the past, but only a few weeks of knowing him just a bit better and I could see he didn't deserve it.

"Wait, I thought you quit law to open your business—how is that washing up? Does she know how successful Silver Ridge Brewing is? Has she ever apologized?" *Is she crazy?!*

I didn't go that far, but those criticisms, at least the ones about his work, seemed entirely invalid unless she was simply determined to be unimpressed by him. The man was a lawyer, and from what I'd heard, a very good one, until he quit to pursue his passion. He still did small things, mostly pro bono, for people in the community, because he was just that good of a guy. Again, he was actually that nice, that good.

He laughed genuinely this time. "Oh, definitely not. She wasn't from here, and I think she was sick of it. She'd met someone through work who lived in Denver or somewhere else and wanted a city life. I never have. I actually heard she was engaged the day I met you." He swallowed thickly, like that held significance.

Ironic that we'd both had terrible days and that our first interaction had set an irrevocable tone. Or so I'd once thought. So much had changed.

But here we were, sharing our biggest hurts over margaritas and guacamole. "I had a pretty awful day that day, too. And..." *Ugh,* I didn't want to apologize for it, but I needed to. "I'm sorry I snapped at you."

He didn't seem to need me to explain and shook his head as though anything else proved unnecessary. I took the pass, though now that we'd broached the subject of that first meeting, at some point, I'd need to explain myself—knowing what he'd faced that day, I needed him to understand my rude, out-of-nowhere rejection of him hadn't been because of him but because of me.

Brodie brought our plates piled with food, and we dug

in. As I ate, the light, floaty feeling of downing almost an entire margarita on an empty stomach shook loose words I wouldn't have asked otherwise.

"What did she mean by 'soft'?"

He cleared his throat, his brow furrowing as he chewed before replying. "I think she meant it in a few ways. At the time, I was probably twenty pounds overweight from being sedentary and stressed, and in retrospect, probably depressed, too. And I think she also wanted someone who was more of an alpha-type personality. Someone who'd get jealous or possessive or just be a jerk to her sometimes. I'm not sure I can explain it, but based on the guy she ended up with, I think that's some of what she meant, too."

My mind whirled. It didn't surprise me that John wouldn't describe himself as an alpha male, but he had a backbone. Or he sure did with me, and I'd seen him in a few instances at the chamber or other places where he'd held his ground. And who broke up with someone because they weren't *physically* hard enough, like muscular enough? Talk about superficial!

Wouldn't be a complaint now.

The words whispered through my mind as my eyes surveyed his shoulders, the planes of his pecs where his shirt rested below his clavicle, and the way the cuff of his polo framed the curve of his well-developed bicep. *Whoa, now.*

"I—that's awful, John. I'm really sorry that happened. And I'm sure you've heard this a hundred times, but it sounds like you're way better off without her." I hoped he could see that. It'd been years, but I knew how wounds from the past could hang around, aching when we least expected it.

He smiled and picked up his fork, spearing some of the

fajita chicken. "I know I am. And after it all shook out, the broken heart healed and I learned a lot."

"What'd you learn?"

His smile kicked up on one side as he chewed, swallowed, then spoke. "Women suck?"

I gasped and threw a balled-up napkin at him, but laughter tumbled out of me.

He tossed it back as he chuckled, shaking his head. "Fine. I think I learned to be cautious. To put my energy toward things that matter. And I also learned I will never, ever get married without a prenup."

My brow raised. "Really? She taught you that, not your law degree and a decade working in family law?"

He rolled his eyes, but a reluctant chuckle escaped. "Fine, maybe it was that. And not so much that I expect a marriage to fail, but... well, it simplifies things. Protects everyone." He paused as though filling in a blank I couldn't hear, then continued. "And in the last five years, I may not've had any big romances, but I think my life has been pretty good."

His eyes flicked around the room like maybe admitting that had been more personal than he'd meant to be, but I rushed to reassure him. "I can only judge from what little I've seen, but based on all the evidence, it seems like you're doing just fine."

The shy smile that pulled at his lips sent restlessness through me, so I shoveled a giant bite of enchilada into my mouth to keep from saying something insane like, *you know, you really are stupidly handsome, too.*

Honestly, it was a wonder he hadn't found someone else. Based on this conversation, I'd guess it was primarily founded in his not wanting to. He'd been burned and had then focused on his family. He'd kept himself from that risk, and I certainly related to that.

"I appreciate your encouragement." He poked at his food for a minute before adding, "And I appreciate you coming to dinner."

I finished my bite and nodded. "Thanks for asking me. I know I dragged you into this and it's kind of blown up into more of a thing than I imagined—"

"That wasn't your fault, remember?"

"Fair enough. But still. I'm going to work on not being so reactive to you. And..." A wave of nervousness washed over me out of nowhere. I'd been completely comfortable, but what I wanted to say—what I *needed* to, had my heart fluttering. "I think we should do it again."

His gaze hooked into mine, and the moment stretched, each beat of my heart lengthening the rope of tension tying us together in this little red booth. I meant the words to mean we should get together again to keep up the appearance of being together. But yes, oddly, some part of me meant it as just... us. Together. Because tonight had been hard at first, but the more I relaxed, the more fun I was having.

The realization hit like a bolt of lightning to a rod. *John is my friend. I* like *him.* It shouldn't have been such a revelation, maybe, but it felt monumental and yet like the most natural thing in the world.

Like maybe, this is what it always would've been like if I hadn't come at him with all the baggage I'd hauled from Colorado to Silverton weighing me down and a chip on my shoulder against handsome men to boot.

"I agree. We should. We have a lot of details to work out."

I nodded, only slightly disappointed he'd kept things

focused on our arrangement. "We do. We only have another few weeks before they descend." I widened my eyes in a dramatic show to match the intonation I'd given that last word.

He grinned. "Now that we've gotten through some of the harder conversations, I think we're on the same team."

I'd had the thought before, and yet I couldn't ignore the swirl of nonsensical feelings that statement gave me—hope, relief, anticipation...

My heart and mind were still untangling the sensation, so I simply said, "Yes. Glad to be on the same team."

CHAPTER EIGHTEEN

John

It was Brodie's fault, really.

Our well-meaning waiter had simply refilled our margaritas. And since Dahlia and I had mutually signed our peace accords via sharing some of our worst moments and being empathetic, we either hadn't noticed, or hadn't cared, or maybe, we'd just been having too much fun.

That had to be the reason I placed my hand on her back as we left the restaurant, enjoying the fact that for once since we started this, she wasn't wearing her full-body puff coat. It must've been why, instead of staying there, that rogue arm found its way around her waist and before I knew it, we were walking with matching strides across Main Street and around the corner.

And it absolutely had to account for why, when we reached Bloom and she turned to me with those eyes and those lips and that face, I had the impulse to lean in and kiss her. *Taste* her.

Where had that come from? Yes, I'd admired her soft, dark hair and her lush lips and those eyes that kind of gutted me even though I hated to admit it, but I'd never truly *wanted* her. That idea had to be courtesy of Brodie and his margarita madness.

I didn't, of course. That would've been utter insanity, and I did still retain some measure of impulse control. Instead, I focused on the grounding bite of the spring evening air and the newfound happiness that Dahlia Price was actually my friend.

"So. We need to meet and talk about... stuff, right?" I asked, because eloquence was my middle name. *Actually, I should maybe make sure she knows my middle name, and I need to know hers.*

She toed the line of the woven welcome mat that sat at the threshold of her shop's door. Oddly, she'd steered us here instead of the door to the building, though I knew she could access the apartment stairwell easily enough.

"Yes. I'll come up with a lightning-round approach or something. We'll go through all the things my parents would expect you to know, and you can do the same for me. Maybe next Saturday afternoon?"

"Sounds good. Let me know when and where, and I'm there." I hesitated to leave, wanting to spend another minute with her. Wanting to touch her in a way that wouldn't be creepy, but just to have a moment of connection.

That was all the margs talking, too, of course. Never mind the little buzz I'd caught had worn off once I'd finished my meal...

"Okay. Yeah." She held the strap of her purse like I'd seen her do a hundred times before, but then she moved.

Stepping closer, she extended a hand. "So, um, yeah. Here's to a beautiful friendship."

And then it happened.

My heart flipped at her small, embarrassed smile, but I didn't hesitate to accept her hand. Our palms pressed together, and it might as well have been our first contact. Not that we'd touched all that often before, but this felt markedly different. More than the first reluctant handshake or the second when we'd taken a step forward but hadn't exactly been ready to form a team.

Maybe because it wasn't forced, or because she'd initiated it and wasn't currently under duress. Maybe because we'd formed a small bond tonight, and that had changed things. Possibly, it came from the nature of our *skin* touching—an intimate affair, especially considering sometimes strangers did this. But the touch of her hand in mine, the tips of her fingers curling around the heel of my palm, felt anything but strange or repellent.

Not to be dramatic, but it sent my thoughts scattering. I'd felt a little something the last time we'd shaken hands, been caught up in her gaze and nerves before seeing my folks, but this?

My eyes jumped from the picture of our palms pressed together, our hands shaking slowly, to her eyes, which were studying me. The second our gazes met, she dropped my hand and stepped back.

"Okay, so, see you Saturday?"

Clearing my throat, I nodded. "Yep. See you soon."

And then, I walked back to my car, fully aware of just how much trouble I was in.

Six days after our impromptu dinner, I couldn't stop thinking about Dahlia. This shouldn't have come as a surprise considering the ticking clock counting down to the wedding and more pretending to be engaged, but the brewery had a lot going on, and soon, we'd be interviewing chefs now that our licensing and everything we needed from the county had come through for the pub portion.

Life was about to get even busier while Liam and I picked up the slack during the hiring phase and prepared for opening in early summer, but all of that would be after the wedding.

The wedding that was in two weeks, and her family's arrival in just over one. *Next* weekend. I didn't know exactly how much interaction I'd have with them prior to the big day, but I figured I should be ready for anything. Knowing that Devon had hurt her and I was essentially her best shot at staying away from him, I'd cleared my schedule just in case. She needed me to pop over for a lunch date or be seen helping with flower arrangements? Done.

So, in truth, I wasn't just thinking about Dahlia like a concerned friend. I was thinking about her in all kinds of ways I never had before, and it was all thanks to that stupid handshake and her dark eyes and, well, might as well blame Brodie one last time, right?

"Are you still doing that? Where's your head?" Liam chuckled and gave me a look like he thought I'd lost it.

Maybe I had. I'd been standing here counting packs of coasters—a job that should've taken about five minutes—for this side of fifteen. My mind? Not on the numbers, that's for sure.

On a dark-haired woman I probably shouldn't be thinking about.

"Just distracted, man."

"Have anything to do with that fake fiancée of yours?" he asked, sliding onto a bar stool across from where I stood behind the counter.

"That transparent?" I asked, not looking up.

"Nah. I guessed."

I snorted and he snickered.

"Fine. Yes. You're obvious. You're distracted all the time right now. And for an engaged man, you seem startlingly deprived of affection, can I just say."

Flaring my eyes at him, I tossed the last pack of coasters into a box and slid it under the bar. "Since she's my *fake* fiancée, that's not really part of the deal."

"Considering you like her and she likes you, I don't see why it shouldn't be. But I know you're not about to suggest it, and my guess is she's preoccupied with the whole... ex and family stuff."

This guy. A few days ago, I might've balked at the claim that I liked her, but crap. I couldn't deny it after spending the last few days thinking about all the ways I'd like to kiss her. *Busted.*

And with Liam, I could be honest. Same with Aidan, but unless one of us showed up at the other's house or he came by the brewery, I hardly saw him. Between navigating life with Maddie and the sharp increase in demand for him as a landscape architect over the last year plus the natural uptick in his schedule over the spring and summer, I didn't have as much time with him. Bummer for sure, but I knew he'd be here whenever I needed him, just like Liam. And thankfully, Liam was here and not scared by these shenanigans I'd gotten myself into.

Once I'd admitted it to myself, it wasn't quite so awful saying it out loud. "Correct. I'm not about to say, 'Hey, Dahlia, I know we hated each other until like ten seconds ago, but any chance you wanna make out?'"

He cracked up, and I didn't stifle my smile. It felt good to poke a little fun at the situation instead of living with this tightness in my chest. It wasn't just worry over how things would go or anticipation for when I'd see her again. Truth was, I liked her. I'd resisted as long as possible, but now that we'd busted through the tendency to snap at each other and cast mild insults, now that she knew me a little and I knew more about her, I freaking *like liked* her, as my second cousin slash sort of nephew Luca would say.

That wasn't a surprise. I'd thought she was the most beautiful woman I'd ever seen the day she walked into that first chamber of commerce meeting. And no, I wouldn't have hit on her *right then*, but I probably would've tried to find out if she was single and feel out if she was interested. Again, not that day, because I'd just had my heart smashed again by my own ex, but her quick rejection of me had stung.

Obviously, it had, or I wouldn't have continued to rise to her provocations and provoke her right back. But like she'd mentioned, she'd come at that moment from a really hard place, and knowing even a little bit about what she'd been through, what she'd left behind, I couldn't blame her.

I couldn't blame her *now*. But for a long time, I sure had. Those sharp words, that look of disgust, had sent me into a defensive posture I wasn't proud of. I'd let my past with Tina and that first impression lead me to believe she was poison in a book-loving dress.

Sure, I wished it hadn't gone that way—that she hadn't lumped all men in the big bad wolf category like her abusive ex, but again, now that I understood a bit more, I couldn't blame her. It would've been neat if I hadn't been feeling particularly sensitive and small at the time, too. I might've laughed it off or even called her on such a bold, rude statement. Instead, it had hit an unseen target.

All the things that came after had been so petty and stupid. I'd maintained a kind of righteous indignance at the whole thing, telling myself it only went that way because she started it. And it had proved easier to focus on the dislike, the irritation for her being so unreasonably rude to me, and to keep that going than to risk drowning in the reality that this beautiful newcomer had seen something unworthy in me before she even knew me.

So. Yeah. I was literally a seven-year-old mentally yelling *she started it!* as I continually acted a fool in front of her.

Until now.

Really, until a couple months ago when she'd pulled me off the street and into her life. But here I was, and I had no desire to leave, even if that made me a little stupid. Even if I saw the end—the anniversary party for my folks—and knew I was barreling toward bigger, more brutal feelings by the time we got there. But there would be an end, and I could focus on that. I'd help her, do my best to keep her safe and make her feel good in the face of so much bad history, and then we'd... be done.

CHAPTER NINETEEN

Dahlia

Quinn's leg bounced up and down while she sipped a margarita. Julian was traveling, so we'd all descended on her home slash palace.

"Dang, woman, what's got you so antsy?" Maddie asked, eyeing Quinn's rampant restless energy.

"First, Cara's on a date and I'm... not handling it well, and second, I want Dahlia to voluntarily update us about her fake fiancé instead of us having to pull it out of her." She took another sip.

Sarah giggled and she and Sadie toasted their drinks—a cranberry lime mocktail for both since Sarah was pregnant and Sadie didn't like to mix alcohol with her anxiety meds—then turned their attention toward me.

Calla piped up next. "Why are you so nervous about Cara's date? She's super responsible."

Quinn sighed. "She is. But she is also out on a date with a teenaged boy, whom I do not trust."

"This one particularly or just the general population?" Sarah asked with a grin.

"The whole lot, obviously. Plus, she's beautiful and smart and amazing, so boys are going to want to get close to her, and I won't be there to karate chop them back behind their boundaries." She swiped at the air dramatically.

We all laughed, and my heart squeezed. She was such a good mom. It did me good to see someone like her parenting someone so special as Cara—it reminded me that I could be a mom and do things differently than my parents had done with me.

"What does Julian say?" Sadie asked.

Quinn's crusty expression softened into a private smile. "When she mentioned she'd said yes to going with this kid to the dance a few months ago, he said something like, 'This Billy Crandall kid is lucky.'" She snickered. "When she told us they were going out this weekend, he said something like, 'Be smart,' and then before he left on his trip yesterday morning, he slipped me an envelope."

"Oh, goodness. What was in it?" Calla was already grinning.

Quinn laughed and her smile could've lit an entire city grid. "It was the creepiest list of information I've ever seen and probably shouldn't admit to possessing. Like, full-on background check, the kid's transcripts, his after-school activities, medications list... *way* too much information about this poor child."

My mouth dropped open, and Sadie covered hers in shock. Calla shook her head and chuckled. Sarah's eyes were wide as margarita glasses. "Who got him that? It wasn't Saint Security, was it? I didn't see any requests for that kind of thing, but I don't think we'd—"

"No, no, sweet baby mama, your guys are all above board. I texted Julian to ask him exactly that, and he said it came from... other sources." She flashed her brows like this was salacious.

"Is Julian secretly a spy?" Calla wondered.

"You know, I could see it," I said. "He'd have access to a lot of people and places. But I feel like Quinn would know, and she's not a great secret keeper, so he wouldn't have married her for the liability."

Everyone looked at me, and Quinn burst out laughing. "I mean, she's not wrong."

"Sorry. This imagination gets away from me sometimes." I shrugged.

"But that brings us to you, friend." Quinn raised her brow and then her glass in an air toast.

Tiny bubbles of anticipation and almost giddiness burst in my belly. I'd been running laps around the last few interactions we'd had, especially that last one, and I wanted to talk about it, even if it went against my typical MO.

"Oh, sure. The gist is that I'm good. John and I had dinner last weekend, and we're on the same page about stuff. We cleared the air a little." Which was kind of astounding when I sat back and gave myself space to think about it. "And we're friends now."

"Friends?" Sarah asked.

I nodded, all decisive clarity and none of that murky mess of feeling that had actually taken up residence in my mind. "Yes. We even shook on it."

My stomach flipped thinking of the contact. I'd felt floaty and happy and borderline infatuated by the time we left Guac, and once we reached my building, I'd gotten nervous he might try to kiss me. Or maybe the nerves had to do with how much I *wanted* him to kiss me and, in truth, I had no idea if he'd want that. Plus, those thoughts were so out of the blue, but he was honestly kind of adorable and I'd had so much *fun*.

I'd led him to the shop door to keep it... more focused on the arrangement and the new friendship. That had been worth celebrating in itself, truly, and all those other floaty feelings could be chalked up to a margarita on an empty stomach while sitting across from a man too handsome for my own good.

"Yeah, seems like all that going on over there is about friendship." Quinn's quip made everyone chuckle.

"So you're still fake engaged, but you kind of like him?" Maddie asked, eyeing me like she might figure it all out by looking closely enough.

A thrill raced through me. "Uh, well. Honestly? Yes."

Sadie and Calla grinned while Sarah clapped. Quinn chuckled like this pleased her, and Maddie just smiled at me. I shook my head, trying to ignore the fizz that'd entered my blood stream now that we'd shifted from talking about Devon to John.

"I'm just getting to know him. We've technically known each other for years, but we're meeting tomorrow to do a twenty-questions type of thing so that we know all those basic details and no one at the wedding will suspect."

"Um, wait. Are you trying to pretend you didn't just admit to liking him?" Calla asked.

I huffed. "No. But I'm not about to take advantage of this situation. He's helping me and he'd do it for anyone. I didn't want to ask him and kind of hated that it was him at first, but I know he's a good man, and I'm not going to push him to see me as something more when we only just started accepting one another's humanity."

Quinn smirked. "I don't think you'd be pushing him."

My mouth opened but no words came out. *What did that mean?*

Maddie jumped in before I could figure it out.

"I like that you're teaming up with him. Everything I know of John tells me he's the man for this job and he'll handle it. I'm worried for you guys and his family, but they'll deal with it. And in the meantime, you have all of us, plus John and Aidan. Your ex isn't going to have a chance to isolate you, let alone think he can try to get back together with you."

I sighed, long and slow, willing her words to be true. "I sure hope so."

CHAPTER TWENTY

John

Dahlia had changed our dinner slash meeting slash figure out who the other person is brainstorm tête-à-tête to my house. We'd planned on hers—she'd offered, and then about three hours ago, she'd asked if we could meet here, at my place, and she'd bumped the time a half hour.

A very small part of me wondered if she'd bail on me and didn't want to have to answer the door when I showed up and outright turn me away. But right on adjusted time, she rang the bell.

I glanced around the living room, wishing I'd thought to pick up flowers or something to make it a little more feminine and warm, and then realizing how stupid that was considering Dahlia was a professional florist and the only place I'd buy flowers would either be her shop or the grocery store, and both seemed wrong.

"Hey, sorry I had to change the plan. I had a leak in my

sink that actually spilled out into the kitchen and, long story short, they turned off my water for a few hours. They got it back on, but I wasn't sure if they would, so I wanted to be sure." She bustled through the door without stopping, heading right for the counter with the bags I should've taken.

She looked really good. A little flustered but really, *really* good. Her cheeks were flushed from exertion, hair curling around her temples and pulled back from her face up top but falling around her shoulders in the back.

"I'm glad they got it back up and running. Have you always lived there?" I asked, watching as she unloaded the takeout. She'd insisted on picking it up since I lived a few minutes outside of downtown and she'd be coming from downtown, though if I'd known what she'd been dealing with today, I would've simply cooked.

"Yeah, I lucked out when I rented the shop—the previous tenant had been gone for a few months and they were more than happy to let me move in. It's old and has its issues, but I love being right downtown and so close to the shop." She unloaded takeout containers and then froze like she'd realized something was wrong.

"What is it?"

Her cheeks brightened with embarrassment. "I didn't mean anything by that, by the way. Your house is..." She looked around, then seemed to register the space and her brows rose. "Really nice. And it's not all that far from downtown."

Was she really apologizing for that remark? We were truly turning over a new leaf if she was attempting to make amends for sharing a basic opinion on her own living situation.

"There's nothing to apologize for. I'm glad you like your place, and I'm not offended you like living downtown."

Her gaze returned to meet mine, and she wore a soft expression. "Seriously, this is really nice, John."

"Thank you. I've only lived here a few years. It's all a little... utilitarian." I took in the gray walls and dark brown couch with cream pillows. It all looked okay together. My mom and sister-in-law had helped me pick some stuff out, and the rest of it had made the move from my last place.

She smoothed her hand across the granite counter where we stood. "The kitchen's great, too. But, hey, can we eat?"

I covered a grin and nodded, reaching for plates and silverware. In another minute, we'd sat down at my small table. Again, nothing special, but I'd slapped some place mats down in my rush to tidy up and make it all seem a little less... boring.

"So what's your Elk Street order?" I asked, eyeing her plate.

She slid the food from the container to her plate. "I get the salmon with roasted cauliflower and salad. I don't know why, but I'm obsessed with that cauliflower."

"Obsessed? That seems like a strong statement for a vegetable." I'd never tried the cauliflower, as it just wasn't something I'd ever choose to eat. Nothing against a good vegetable or anything, though.

She chuckled under her breath and then speared some. "Try it. I promise you, it's better than any bland, butter-soaked version you've tried."

In a move that felt like I'd departed my regular life and entered an alternate universe, I leaned forward and took the bite of food from her fork. With my mouth. So she'd basically fed me.

The spice and flavor of turmeric and cumin hit my tongue, and my brows raised as I chewed. Surprisingly delicious. But the best part was her face, which was absolutely beaming. It had to be the most genuine smile she'd ever directed toward me.

"If I'd known eating cauliflower would make you smile like that, I would've done it a long time ago," I said, the unearthly sensation of the evening heightening with my comment.

Her cheeks pinked again. "Well, I'm right, aren't I?"

I nodded. "Yes. Never would've guessed it, but that's some amazing cauliflower. It'd go well with an IPA."

Her eyes crinkled as she chewed a bite, and it was stupidly charming.

"Do you always think like that? What beers would pair with food?" she asked after she'd finished swallowing.

I nodded. "Yeah. Hazard of the trade, I guess. I'm in charge of hiring the chef for our pub, and I've been reading up on beer and food tastings basically since we started. I'm no expert, but I'm trying to have a little basic knowledge."

"That's smart. Plus, you're pretty passionate about beer, so it makes sense you'd want to know more about that aspect of it."

That comment spread through me like a hot sip of coffee on a cold morning. It wasn't a put-down, but an observation, and it seemed like she liked it. Or, maybe that was a bit much, but it didn't seem like she found my love of beer to be problematic.

"Thanks. Yeah. I'm guessing you're similar with flowers. I feel like between you and Aidan, you probably know everything there is to know about growing things and making them beautiful."

Good. Grief. Why did everything I say sound so oddly

canned? I hadn't realized how nervous I was until just now. This moment, feeling that usual pull toward her—to look at her, talk to her, touch her.

She grinned, the expression hitting me between the ribs before she spoke.

"That might be true. Though I know very little about *growing* flowers. I can teach you how to arrange them or tell you what they mean, but not how to actually make them sprout from the ground. That's all Aidan."

We chuckled, the moment of shared affection for my cousin further warming my chest. Why was it such a pleasure to hear her talk like this? Why did it send my heart skittering?

Maybe because we'd *never* talked like this. Last weekend at dinner, yes, but any other conversation had either been fraught with the *wrong foot* reality of our first meeting or half discussions of our plan to move forward with this whole fake engagement.

And speaking of, I finished my meal, the reality of how much ground we had to cover weighing on me.

"I think we need to get serious or we're in danger of talking all night and never getting around to the nitty gritty." Okay, so maybe *all night* was an exaggeration, but we'd set out to do this last week and had gotten waylaid by our various pasts and confessions therein.

"Good idea," she said as we cleaned up.

A few minutes later, we'd discarded the takeout containers, stuffed the dirtied plates into the dishwasher, and I'd suggested we sit on the couch and sip a beer to get comfortable with each other.

"If you like beer, that is. No problem if not. I have wine, maybe, or gin, but—"

"I like beer, and I'd love one. Thank you." She tucked

her grin away and turned for the couch, and I mentally facepalmed as I grabbed two bottles of the Silver Ridge IPA.

"I should've offered you one with dinner, sorry. Obviously, I don't do a lot of hosting at home."

"No? It's so nice, though. Do you just... go out?" Her gaze swept across the stone fireplace that made up the central focal point of the room.

I handed her a beer, then sat on the opposite end of the couch. "Believe it or not, I'm not all that much of a social butterfly these days. Most of the time, I end up at Aidan's or Mike and Jenny's. Or, yeah, we go out." I didn't want there to be any confusion—I was not out on the town with different women. She had to realize this by now, but if not, I needed her to know it. "No one will be expecting me to take them out, or anything."

"Okay..."

I huffed. "I just mean, I wasn't dating anyone else when all this started. And I gather you weren't either. So as far as that part of the story goes, we should be in the clear."

"Ah. Yeah. Good." She took a swig of the beer, then added, "This is really good."

I wasn't above the wash of pleasure her compliment gave me. No, I didn't personally brew the beer anymore, but it'd started with a handful of basement brews Liam and I had thrown together. Knowing it was damn good beer now never ceased to please me.

"Thanks. So, did you really make a list?"

She pulled out her phone, which made me realize how nice it was that neither of us had been glued to our devices. My ex's tendency to be constantly available to her work and friends and family had meant she had the phone glued to her hand at all times. I'd excused it, certain it meant she was just being a *good* friend, *good* employee, *good* daughter, but what it led to was the two of us sitting in different dimensions while at the same table.

"Are you ready? Let's do this quickly and then anything else we need to discuss can grow out of it." She swiped at her phone, apparently reading the list.

"Sure. Let me have it."

She sipped her beer, then straightened, and a thrill ran through me. It only *just now* occurred to me that this was my chance to finally get to know—*really* get to know—Dahlia Price.

CHAPTER TWENTY-ONE

Dahlia

Excitement fluttered through me, and I launched in. "Favorite color."

"Dark blue."

"Favorite food?"

"Burgers."

"Favorite place?"

"Uh, this spot on the Sego Lily trail, or my back yard."

Interest piqued, I raised my brows.

"You want to see it? I may or may not have had some landscaping help from this guy I know."

The little half-smile he wore had me biting my lip and staunchly ignoring what was happening in my belly. The flips and drops and fluttering had to stop. "I'd love to. But show me when we're done here or we'll never get through this list."

He nodded his assent, and I continued. "Favorite thing about your job?"

His brow furrowed for a second. "Working with Liam, and providing something that makes people happy."

The more I knew about John, the more I liked him. For the hundredth time in the last few weeks, I wondered what it would've been like if I hadn't started a fight the first time I laid eyes on him. We had so much in common.

"Favorite part of your job?" he asked, the softness in his tone betraying just how sensitive to me he was.

He couldn't possibly know what I'd been thinking, but he could tell something heavier than my twenty questions had tumbled into my thoughts. "You stole my answer."

"You work with Liam, too?"

The wink he gave me disarmed me completely, though I wouldn't have snapped at him for that. But in the past, with an adjustment of tone or posture, it would've been right in line with all our nonsense.

"I'm sure he's great, but no. I actually like working solo a lot, though I am forever thankful for my team. But what you said about liking that you make something that makes people happy—that. I *love* that."

He nodded, totally getting it, and my heart flipped. Being in a service industry, making a product... it was prevalent enough around here, but I'd never dated someone who could relate. Not that I was actually dating John, but having him understand that entrepreneurial side of things felt honestly kind of awesome.

Devon had been in real-estate, and I'd always thought that since he dealt with consumers and had a customer service element to his work, he'd get it. But he definitely hadn't. His drive was to make money and build his reputation and clout.

While there's nothing inherently wrong with having goals to go into politics, or even to make a lot of money, there'd been a patent disregard for those same people he'd be relying on to vote for him when the time came that never made sense to me.

Though in retrospect, I shouldn't have been surprised. Everything about Devon had been for show.

"And wait, what's your favorite color and food and place?" John asked, mercifully derailing my thoughts of my ex.

"Oh, right. Uh, I love the bright green of a daisy stem or the sort of sagey green of eucalyptus leaves."

He smiled. It wouldn't have been something to note, except it sent my stomach tumbling, the way it flashed across his face as though he liked my answer. Like something about my answer genuinely made him happy.

What a weird thought. No idea why, but it felt so clearly like he enjoyed my answer, and it left me a little flustered. "And uh, you already know I love baked goods of all kinds. If I had to name a favorite, I'd say cinnamon rolls in winter and donuts in the summer."

His smile widened and my heart thumped. *What is this man doing to me?*

"And place?"

"Ah, that's easy. My worktable. Or the front doorstep of my shop."

His head tilted to one side. "Why those places?"

My answer wasn't poetic, but I wanted him to know. "The doorstep's where all the possibilities are. Before someone steps inside, there's a moment when they don't know what it looks like or what I can do for them. And if you stand on my doorstep and look east, Silver Ridge Peak is..." I shook my head, finding the towering heights of the mountains surrounding our little town impossible to verbalize.

"That is a good spot," he said, another soft look on his face.

"Are you thinking I'm a weirdo for liking my front step?" I asked, feeling the odd combination of slightly embarrassed and mildly defiant.

The shake of his head came immediately. "Not at all. I'm thinking I've been right about you all along."

I straightened. "Really."

It wasn't a question—more of a statement of disbelief. I'd thought we'd gotten past all those first impressions and bad feelings. What about my answer to "What's your favorite place?" had made him go back to all of that?

"Yes. Like I said at my parents' house, you're a romantic. I've always thought it, and now you've confirmed it."

"Because I read romance novels?"

He chuckled but shook his head again. "No. I mean, sure, that's probably something that contributes, and I'm guessing it's up there in the 'What's your favorite hobby?' category, but it's the way you think about things."

"Do tell." My defenses were rising, so accustomed as they were to shooting up to protect me.

"You see the possibility in things. Yes, you're a savvy businesswoman, and from what I can tell, you're an excellent florist. But at your heart, I think the thing that drives you is that romantic side. You like the flowers because they're a key that unlocks possibilities for a moment, a memory, and I think that's..."

For some reason, everything in me had frozen, his words —whatever he said next—an essential truth I needed before any more thoughts could complete their journey through my synapses.

"What? What is it?"

"Amazing. Miraculous, even."

Throat thick, I swallowed and cleared away the emotion that'd tightened there. I'd lost that little romantic heart for a while there, and maybe that was part of why all of this with Devon resurfacing had me so upset. I'd thought I'd made so much progress away from that place, that I'd rediscovered myself and that wildly hopeful heart again. The idea that I was miraculously hopeful felt like a conviction and a blessing all in one.

"That's... a nice thought."

"I wasn't trying to be nice, but sure." He frowned but seemed to shake off whatever had caused that. "So the wedding's in two weeks, but your family arrives next weekend?"

"Uh. Yeah. And I should probably tell you, or, ask, um, because they're, uh, planning on a little thing early in the week I'll have to attend." *Wow.* Why had nerves just hit me like a delivery van?

"Do you need me to come? I have a pretty light schedule, so I can—"

"No, no, I don't want you to upend your life for this."

He gave me a look I couldn't quite decipher. "We're already this far in, Dahlia. It's okay to ask me for what you need."

I sighed, a rotten, twisted feeling weighing in my belly. Reality was, I didn't know what I needed from him, but I was beginning to think it was a lot more than I'd initially led on. And maybe more alarming than that was that I'd started feeling glad I had the excuse to ask.

CHAPTER TWENTY-TWO

John

I hadn't expected to feel so angry with Dahlia's family the first time we met, but as luck would have it, they came to me before I had much of a chance to prepare myself. She'd texted a few short bursts about five minutes before she walked into my office, her mother and oldest sister close behind.

"So, this is my... John." She smiled, but her eyes screamed panic as she walked toward me.

Shooting to my feet, I leaned in and accepted her kiss on my cheek, doing my best to show her this was fine—we'd be fine. The two women behind her both had dark hair and were clearly Dahlia's family based on their shared features, but their designer handbags and thousand-dollar sunglasses contributed to a much different vibe.

"Such a pleasure to finally meet you both, Mrs. Price. Rose." I held out a hand to them and her mother glanced at it, then tucked her hands closer into her chest as they clutched her small purse. Rose smiled and batted her lashes but didn't reach for my hand either.

O-kay.

Letting my hand drop, I turned toward Dahlia. "This is a fun surprise. I thought you all were arriving tomorrow?"

"Tomorrow? No, we'd always planned on today so we could acclimate. Azalea is arriving Sunday afternoon. We're going to the spa Monday through Wednesday, and we were expecting everyone to join us, but I take it you weren't planning on that?" Mrs. Price addressed Dahlia with the question.

"Uh, I'm not sure. I thought the spa was tomorrow and Sunday?"

The tenor of Dahlia's voice was off—nothing I'd heard before. It sounded small and stifled, and I instantly hated it.

"Why would you think that? We've always planned to go to the spa Monday through Wednesday. It's like you don't even attempt to pay attention to the emails I send you." She paired this with a shake of her perfectly coiffed head and flicked her hand out to glance at her watch. "On that note, we should go get settled at the resort. You probably want to get dressed for dinner."

I exhaled slowly, biting my tongue. It would not help Dahlia for me to lash out at her mother, but good *grief*, I wanted to. Who spoke to their daughter like that, especially in front of someone they hardly knew?

"Dinner?" Dahlia asked.

Her mother huffed. "Don't tell me you've forgotten. Half our friends are arriving early this weekend, too. Your aunts, the McNairs, the Dodges."

She tossed these names out like they should impress me and remind Dahlia. I wondered whether she knew who

Dahlia's friends were—something told me no, or they'd be working much harder to be on their daughter's good side and weasel their way into Julian Grenier and Maddie Reynolds' good graces.

Dahlia's hand curled into a ball, and she shoved it into the pocket of her jeans. "Uh, I wasn't aware of dinner tonight. I—we made other plans."

Her mother's lips thinned into a displeased line. I jumped in, the impulse to shield Dahlia no longer something I could stop. "Yes, my fault. My family has an important event this week and since Dahlia will be so focused on the wedding, she was kind enough to give us tonight so we could celebrate it together before your festivities begin. And, I apologize, I meant to say congratulations earlier. The Silver Ridge Resort is a beautiful venue."

Rose's cheeks pinked, but it was the mother who spoke again. "Of course it is. And Rose will make a gorgeous bride. Will the flowers be ready?"

Dahlia nodded—up, down, but didn't say a word.

This was all so far from right. Dahlia was fiery and spirited. She held her own. Though maybe she'd only been that way here. She'd come out of an abusive relationship, but clearly, the family dynamics were problematic, too, if this was a typical exchange for them.

"Fine, fine. Well, we're off. We'll expect to see you Monday, I guess, if you can manage to clear your schedule for your oldest sister's wedding," she said, looking what I could only call disgusted as she glanced around my office.

I scowled at her back, then watched them go. Liam walked in and they backed away from him like he was Bigfoot himself and not a handsome, bearded man who'd greeted them with a smile.

Who *were* these women?

"So that's my mom."

"Yikes." No getting around it. Might as well just have it out here.

"Yeah." She slumped into one of the chairs across from my desk, and I sat in the one next to her.

We hadn't touched all that much, but I needed the connection and I hoped she'd accept it. Reaching for her hand, I linked our fingers. Her eyes met mine in question and I leaned over, cupping our joined hands with my free one.

"I'm starting to get this whole thing a little more, and I was in the room with her for two minutes. Dahlia, I don't want to sound like I don't think you can handle your family, but I want to be there for you. If you need to do the spa thing, take me with you. Or, I guess maybe it's a girls' thing?"

She shook her head. "No, it's everyone. They rented a ton of rooms. I honestly thought it was Saturday and Sunday. I figured I'd go, and then I'd have a few days to recover before the wedding."

She closed her eyes, teeth gritted, and breathed. When her lips pressed together, I could tell she was fighting tears.

I'd only felt this feeling a few times before in my life. Once a few years back when someone had railed on Aidan for being a grump at the store and accusing him of using his wife's death as a reason to be a jerk. Once when a much bigger kid shoved Luca into the dirt at the park and my nephew cut open his lip. And once when some lady had made my mom cry, because you do not make Nancy Wallace cry on my watch.

But right now, it boiled up from the depths of me. The need to defend her, protect her, and destroy anyone who threatened her peace practically exploded through my chest, burning me like magma erupting.

I pulled her to me, hugging her around the shoulders from where I sat as she fought with her own tide of emotion.

"I'm not going to cry about this," she said into my shoulder, her voice shaky.

"You can cry if you need to," I said, breathless with the need to do something. This wasn't even her jerk of an ex. This was her own family.

She inhaled sharply and leaned back, swiping under one eye and blinking away more tears. "I don't *want* to cry. I'm not weak and I don't want your pity."

The lava-hot anger cooled at her words. "I don't pity you, Dahlia. I pity *them*. All I feel for you is the desire to get you through this mess." Well, maybe not *all*...

Her beautiful dark eyes hooked into mine and her body moved with a long inhale. After a few more seconds, she nodded. "Thank you. I'll—I'll figure it out."

"*We'll* figure it out."

She might've been used to managing her family alone, but from now on, she had me, too. The more details filled in, the more convinced I became that her grabbing me off the street hadn't been an accident or coincidence. It felt a lot like fate.

And since I couldn't exactly insult her parents and make everything worse, I decided I'd do what I could to make this a little bit better. I'd remind her just how many people cared for her and wanted the best for her.

CHAPTER TWENTY-THREE

Dahlia

John's sudden plans for us tonight might've struck me as odd if I hadn't already been off-kilter from the lovely chat with my mom and Rose. I'd left his office with a mix of dread and embarrassment coating me and decided I needed a minute to myself before we went to whatever family dinner he had planned.

Probably for the best I hadn't known about any family gathering. Or, honestly, maybe he'd told me about it and I'd been so focused on my own family that I'd just spaced it. All the more reason for a jog. I hadn't gotten out for many lately, usually sneaking in a workout at Grit and calling it good. But sometimes, breathing in the mountain air and plodding my way through the winding greenways of Silverton lightened my load.

Back home, I cleaned up, eyeing the kitchen faucet's incessant drip as I bustled around getting ready and finished swiping on mascara right when John knocked. Despite the draggy feeling that'd shrouded my afternoon, I liked John's parents, and I was looking forward to officially meeting his brother's family.

"Hey, give me one sec," I said, flinging the door open and hustling back to the table where I'd left the small bouquet.

"No problem."

He'd stayed in the doorway, eyes taking in the tiny apartment I'd made my home, a soft smile on his face as I held up the small arrangement. "Didn't want to show up empty-handed."

Our eyes locked just as I arrived at the doorway, and he reached for me. His warm hand rested on my upper arm, and in what felt like a slow motion or freeze-frame approach, he dipped his head and pressed his lips against my cheek, the stubble on his chin scraping just slightly.

I sucked in a breath, surprise and more than a little delight at the gesture releasing butterflies into my chest. He withdrew, squeezing my arm gently before dropping his hand.

"Shall we?"

I nodded, suppressing my grin and feeling so much like a girl heading out on a date with a boy she liked, I hardly knew myself. I should be worrying about my family, or even his, but right now, I was admiring John's plaid button-up and the jeans that did great things for his backside. I was relishing the way he'd rolled the sleeves and bared his forearms, then how he held the door for me, then how the interior of his car was so clean and smelled actively pleasant.

What is going on? I didn't spend a lot of time sniffing men's cars. I'd even been in this car, though at the time I'd brought a storm cloud with me, so maybe that was why. Or, maybe it was thanks to what was growing between me and John—what he'd done for me earlier. He'd stood by me, been remarkably polite to my rude mother, and he'd consoled me after.

"You look beautiful tonight."

His voice cut into my thoughts, flipping my stomach and tossing to the wind all my resistance to simply gazing at the side of his face.

The sharp line of his jaw was just covered with stubble. It gave him this rough edge he didn't always have, and I liked it a lot. Feeling the brush of coarse hair against my cheek made me want to feel it at my chin for a real kiss.

Whoa, girl.

Clearing my throat, I finally responded, "Thank you. You look very handsome."

The side of his mouth I could see kicked up into a smile, and he let out a breathy chuckle. "Thanks."

"Why are you laughing at that?"

He kept his eyes steadfastly on the road. "I was just marveling at how far we've come."

The crease in his cheek that made up part of his smile held my attention as I thought about that. We really had, hadn't we? A few months ago, we could hardly stand to be in the same room together, and now here we were, cooperating and willingly spending time together.

Or, mostly willingly.

Though, in truth, I was very happy to be with him. Just seeing him when I opened my door had made me want to fling my arms around him. He'd given me a hug earlier, an arms-around-the-shoulders thing that mostly made me want to burrow closer and press fully against him to absorb all his warmth and comfort.

Maybe at some point, some way...

Wait. "Are we not going to your parents' house?"

He slowed the car at the security gate to The Ridge neighborhood, where many of our friends lived. The guard waved us through when he saw it was us—the beauty of a small town at work, to be sure.

"We aren't." He still didn't glance my way, ever-focused on the road like his life depended on it.

And then it hit me how it *did*—how it must've felt that way after losing Aidan's wife years ago to a car accident. Something about that battered my heart and made me want to hug him as he pulled into a spot on the street in front of Maddie's house.

He parked and turned to me. "Sorry. Didn't mean to sound snippy. Just... driving."

"No, it's fine." Wherever we were going, did it matter? I wasn't with my family, and that was paramount. He'd gotten me and my bad attitude for his dance chaperone gig and maybe technically the family dinner, and I'd have him for the spa trip, then the wedding, probably some part of the rehearsal, although we hadn't talked through next weekend yet. But I needed to add something. "I'm just sorry you're not getting more out of this."

"I'm getting plenty out of this, Dahlia. Don't worry about that."

I sighed, too charmed by his soul-deep generosity and kindness to say much other than, "Okay, but... why are we at Maddie's? What's going on?"

He gave me a fakely alarmed look. "We're at Maddie's? Oh, no, I meant to take us over to the resort so you could have dinner with the Rockefellers and the Carnegies—oh, and the Kennedys, of course."

I shoved his shoulder and rolled my eyes, though something pleasant and hot glowed in my chest. His making fun was so gentle and silly, nothing like what I'd experienced before. Still, I couldn't let on. "Rude."

He raised a brow. "You'll live."

I laughed and shoved the car door open, shaking my head at his silliness and secretly loving it. We'd never been like *this*. It was like he'd always held something in reserve, or maybe that edge between us had been too big, and now it was gone. I didn't know what it meant, but it made me excited for the evening ahead. I liked his parents, but knowing I'd be at Maddie's house, in a place I felt comfortable and with one of my best friends and my good friend Aidan, most likely? *Perfect.*

"Do you think your parents have any idea how many super fancy friends you have?" he asked, glancing at me as he held out a hand.

I took it without a thought, happy to be connected to him in this way. The contact made my fingers feel fizzy and a tingling sensation climbed my arm, but I focused on the question. "No. They don't. I've made sure I don't ever mention first or last names, but honestly, even if I did, I don't think they'd ever put it together. They wouldn't imagine me even having them as clients, let alone friends."

His baffled expression made me want to kiss him.

Huh. Sure enough. More and more, this man was drawing me in and he didn't even realize it.

"I don't get it. How can they not recognize how talented you are?" He squeezed my hand for emphasis.

Ugh, and again. There he went, being basically perfect and not even realizing it. How was he single? "That's very sweet."

"Nah. I'm not sweet. I'm honest. And they're missing it." We stopped on the porch and his gaze hooked into mine.

My heart fluttered and my pulse jumped.

"I hope it's okay, but I put together a little something as a distraction tonight."

And just as I was about to ask what, Maddie's door flew open and she beamed at us, noise spilling out around her. "Come in, love birds. The gang's all here."

She ushered us inside, and before I stepped fully into the gorgeous living room, I stopped. In one corner stood my book club friends, and in another, a small contingent of Saint Security guys I knew. Quinn and Julian, Calla and Wyatt, Sadie and Warrick. Mouth agape, I turned to John. "How... how is everyone here?"

He squinted and his lips pinched in a move that looked like he was hiding a smile. "We needed plans and I thought hanging with your people might be better than hanging with my folks."

I didn't hold back this time. Throwing my arms around his neck, I clung to him and cleared my throat to keep the surge of gratitude at bay. "Thank you."

He leaned away and shook his head, the smile in his eyes making my stomach flip. "Hey, I just put out the call. Everyone showed up because of you—because they love you and wanted to see you."

I crushed my teeth together to stay the tears. "This is so nice..." My voice came out watery. He'd done all this for me, and I knew it'd been *him*. I'd been getting little texts from the girls, reminding me they were rooting for me, but the insanely busy schedule had meant I hadn't seen them in person as much as I normally would. Being here with them... this met a need I hadn't been able to verbalize.

He held me by the shoulders and grinned down at me. "Don't cry, Price. Go talk to your adoring fans, and I'll be here when you're ready to go."

Good grief, he was too much tonight. Or maybe I was

feeling small after seeing my family and needed the buildup. But the thing about John was, he meant it. He was sweet and thoughtful and kind and... how had I never appreciated these things about him? Because none of this was actually surprising, only surprising that it was directed at *me,* and now, I shouldn't be shocked by that either.

Some wild hair in me made me say, "Are you an adoring fan, too?"

His smile widened. "Absolutely."

CHAPTER TWENTY-FOUR

John

The sheer joy that exploded out of me when Dahlia hugged me to her and tearfully thanked me, like calling a bunch of her friends and throwing together a little Friday night get-together resembled some kind of heroic act, was shockingly fleeting.

"You know, you could just go join the conversation." Aidan nudged me with his big stupid shoulder.

"I'm not about to interrupt them." Tempting though it was.

He stood by me, watching with me as Bruce and Dahlia chatted. She laughed and gave him all her prettiest smiles, the effect of which was to set my simmering jealousy to a ridiculous, uncharacteristic boil.

"You realize they're friends, right? Just like I am with her, and she is with Wilder or anyone else."

I narrowed my eyes at him, then turned back in time to

see Bruce curl an arm around Dahlia's shoulders and give her a side hug before releasing her. Kieran smiled along with them, as did Tristan.

"You are engaged to Maddie. Wilder is a taciturn, quiet father-to-be, and that's completely different. And I don't even know Tristan." But Bruce? There was no measuring up to Bruce.

"Hey, seriously."

Aidan's tone made me turn, albeit reluctantly.

He gave me a stern stare for a minute before continuing. "She doesn't need a jealous fake fiancé."

My jaw clenched. "I know that. Obviously, of all people, I know that."

"Then why are you standing over here stewing about her talking to someone else?"

Did he have to be such an observant jerkface? I really didn't need his serious dad-mode talking-to.

"I'm not trying to. This—" I cleared my throat, not liking the whiny tinge to my words. "It snuck up on me. I thought it'd be different, but now..."

One dark brow rose. "Now?"

With a sigh, I admitted it all. "Now it's more than fake for me. And I'm staring down two weeks until it's over. I'm trying to figure out how I'm going to keep my crap together and not walk away from her destroyed. And it's a hell of a lot easier to focus on her flirting with Bruce than it is on how much I want it to always and only be me."

The smile that rapidly turned into a Cheshire grin on my serious cousin's face took me by surprise, as did his rough hand on my shoulder shaking me. I scowled at him, but he kept on grinning.

"This isn't all bad. You get that, right?" he asked.

Shifting on my feet, I crossed my arms over my chest.

"The impending destruction of my pride? Sure, sure, not bad at all."

He hooked an arm around my neck and jostled me like we were ten and twelve and not skirting forty. I shoved him away and gave him a mock glare, but the whole conversation had taken the pot of my boiling envy off the burner.

"I'm not sure ego is the right word here, but sure. I get that it's scary. Let me just say I'm glad you're doing this—specifically *you*—and I think, based on the way she keeps glancing over here, keeping you in her sights, she is, too."

A thrill slipped through me. "She is?"

He just grinned and patted my shoulder, because when I returned my attention to Dahlia, she was deep in conversation with Quinn, Sadie, Sarah, Maddie, and Calla, and Bruce was sauntering in my direction.

Okay, *fine*, he wasn't sauntering, and I was being an ungenerous little twerp.

"This was a great idea, John. I don't know everything that's going on, but your girl seems really happy. Thanks for including me."

Bruce extended his hand and I took it, shaking amicably and attempting to ignore the thrill that hearing him call Dahlia *my girl* gave me. "Glad you came. The book club is really important to her."

He nodded, glancing around before returning his attention to me. "I'd like to get with you about doing an event at the brewery for the Saint Security one-year anniversary, if you think you'd have time this week?"

Unexpected, but I was always happy to have more events in our space. "Definitely. I'll be in the office Wednesday through Friday—swing by any time, or give me a call."

"Will do."

With that, he gave me a chin nod that should've seemed stupid in the context of our conversation but just seemed kind of cool and subtle, and wandered off to fill a plate from the huge spread of food everyone had thrown together and lined Maddie's countertops. He'd made no attempt to claim Dahlia and had called her *my girl.* Wanting clutched at me and my stomach clenched at the thought of Dahlia as mine.

As really, actually mine.

Maybe the time had come to let go of the showy jealousy when I thought of Bruce and accept that he was a good guy. And maybe, finally, admit that Dahlia and I were good together. Maybe even great.

I milled around, chatting with Kieran and Tristan, then the Saint brothers. Julian stood nearby and glowered, but he nodded occasionally and even chuckled once or twice at something Warrick said. Soon enough, I couldn't help but search out the woman who'd plagued my brain for months now.

My eyes found her and my breath hitched. She had her head thrown back, eyes closed in a smile, and her laugh could be heard from where I stood—or at least, their little group's cackling could. Like moths to flames, each of the counterparts to the group fluttered closer.

First, Warrick wrapped his arms around Sadie and practically drowned her in his embrace, but her smiled widened and she quickly turned to accept his bear hug with enthusiasm. Wyatt slipped his hands around his wife's waist and kissed her neck, the gesture hot enough I blinked away from them in time to see Wilder slide his palm to the back of Sarah's neck and kiss her temple. Julian leaned over Quinn's shoulder and said something that made her mischievous eyes sparkle, and then finally, Aidan.

My throat tightened as I watched him take Maddie's

hand, their fingers twining. It wasn't the move, but the expression on his face and then on hers. Relief and pleasure, anticipation and homecoming. Unadulterated love.

I remembered him with Viv. They were great together. And I remembered, all too vividly, the aftermath. The ghost of a man he'd been for so long until he'd pulled himself out of the depths for his son and himself and he started living. And right about then, Maddie showed up.

I'd encouraged him to go after her, loving the idea of my quiet, humble cousin connecting with someone plucked from the pages of one of my gossip mags. But then, his heart had gotten involved and I'd pushed against it, almost begging him not to give her another chance. The stubborn man had, and this moment, like so many before it, reminded me what a good move that had been.

The incredible risk and quiet heroism it took to try again after so much loss threatened to gut me for some reason. Actually, no. I knew why.

In my heart, down at the root, I could feel how I'd let myself cower and fear. I'd used distraction, deflection, and deprivation as the tactics to keep myself safe from possible heartache, and now here I stood on the precipice of falling for a woman I couldn't have. She didn't want or need a relationship and ours was a temporary situation.

But maybe I could channel Aidan for a while. Maybe I could be brave and enjoy Dahlia being my girl for the next few weeks, enjoy this glimpse of what life could be like so that someday, I'd be brave enough to try again.

Dahlia grinned as her friends each stepped away into the arms of their partners, and then she turned to me. Those eyes said she wanted me close, and I might not pretend to understand women and especially not Dahlia Price most of the time, but this message I received.

This was the opposite of *not interested*.

I huffed out a breath, the force of her dark gaze sending my stomach to my toes and my heart to my throat. Why was that look in her eye directed at me sending my pulse through the roof? Why did everything feel like it was moving too fast and in slow motion all at once? Like a gauzy dream and vivid fantasy as she waited for me.

And then, I summoned that courage I'd been pondering and went to her, sliding an arm around her waist and curling her close.

"You doing okay?" I asked, voice low.

"More than." Then she leaned up on her toes and pressed a kiss to the corner of my mouth.

I could be brave now, but there was nothing that would compare to this—to her. Real or no, I'd never find someone like her again.

CHAPTER TWENTY-FIVE

Dahlia

Wringing my hands as John drove up the canyon road, I did my best to appreciate the passing scenery and not let my mind spiral out with dread. He'd turned on music and stayed relatively quiet, leaving me to my anxieties.

I hadn't actually seen my family again since my mother and Rose's brief visit to John's office. Not anyone. Friday night had been amazing—seeing my friends had restored me. It'd reminded me of the life I'd built here, of how many people I had in my corner, and it'd refueled my soul like good fresh soil and fertilizer.

I'd had a busy Saturday, and I'd leaned into the work in order to ignore the reality that I was leaving town to head up into the mountains days before a major wedding—never mind the fact it was my sister's wedding. I had my assistants hard at work while I was gone and I planned to leave first thing Wednesday so I could get back and get everything done. And maybe, just maybe, I'd tried to think about something other than the family drama and John... because all I really wanted to do was think about him.

Especially because he sent me another batch of those perfect donuts in the pretty pink box with a note that said something about me being sweet and taking care of myself and being proud of me, then signed *Your lucky fiancé, John.*

I mean, seriously? How was I supposed to focus on flowers?

"I can practically hear you thinking," he said, gaze jumping to me, then back to the road as he drove.

"Sorry. Just running through everything I still have to do for the wedding." The list was long and no doubt whatever happened in the next forty-eight hours would mean adding to it. And I wasn't about to tell him I was still thinking about those donuts or how much I wished he would've delivered them himself so I could share one with him and then kiss the frosting off his gorgeous lips.

Sheer wistful wanting raced through me and nearly made my breath come up short. I'd gone from foolishly thinking I disliked this man to wanting more of him in what felt like seconds, and yet I had no shame over it because it made sense. He was everything I should want, and as it was clearly turning out, everything I *did.*

"What should I know?"

His question was gentle, but I still inwardly cringed as I recalibrated to focus on the issue at hand. We'd talked through a lot the last few days, swapping texts when new questions popped up I thought might get asked. And frankly, the more I knew about John, the more I liked him. Pair that with his monumental thoughtfulness Friday, the donuts Saturday... I was a goner.

But this—his gentle way of asking me what I needed and how he could help—this skewered me most. I didn't want him to see me near Devon at the wedding and I didn't want to need his help with my family, but here we were, barreling toward thirty-six hours of unavoidable fam time.

"I'm sure there's something I should be able to tell you that will help, but I really don't know what. I haven't spent time with them since I left. They visited once about a year ago and I hardly saw them. I honestly don't know what the dynamic will be beyond what you saw at your office."

His large, warm hand reached for me and squeezed my wrist gently before returning to the steering wheel. "We'll play it by ear, and hey, we get a massage out of it, right?"

I chuckled, grateful for his attempt at being positive while still reeling from the flood of sensation that familiar, lovely touch had caused. "Yeah. And facials and all kinds of stuff. You a big spa guy?"

I could only see half his smile since he looked straight ahead, but even that made a tiny stitch in my chest loosen.

"I've had a massage one time and really liked it, but I've never done any of the other stuff unless you count pedicures by my nieces. They aren't *great* at precision with polish, but we've discovered that if they use glitter nail polish, the execution is less important."

Of course he was the kind of uncle who let his little nieces paint his toes. *Of course he is.* "Please tell me you're going to get sparkly toenails if you get a pedicure this weekend."

"Oh, definitely. I was going to ask if I could wear my old Birkenstocks to the wedding, too. I find a nice faux-leather sandal works really well with a tux." He glanced at me and winked.

A laugh tumbled out and another few stitches unraveled, his silliness alleviating the tightness by degrees. And then, we crested out of the canyon and into the upper valley road that led to the spa and my mouth dropped open with awe.

We'd gone up in elevation another thousand feet and were at the back of Silver Ridge Peak now. From this side, it looked just as impressive. Thanks to the springy weather we'd had for the last few weeks, snow had melted off along the roadway and tiny light and dark purple crocuses and daffodils bloomed like someone had scattered their seeds with a generous hand.

The sky stretched endlessly in front of us, and the pastures dotted with Wyatt Saint's cattle spread out in all directions. If you could ignore the altitude and the mountains behind and to each side, you might think you'd stumbled into a verdant plain. The silver river cut through the land, zigzagging along next to the road as we drove.

I loved Silverton so much, but this space felt special. Sacred, almost.

"I should come up here more often. I always forget how gorgeous it is," he said, the wonder in his voice matching my thoughts exactly.

"I can't believe I'm going to say this, but I'm actually feeling kind of... glad. That's not quite right, but I'm... hopeful? Maybe?"

He chuckled. "Is that a question? I'm not sure I can tell you how you're feeling." He navigated into the long driveway, the only hint that we'd be finding the spa soon being the stonework sign that said, "Escape."

"I maybe need you to do that, though. I'm not sure I can be trusted," I joked, enjoying the way every mile out of Silverton we drove seemed to loosen me up. Ironic considering we'd be facing down the very thing that'd stressed me out so much the last few months, but I'd take it. After dreading it for so long, there was a kind of relief in knowing in a matter of days, however it went down, this mess would be over.

The spa's beautiful structure appeared. I'd been up here to do the flowers for various bridal showers and other events, but I'd never attended myself. When it first opened, it had a small guest house feature, but in the last three years, the owner had expanded significantly. With no other lodging available in the immediate area, and through some high-profile visits like Maddie and even more so, her friend Juliet, plus Calla and a host of other local and visiting celebrities, she'd become a destination spa.

No wonder my mother had to have it as part of the wedding week.

John pulled into a spot and parked. We both breathed in the view ahead, finding courage from the vista of the mountains and the open fields. The spa itself had clusters of pines and aspens at different points, but still plenty of open space to see the sky.

"You ready for this?" he asked, drawing my eyes to him.

Looking at those hazel eyes in that handsome face, I answered with the truth. "I have no idea, but I'm ready to get it over with."

He grinned. My heart did something twisty and strange in my chest, and then we got out. We carried our own bags, though he'd offered to take mine and I'd refused, and entered the reception area. Before we could set them down, a bellman hustled to us, commandeering our bags and apologizing profusely for not meeting us in front to park the car.

"No problem—we were happy to park ourselves," John said, shooting me a look with raised brows.

Genevieve Draper smiled warmly as we approached the

natural wood reception desk. "Welcome to Escape Spa. I'm so pleased you'll be staying with us, Dahlia."

She rounded the corner and kissed my cheek on each side. She'd done this each time I'd visited after the first, so I'd been prepared for it. That inaugural visit had seen me scrambling and feeling like a little country bumpkin next to her glamorous greeting, but at this point, after being surrounded by world-famous pop stars and actual billionaires who were, as it turned out, fairly normal people, I'd lost that sense of smallness.

"I'm excited to experience the spa. It's just so beautiful up here." I glanced around at the stylish, warm lobby, and wished I wasn't facing the cold reality of my family ruining the charm. If it were me and my girlfriends, or just me and Azalea, or even just me and John...

Whoa.

"The view is spectacular," John said, then stretched out his hand. "John Wallace. I think maybe we've met once when you first got up and running."

"John, yes. We have. So nice to have you as well." She slipped back behind the counter and tapped on her computer. "I have you in a king room with a garden view. Room four-oh-eight. If you find you need any additional pillows or anything else, please just call the front desk. We're staffed twenty-four seven."

I blinked. King room. *Room.* I'd assumed my parents would get two rooms when I mentioned John was coming. Something told me they'd do whatever they could to keep us apart, including get two rooms, but apparently not.

"Uh, just the one room, then? I wasn't sure what my parents had booked." I hoped my discomfort didn't show through as much as I suspected it did.

Genevieve proved the consummate professional, as

always. "Let me double-check." She tapped on the keyboard, eyes studying a screen we couldn't see, then tapped one last time. "No, just the one room."

"Well, that's good news," John said, his arm wrapping around me. "We weren't sure whether they'd be more old-fashioned and book two rooms. Perfect, right, love?"

He grinned down at me, his eyes doing their work to calm me even though I knew I owed him an explanation.

"And I hear congratulations are in order?" She eyed us, a pleased grin on her lovely face as she turned her back to us and reached for a key in the mailbox-style wooden cubbies behind her.

Such an odd little detail, but I'd always liked the fact that she used metal keys with big, ornately carved wooden flowers and leaves as keychains. It helped contribute to the *unplugged* emphasis of the spa.

Nerves looped and twisted in my gut. "Yes, my sister's wedding. We're all so happy for her." With the possible exception of me, but oh well.

"Of course, but I mean on your engagement!" Her excitement overflowed out, and for just a second, I felt it, too.

"Thank you. We're really happy," John said, his arm tightening around me as he accepted the key from her.

My pulse ticked up at his nearness and I was reminded again that we hadn't talked about *that* part of things, though we'd been more affectionate lately, and especially Friday night. Based on the one-room situation, the time had come. Because we would be in one room together—of course we would as an engaged couple—and probably one bed.

And somehow, I hadn't even thought about that until right. This. Second.

Honestly, I'd been so sure we'd have two rooms. But

why? Why would I think that other than the fact that putting us in one seemed like a tacit acceptance of our engagement, and I was fairly certain my parents hadn't gotten past the denial portion of their grief?

"Wonderful. Well, down the hall to the left, you'll find the elevator, or the stairs are just past. Enjoy your stay." She smiled, then picked up the phone when it rang as we stepped away.

We didn't speak as we followed her directions, then entered a waiting elevator. It was small but didn't seem unstable, and now that my legs had turned wooden, I was grateful we wouldn't have to climb four flights of stairs to our room.

Leaning against the back of the elevator, we both stared forward. His elbow brushed my arm and sent little tingles in all directions. What should I say?

The *ding* and jolt of the doors opening made the first sound, and when he gestured for me to precede him, I swallowed hard and searched my mind. It wasn't like I'd engineered this, and he didn't seem upset. We both stayed quiet because we were sorting things through.

I didn't want anyone overhearing, and since I had no idea where my family's rooms were or if they were even here, I resolved to just get it all out there—the surprise of one room, how we'd handle one bed, all of it—as soon as we entered our space.

But when I rounded the corner, John a few steps behind me, I heard an all-too-familiar voice.

"Well, there she is. Dolly, you look stressed. Can I buy you a drink?"

CHAPTER TWENTY-SIX

John

This guy.

"Devon. What are you doing here?" Dahlia's voice came out shaky.

I stepped up behind her, sliding my hand around her waist to remind her she wasn't alone.

"I'm the best man. Why *wouldn't* I be here?" He gave her what I assumed he thought must be a charming grin, then turned to me. "And you again."

"Me again. Me consistently and indefinitely since I'm her fiancé." If a hard edge laced my tone, so be it. He'd offered to buy her a drink while her fiancé stood immediately next to her and still didn't seem to register my role, or more importantly, his *lack* of one in Dahlia's life.

Devon smirked in a way that had my teeth clenching. With a light chuckle, he winked at Dahlia. "I'll see you in a little while. We'll catch up."

He walked away and I turned to watch him go until he rounded the corner to the elevator bank. Dahlia was moving toward our room and only the cold air rushing in where her body had been against my hand made me do the same.

She'd taken the key from my hand as I'd stood there mindlessly and she opened the door quickly, then marched in, dropped her bag along the way, and walked to the sliding glass doors. With jerky movements, she unlocked the door, pulled it open, and walked out onto the small balcony.

As frustrated as I had gotten, she had to be more so. I didn't have a history with the guy and I wanted to smash his face in—and I was genuinely a non-violent person. I couldn't imagine the riot of emotions circling Dahlia.

So, I gave her space. I unpacked a little—hung up the two nicer shirts and suit I'd brought and tucked my toiletries into the bathroom. After operating on *go* mode the last few minutes, I glanced at her to see her still gazing out. A soft spring breeze ruffled her hair over her shoulder and I could just make out her profile.

My chest ached. She was so beautiful, and she shouldn't be standing there thinking about... well, about anything other than how stunning the view was and how much she was looking forward to a massage. And how much fun it must be to be here with her fiancé.

Yeah. Right.

She shifted and I snapped my head in the opposite direction to avoid being caught staring. My gaze landed on the bed—the *one* bed. Standing here staring at the bed I'd be sharing with Dahlia in a matter of hours wasn't the best idea I'd ever had, so I let my feet carry me to her. If she didn't want me out there with her, or if she didn't want to talk, I'd leave—go look around or something.

She turned just as I stepped onto the balcony and didn't

exactly smile but didn't seem perturbed by my arrival. And one thing I knew about Dahlia was that if she *was* upset, she usually had no qualms about letting me know.

Although that thought made me realize that wasn't true—at least not for her friends. From what she'd said, she hadn't told them anything about her past. So actually, she was a master at hiding, or deflecting.

"I can leave. I just wanted you to know you're not alone." I'd said it before, but something told me it could bear repeating.

She swallowed. "Let's go in."

I followed her, then shut the door. "You okay?"

She whipped around. "I'm fine. I'm actually completely fine. And any time I've second-guessed the need for us to do this has now been canceled out by that interaction. I didn't realize he'd be here, didn't want him to be here obviously, but it's better this way. He can see we're staying here. He can see he has no room, that he'll get nowhere with me. And hopefully, my parents will get that message loud and clear, too."

"Exactly. I never questioned your need to do this, honestly, but everything's adding up even more. I'm sorry that's the case, but we're going to convince everyone." Stupid—so stupid, really—but I stepped closer and brushed her hair back, over her shoulder. "We'll make everyone believe there's never been a more blissful, perfect couple in the history of time."

She laughed at the absurdity of that, but at least it was a real smile, before she sighed and her eyes flicked to the bed. "And of course, there's only one bed."

"Of course?" Had she guessed that'd be the case?

"I foolishly thought they'd get us two rooms since they're so unsupportive and I feel stupid for not even considering this, but I mostly mean that *of course* there's only one bed because this is always how it goes."

When she saw my confused look, she explained. "In books. A fake relationship trope almost always ends up with forced proximity and only one bed."

"And how does that work out for everyone?" Why had my pulse jumped?

Dahlia's cheeks flushed. "Uh, well, they're romance novels so... usually pretty well."

Her nervous chuckle made something click in my head. Standing here imagining what it meant for an only one-bed trope to work out well in the books she read might be a little messed up considering we were in the same situation.

As though she'd realized the same thing, she rushed to say, "Not that that's us. It's just, I have this bad habit of assigning people into romance tropes and... yeah. It's fine. We'll be fine. I'm fine. I can sleep on the love seat."

An overstuffed chair sat in the corner next to a small table, a stylish reading lamp arching over the back. *Cozy.* But definitely not a couch and not a place anyone slept in.

"That wouldn't fit one of my nieces, and it definitely won't fit you. I can take the floor—"

"Don't be silly. You're not doing me this huge favor and then sleeping on the—"

I stepped closer to her again. "I'm not being *silly*. We weren't anticipating the one-bed situation, and I'm not going to force you to sleep in the same bed with someone you hated a few months ago."

She reared back. "I never hated you. We've been over this, John, and you're not sleeping on the—"

"Well, you're not sleeping there either."

She set her jaw. "Fine. We'll both sleep in the bed, and

even though you are tall and muscular, I assume you will not take up more than your half."

Heart thrumming from the exchange, the subject matter, and the thrill of seeing a little fire back in her eyes, I nodded. "Yes, ma'am. I'll stay on my half if you stay on yours."

With her arms crossed, she nodded. "Good. Fine. And now, we need to talk about"—she cleared her throat—"touching."

I coughed, the words unexpected and strangely thrilling. We'd been close in a lot of ways, but standing here next to the bed we'd be sharing later thinking about touching her had my pulse jumping. "Touching?"

If my voice sounded a little froggish, I could forgive myself.

"We'll need to hold hands, at least. Arms around shoulders or waists. Maybe a kiss or something. I'm not sure. I can see someone toasting us and we can't hesitate. I just don't want you to be uncomfortable with anything."

Hoping my face stayed neutral, normal, I nodded. "Of course. And if we were actually engaged—I mean, if we were together, I'd—" I cleared my throat and squinted out the glass sliding door toward the stretch of land beyond, internally panicking.

"You'd... what?"

The normal edge of impatience or resignation didn't tinge her voice. Instead, she sounded almost breathless. Likely my imagination at work, but if that was the case, it'd done a fine job of things. Her cheeks looked a little pink, her mouth open just a little, as if waiting there with bated breath.

Yes, I'd glanced at her mouth. When I registered what I'd done—how she'd been looking at me while I'd done it, and she *must* have seen my eyes drop there, like they'd done a thousand times before but undetected, I snapped my eyes back to meet her gaze.

A stab of that boldness I sometimes felt when faced with her, a lick of that *wanting* paired with the fire that burned between us when we butted heads, reared up and took hold of me. "I'd want to touch you. All the time. I'd want everyone to know you were mine, and I'd spend every minute reminding myself we were in public and I needed to keep this thing between us under wraps until we were alone."

Her mouth shut and she swallowed hard, her lashes fluttering as her eyes flickered between mine.

Panic shot through me, a real sense that maybe I'd said way, *way* too much looming large over me like a fast-moving storm...

"Oh." That one word from her broke the tense silence.

And yes, that time, it was breathless. And honest to every good thing, it sounded like, "Yes, please." Don't ask me why I heard it, but I did, and I wanted very much to acknowledge it.

Fortunately, a wisp of sanity remained and I paced away from her, facing the door again. "Sorry. Yeah, just, uh, you know, saying I'm comfortable with hand-holding or whatever. We've already done that. And a kiss is fine. If we want them to believe it, we've got to sell it."

She cleared her throat and I refused to look, refused to indulge myself and see if the blush had deepened or if that look in her eyes was still there.

"Right. Yes. Glad we're on the same page."

I smiled to myself, something simmering beneath the surface that I couldn't quite verbalize, so I nodded. "Yep.

We're good. Do whatever you think you need to so they buy it."

And if I enjoyed it—if we *both* enjoyed it, based on the last few minutes and the way her breath had hitched when she noticed me looking at her delectable mouth—well, then. What a nice engagement gift.

CHAPTER TWENTY-SEVEN

Dahlia

The patchwork of anticipation and dread had me off-kilter while we got dressed for the cocktail hour my mother had scheduled. Fortunately, she'd given us just enough notice and we'd planned our attire accordingly—otherwise, I would've packed sweats and comfortable clothes and maybe one decent something for dinner each night, but not *cocktail attire*. Apparently, it was catered and everything.

The dread made sense. My family was here, my ex was here, and I didn't want to spend time with any of them. The anticipation.... Well, that had to be due to seeing Azalea for the first time in well over a year.

As I swiped on the finishing touch of mascara, I nodded at my reflection as though we were in conversation. Because also? I was looking forward to showing up with John. He'd been nothing short of wonderful all day—or in truth, much longer. And I... well, the more time I spent with him, the more I liked him.

Discussing physical boundaries had sent a kaleidoscope of butterflies through me and I knew touching and being touched by John Wallace wouldn't be a hardship. The few times I'd experienced contact with any part of him had been nothing short of either comforting or electric, and sometimes, improbably, both.

After slipping into my dress that my friends had consulted on via video call as I'd packed, I pulled the zipper up, up, but it stopped. I tugged at it from behind my back, arching impressively and making me wish I went to Warrick's gym more often and was generally more flexible. He did love to harp on sticking around to stretch, but I rarely did lately, too antsy to get on to the next thing. After a few more contortions, I surrendered and shoved open the bathroom door.

"Any chance you can help me?" I held my hair out of the way and turned, presenting my back to him.

"Sure, what do you—"

When he didn't continue, I glanced over my shoulder to find his eyes shifting around, looking anywhere but at me.

"Can you do the zipper? I can't reach." My voice came out quieter than I expected, but his silence had thrown me.

He cleared his throat, and his gaze met mine. "Zipper? Of course. Sure. No problem."

I turned away as he stepped forward. My stomach flipped and plunged, my cheeks heated, and my hands pressed over my belly and heart as though to steady myself. "Thank you."

His knuckles brushed my upper back where he held

one edge of the material, and then I felt the drag of the zipper up the last ten inches until it fully joined the two sides of the dress. My breath hitched as one finger traced the line of the dress along my back, then over the cap of my shoulder before his touch disappeared. I'd never been happier about my choice of off-the-shoulder neckline.

"All set," he said, the graveled texture of his voice sending my pulse higher.

I turned slowly, eyes snagging on his lips before they met his eyes. "Thanks."

"Anytime."

The burnished gold rimming his hazel eyes caught me, held me, and I couldn't look away. He wore a jacket, collared shirt, and tie, none of which I'd had time to admire, and yet it was those kind, captivating eyes I couldn't escape. Except just now, *kind* wouldn't have described them.

Something more like... hungry. *Needy*.

Wow.

As handsome as he was, I'd never thought of John like this. I could admit I'd thought about kissing him, especially in the last few weeks, but the last hour had shown me a side of him I hadn't been aware of. Maybe it was because I'd only felt the hint of such things in books—I'd never once felt this tingly, heady sensation like anything could happen paired with *I really hope something will happen*. Even Friday's interactions, as coupley as they'd been, had felt sweet. Exciting, yes, but still covered in the glow of what a nice gesture John had made by setting up the evening with friends. I'd kissed his cheek—*almost* his mouth, but that had been in thanks.

Okay, it'd also been because I wanted to actually kiss him, but I also didn't want to be the one to do it. I wanted more of him, and yet I didn't know how to get it in the odd context of our fake engagement.

It'd been so long since I'd wanted someone to touch me, let alone kiss me. I'd been welcoming John's touch for weeks now, finding courage and strength in his arm around my shoulders, his hand in mine. The thought of *more*, the thought of him wanting more, too, and not just doing it for show, thrilled me down to the pointy tips of my high heels.

Amazingly, those thoughts bolstered me. Instead of nerves over seeing my family and Devon, I felt a buzzy anticipation for how we'd handle it all *together* and how this night might change things. Not just for me and how my family and ex saw me, but for me and John. The two of us.

"Ready?" I said on a whisper, my voice hiding behind all the thoughts about John's sensuality I never would've imagined having.

He blinked once, as if ending a trance, then nodded, and his congenial smile found its place. "Let's do this."

Apparently, the name of the game was *pretend we're all happy about Dahlia's engagement*. At least that's how Rose and Conrad played it off, as did my parents. My aunt and uncle, two cousins, and the handful of other bridesmaids and groomsmen also seemed to greet me with beaming smiles and kissy faces such that by the end of our ten minutes rolling through introductions, I'd ended up far less stressed and much more confused.

"So... this is going well," John said, the hint of wariness

in his voice betraying he thought it odd, too. He just had no idea *how* odd.

"I... honestly have no idea what's happening," I said before taking a sip of champagne. When I glanced back at John, he watched me with a small smile I couldn't decipher. "What?"

"Just enjoying the view."

My stomach did a row of backflips. "The one from our room is better," I said, tucking my chin down and taking another drink.

He tilted his head side to side like he wasn't sure. "Not for me, I guess."

But before I could get too swept away in it, Devon arrived, slinging an arm around John's shoulders roughly enough that John's champagne sloshed over the side and ran down the stem to drip on the floor.

"Aren't you going to make a speech?" he asked, his words a little off.

"A speech? I hadn't planned on it," I said, giving John an *I'm so sorry and I have no idea what's going on with him* look.

Devon smirked, then gave me one of his classic scowls like he found me disappointing. "Of course not *you*. I mean our man John here. He's the belle of the ball, after all."

John slipped out of Devon's weirdo grasp and stood at my shoulder. "Since I'm the new guy, I figured I'd just be along for the ride." He smiled down at me and winked in a move that did a great job reassuring me.

Just having him nearby, his shoulder brushing mine, relaxed me a few degrees. Being near Devon meant there wouldn't be any real relaxing, but John's focus on staying close alleviated the low-level dread at seeing the jerk.

"Well, in that case—" Devon spun and snatched a fork

from one of the tables that held an array of appetizers, then clinked it against the edge of his glass. It made a shrill *ting* and drew attention immediately.

Forget low-level. Devon loved attention, and if he was pulling attention in response to me being here with John, in response to John being agreeable and awesome, this could mean nothing good.

I reached for John's hand, not liking where this was heading. Devon had taken John's presence and the apparent acceptance of it as a challenge, and he seemed like maybe he'd had a drink or two before showing up tonight.

"First, a huge congratulations to Rose and Conrad. We're all so excited to be here celebrating with you two." He raised his glass at my sister and her fiancé, who grinned.

I'd never *loved* Conrad, but they did seem to suit, and tonight they were especially happy to be together. Good for them. I hoped he wasn't hiding an evil side like his best friend, and wondered, not for the first time, if I should pull Rose aside and just... ask. Just make sure she really wanted to go through with it.

"I'd be remiss if I didn't acknowledge the other big news in the room, Dahlia's engagement to our new friend John Wallace."

The slight edge to his voice might've sounded charming or magnanimous to some, but I heard it for what it was— irritation. My stomach dropped low in a very un-fun sensation that made my pulse tick up in warning.

Everyone else clapped, a few *hear, hear* scattered around the room, and then he spoke again.

"While I couldn't have imagined toasting something that meant Dahlia wouldn't be with me, I can recognize young love when I see it."

His gaze swung to meet mine, and I saw the sneer

before he continued. "But my thought is, if we're already all together celebrating, why not take this whole event up a notch? Instead of one wedding, let's do this up right and make it a *double* wedding. I know you two don't have a date set, so what do you say?"

All attention turned to us, but mine shot to Rose. Her smile fell and she bolted, but no one noticed that except Conrad, who followed her. Everyone else—*everyone*—was watching me and John.

I laughed nervously. John shook his head like he was perplexed.

"Oh, come on, you two! If not now, then when? You don't have a date set, do you? Did I get that wrong?"

A sharp exhale escaped me. "No. We've got a lot to plan around and—"

"Then it's settled. John and Dahlia will be joining in next weekend, and we already know you'll like the flowers, right?" He winked like this was the most fun he'd had in years.

It probably was.

Because what I hadn't told anyone yet was that the whole wedding was what I'd planned for me and Devon. Granted, I hadn't been in love, and I hadn't planned the wedding of my dreams or anything, but the arrangements were what I'd once described to Rose. The location, too. Parts of the menu, and oddly, the dress. It was like she didn't have her own sense of what she wanted, so she'd taken mine.

"Thank you for thinking of us, but we don't want to interrupt the plans as they are. We wouldn't dream of imposing on Rose and Conrad's big day." John's attempt at shooting Devon down proved admirable, though unbelievably, my parents were grinning at the idea.

No way this could happen—absolutely *no way* Rose would go for it, let alone my mother. That was the only thing tethering my sanity in place.

"You know, that's a wonderful idea! I love it, and not to be crass, but it'll be an incredible savings."

My mother winked at my dad, who got this pleased look that made my stomach lurch. The whole room erupted in oddly excited discussion, their words melding together to do nothing more than raise the overall sound in the room and send my blood pressure a few numbers higher.

What is happening? My consolation was Rose. Whenever she recovered from pouting about the moment not focused solely on her, she'd tell them and they'd listen. *Ugh.* That was harsh, but I was struggling to feel very generous at the moment.

Azalea must've agreed, because she came to my rescue when she spoke to Devon. "There's no way this'll fly with Rose."

He sniffed. "We'll see. I know Conrad will do just about anything for me. Oh, and it's a shame you forgot your engagement ring."

He winked at me again and sauntered off like he hadn't just insinuated he'd get his bff to have a double wedding in order to either force my hand or prove that my relationship with John was fake. His pushing this told me he didn't believe we were a couple, and that grated on me as much as his general arrogance.

Watching him go lit a match in me. With the force of a thousand suns, my rage rocketed from zero to stratospheric and I could hardly see straight.

"I need to go. I need to go." I'd repeated myself, grasping onto John's forearm and genuinely unable to form any other words.

He moved, drawing me along with his arm around my shoulders. We navigated the well-wishers and almost made it out without dealing with my parents, but no such luck.

"Will you really do it?" my father asked, the first words he'd spoken to me other than the congratulations he and my mother had offered a half hour earlier.

"Why would you want me to? Why would you think Rose would want this?" I asked, my voice shaking with fury and, unfortunately, now, more than a little hurt. So much simpler to live in a low-level state of numbness toward them when they weren't here. But even that felt frustrating because I didn't want to feel like I'd been burying my feelings toward them all these years. I'd accepted we'd never have the kind of relationship I wished for, but I hated that any of this was happening.

My mother's face morphed from her pleasing social smile to something sharper. "Of course she doesn't, and of course we don't." Her eyes flicked to John. "You know who you belong with, Dahlia, and if we can't convince you, maybe a little external pressure can. His career is going to skyrocket, and this man's little beer business is hardly something to build prestige, let alone a happy life."

John's arms tightened reflexively, but not painfully. More like a pulse to show me he was there, but he wasn't going to try to speak for me.

"I don't understand how you can still believe that I'd ever want to be with Devon for *any* reason—how you can believe you're right about *my life*," I said, my voice only a sketch above a whisper.

"One might wonder the same about some of your choices, hmm?" Her brow arched, and then she turned, a winsome smile stretching across her mouth directed at my aunt. My father turned away, too, and just like that, we'd been dismissed.

Hurt and that same rage that'd been burning through me ravaged my insides and I bit down on a sound that would've been something between a sob and a scream. My jaw ached from clenching, every muscle in my body tight.

"Come on," John said low into my ear and guided me out of the room, not letting anyone else stop us to chat.

CHAPTER TWENTY-EIGHT

John

Her soft hand in mine, I led Dahlia through the maze of people and down the hallway to the elevators without another word. She looked like a teakettle seconds from boiling over and the mission was clear: get her out of there.

My mind brimmed with conflicting, clamorous thoughts, and I wanted to talk them through. I was typically an external processor. I needed conversation and interaction to help me make sense of things, and this horror show of an evening proved no different. But Dahlia needed space to process, too... or scream. Maybe we should've been heading outside, though privacy seemed essential.

Neither of us spoke, though I had to bite my tongue a few times not to ask her what I could do or what she was thinking. She didn't need me provoking her after her ex *and* parents had just done their worst at that.

Her hand stayed in mine, firmly gripping my own the entire time. No weakness or slagging to her—she wasn't about to fall apart. After her ex's little flex and her parents' clear preference for him and his political superstar future displayed yet again, I wondered if she'd start crying or get that zoned-out, overwhelmed look I'd seen on and off the last few weeks.

So far, the only thing I knew was that she needed a minute, and I was going to give it to her. I unlocked the door and we went inside, our hands finally dropping as she paced toward the sliding glass door, then turned and headed back towards me again.

"I'm going to give you some space and I'll be back in about thirty minutes. If you need more time, just text me."

Her eyes snapped to me, but she nodded. Relief hit when I registered the expression there—not one of injury, or pain, or needing to curl up in a ball and cry. Any of those would've been perfectly fine because she should feel however she needed to feel.

But no. What I saw in Dahlia's eyes hit me between the ribs, a sharp jab of that fire I loved to see, and something I could only title *determined rage*.

"Be back soon," I said by way of acknowledgment, and then slipped out. I had no destination in mind other than *not* back down to the Price family-sponsored cocktail hour, and I'd seen signs directing to a few places I wanted to check out. After wandering and effectively avoiding anyone in her family's retinue, I returned to the room exactly thirty-three minutes after leaving her, bracing for whatever I'd find behind the door.

Thing was, I wanted to be empathetic. I wanted to be the shoulder she could cry on if she needed that, or her confidante, or just someone to make her laugh and cut through all this BS. The worst thought I'd had in the last half hour was that I may not know or be able to give her what she needed.

But... why should I care? Not that I was unfeeling—sometimes, I felt too much, really. But why would I worry about being able to take care of her when all of this would come to an end in a matter of days?

The way my stomach sank into a pit at that thought should've been an alarm, but I shrugged off that fear, knocked before entering the room, and found her standing, still in her three-inch heels and stunning dress, facing the windows. I wondered if she'd stood there the entire time, rage staring out the window.

Internally, I debated whether to even ask. Because really, it was just stupid to say words like, "Are you okay?" out loud after her ex had tried to push us to get married during her sister's wedding and her own parents had admitted to agreeing to it if it would ultimately force her to fess up that we weren't really in a relationship.

Mercifully, she broke the silence first without turning away from the view. "Thanks for giving me some space."

"Need more?" I asked, shoving my hands into my pockets when the image of me approaching her from behind and wrapping my arms around her took hold of my mind. *Not helpful, John.*

But, God, what if it would be? What if my touch could soothe her and light her on fire like hers did for me? What if I could bring her comfort and safety the way my heart clawed at me to do? Was it a fundamental flaw in my character to wish I could help her, or was it that part of me that just wanted to help people more generally?

I knew better. If this were someone else, I likely would offer a hug. I wouldn't worry my closeness would prove to be so unbearably charged I might take something more than an embrace, I might reveal something far bigger than I realized.

She turned away and met my eyes, effectively sending my stomach plummeting four floors to the ground. Because rage?

Rage looked *amazing* on Dahlia Price.

She'd be stunning in slouchy sweats or jeans or a plastic bag, but she had literally stolen the words from my brain or mouth or wherever words were supposed to come from when she'd stepped out of the bathroom and asked me to help with her zipper.

That same dress that framed her decolletage like the art she was, the off-the-shoulder style so gorgeous I could still hardly think through the clutch of wanting I felt when I looked at her, only accentuated her beauty.

This was the problem with becoming friends with her and getting to know her. I couldn't pretend I disliked her anymore. We weren't fighting, she wasn't shoving me away, and I wasn't pushing back just to get a rise out of her and yet remind myself I didn't care what she thought of me.

Call it the dumbest logic ever, but a not-small part of me had thought a little too hard about actually marrying her this weekend. Just a flash of vision that had me watching, heart in my throat, as she walked down the aisle dressed in white, a pathway of flower petals at her feet. I'd snapped out of it in an instant, but it'd etched into my memory despite the brevity. I had no plans to get married, no plans to surrender my bleeding heart to someone and wait for her to trample it, but the image had arrived whether I'd summoned it or not.

"No. I think I'm good. I just..." She shook her head, lips pursing as she searched for the words. "I think I've almost burned through all the rage and now I just want some distraction."

"Well, in-room distractions are movies, food, or... uh, pretty sure I can dig up a deck of cards. Out-of-room distractions are better, though."

And frankly, staying in the room with her right now wouldn't be the best choice. Not with the way I felt drawn to her and the stark sense that *going* to her might be a genuine error in judgment. She didn't need me falling all over her while her family and her ex tried to control her.

"If you think we can find some space away from anyone I know other than you, lead the way." She finally moved away from the sliding doors and walked to me, stopping just a foot short of where I stood inside the room.

"I'll take that challenge. I scoped out a few options, but I think I have a good one. Trust me?" I held out a hand on reflex before I thought better of it.

Because if I had, I would've checked the impulse or kept them shoved deep in my pockets. I wouldn't have let that stupid, blind courage I'd foolishly let loose on Friday take the wheel.

But without hesitation, Dahlia set hers in mine and nodded.

"Of course."

Our gazes held and her words soaked into me like ink into fibrous paper, etching into the substance of me. *Trust me? Of course.* I didn't take it lightly that she meant those words—would do whatever I had to in order to keep that trust.

"Then let's go."

Ten minutes later, I'd led her to the roof and dug up a bottle of champagne and a platter of antipasti and a small plate of chocolate-dipped strawberries, all thanks to the kind soul at the reception desk who'd done me a huge solid. I'd have to make sure to give her a good employee feedback card or whatever Genevieve had in place to give her people encouragement.

"Okay, this is kind of amazing," Dahlia said as I approached her where she stood at the railing of the spa's roof.

The whole rooftop was finished with a glass wall to keep the view as visible from all points as possible. Clusters of cozy seating and small side tables centered around fire pits gave the cool evening a comfortable, welcoming vibe. They even had a small bar up here, staffed with one person. I wondered how Genevieve managed to keep this staffed since we were currently the only ones up here, but considering the luxury pricing of the spa and lodging, it made sense they'd be well-staffed.

"Incredible view," I said, refusing to take *her* in like I was the mountains nestling down in the darkness and the stars pricking the veil overhead as the last vestiges of purples and pinks disappeared at the horizon.

"It's so gorgeous. I love our view back home, but it's nice to be out here, a little farther from real life and a little closer to the heavens, it feels like." She turned and caught my gaze with a soft smile that seemed genuinely happy.

I raised the two flutes I'd obtained and the unopened bottle of champagne and her eyes lit. "Drink, m'lady?"

"Yes, please. Oh—" She fluttered over to the teak love seat and sank into the cream cushion of the bench. "You found real food."

She focused on the small table next to the couch that held our charcuterie and strawberries. I worked on easing the cork out of the champagne bottle, then poured our glasses, appreciating how she plucked meats and cheeses and built a neat stack before shoving it into her mouth.

Her groan had me shifting in my seat, sliding a glass her way without looking.

"You seem like you're perking up," I said, glad my voice didn't betray any of the wobbling, off-kilter that'd set in from those sparkly eyes and how our shoulders brushed here on the little couch.

"I think my rage lit everything else on fire and I've come out the other side." She raised her eyebrows like, *tada*, then took a giant bite of cracker, cheese, salami, and some kind of something else—maybe the tomato-bacon jam, which was mind-blowing, by the way. Maybe I could lure their chef away for the pub.

"And what's on this side of rage?"

After swallowing a sip of her champagne, she grinned. Yeah, Dahlia Price, in the same lodge as her family and her nasty ex who'd just tried to pressure her into getting married in less than a week and had her parents' support, grinned at me.

My little sucker of a heart rolled over before she ever spoke, but then she hit me with those sparkly eyes and it straight up dropped. This woman had no small amount of power over my internal organs, apparently.

"I was thinking we just... have fun. I just want to be here with you and have fun. That sound okay?"

Not leave early. Not tough it out. Not suffer through, or

spite her parents by being obnoxious, or hide out with Azalea and make the best of it. She wanted to have fun *with me.* "Course. Of course. That sounds ideal to me."

She chuckled and held up her flute. "Glad we're on the same page, Wallace."

I touched my glass to hers in a toast. "Likewise, Price."

CHAPTER TWENTY-NINE

Dahlia

I couldn't say why exactly my entire mindset had shifted, and I felt more settled in myself, in my bones and soul, than I had in months, but that was the truth of it.

Sometime between hearing my asshole ex try to convince a crowd of my family and my sister's friends that I should be married at the same time as her and my own parents looking down their noses at me for not choosing an abuser with a bright political path as my future husband over someone they didn't know at all and was freaking amazing, the framework of my mind had clicked into place.

It hadn't actually been a sudden shift. I'd felt myself moving, inching toward this realization and relief, but it'd been painful getting here. Like all the therapy and personal work I'd done for years had been forced to *work* for me these last few months since Devon weaseled his way back into my life. I'd had to use those affirmations again, remind myself who I was, and *believe* them. And dang if that hadn't been difficult.

Part of what I'd been struggling against—raging against, really—was the need to summon those tools and use them. Some part of me felt I should be free from needing them, like if I broke an arm, I shouldn't then need to address it with an X-ray and cast. No, this wasn't a broken arm, but it was breaking something—or it'd tried. That metaphor wasn't clicking, but it held true nonetheless.

Staring out the window after John left me in the room, something about the stretch of wilderness and open sky had made me take a full, real breath and the longer I stood there, the more I felt a certainty take root. It was so clear, I'd laughed aloud.

I had a life here, friends here, and Devon couldn't take that from me. John had gifted me with that stark reminder on Friday, and it'd never been more valuable than now. Granted, I was incredibly thankful for John's presence here with me, as I didn't want to face the jerk alone, but still. I didn't need to run around scared or intimidated or dreading what he'd try to force us into next because I was here as an *us*.

And then, John had opened the door after thoughtfully giving me space and... bam. Revelation number two hit. And that had been almost as profound.

I was going to kiss John Wallace. If he gave me even an inkling he wanted that, which I figured he might just do based on some of the heated looks we'd been trading, I'd go for it. Watching him sip champagne and tell me stories about the brewery and insane customer service requests they'd gotten, again I felt that kinship with him.

Well, kinship and almost unbearable attraction.

"She looked at me and she said, 'You have six weeks. It

can be done.'" His eyes were wide like it still made him crazy.

"Wait, this woman wanted you guys to brew her a special beer for her wedding?" I laughed at his expression when it only intensified.

"Yep. *Demanded* it. Like we owed it to her. It was wild." Shaking his head, he took another sip of his drink.

"I hate to ask, but was she famous? I've had some nutty requests and most of them have come from the uberwealthy or famous inhabitants of Silverton, or worse, the destination people." A host of memories scrolled through my mind.

He snapped and pointed at me. "Yes. *Yes.* I mean not famous, but the weirdly large collection of ridiculously rich people that've made their way to our little corner of the world? So many odd things pop up with that population."

"I had one guy order an arrangement, but he wanted it edible. I told him I didn't do that—those little baskets with fruit made to look like bouquets—and he was incensed. Then he kept saying, 'How much?' like offering me more money would change the fact that I arrange flowers and do not nor have I ever stocked cut, prepared fruit for delivery."

He grinned. "Well, how dare you?"

I laughed, shaking my head. "Right? The gall."

His smile widened and the little bubbles from my champagne seemed to have entered my blood, carrying a lightness to my fingers and toes. "It's funny to talk like that though, because until I moved here, I'd never really interacted with people like them. I mean, isn't your partner's brother Jamie Morris?"

"That he is. I grew up with the little dreamboat."

I covered my mouth to hide my guffaw, and while I did, he continued. "Meanwhile, you're best friends with Julian

Grenier's wife, Miss Mayhem herself, and Madeline Reynolds." He ticked them each off on a finger.

"Shhhh." My eyes darted around to make sure no one had heard, then mimed zipping my lips until he did the same. "Aren't you about to be related to Maddie?"

His smile softened then, and it was that—*that*—that made me melt. All that fizzy excitement whittled down into this brutally sweet sensation, and my heart squeezed.

"Yes. Cousin-in-law, technically."

"You and Aidan are really close, though. Closer than you and Mike in some ways, right?" For some reason, it sounded quieter now, like the night had stepped in to surround us, shrouding us in intimacy and closeness.

He set his glass aside and leaned forward, the movement rustling his shirt a little and lifting his warm, clean scent that I unabashedly inhaled. Well, maybe I would've been a little abashed, but he'd set his elbows on his knees and was staring at the fire instead of me being a weirdo.

"In a lot of ways, yeah. He's gotten a lot closer since Viv passed, both with me and my parents. I'm really grateful for him."

I studied his profile. His brows had notched down, the host of memories he must be replaying making that smiling mouth curve in the wrong direction. It struck me then that John was one of those people who always looked like he was smiling, or about to, but I'd so rarely seen that. He'd worn the mask of serious or irritable whenever we'd talked.

Unwilling to shift the conversation away from Aidan just yet, I took a deep breath. "He's so deeply grateful for you, John. From what he's said and what I've heard, you've been there for him through everything. That's pretty rare."

He shook his head just once. "Nah. He's been there for me, too. Plus, he's an easy guy to love."

Something about that made my throat tighten, and I instantly wanted to say, "You're an easy guy to love." The zaniest impulse, but the words lay right there. Because it'd become more and more unavoidable as we'd spent time together that he was truly a generous, funny, loving person. How had his ex treated him so poorly? Of course, he might've changed in the years since they were together, but the fabric of who John was couldn't have changed all that drastically.

"What?" he asked, now leaning up and watching me.

Unwilling to say exactly what I'd been thinking, but having a glass of champagne and only a handful of bites of the charcuterie board to eat, I spoke without thinking my words through like I normally tried to.

"I was just thinking your ex was an idiot." I tucked my lips together, then grabbed a chocolate-dipped strawberry and shoved it into my mouth to keep from saying any more.

It took him a minute, but he eventually asked, "Yeah? How so?"

The scrape of his words told me asking had cost him something. He wouldn't want to beg for more, and I got that, but I also understood the desire to know why someone would think that. Why a relationship that had been painful to get over seemed flawed in someone else's eyes, too, no matter how much that had been validated. It was something he'd been doing for me since I'd roped him into this mess, and I wanted to return the favor.

And maybe more than that, I wanted him to know I saw him.

So instead of hiding behind more chocolate-dipped strawberries, I wiped my mouth and adjusted on the little couch so I faced him. "I think you're the best kind of person, and I think she must've been the most selfish, awful person not to appreciate that about you. I don't know all the details of your... dynamic—" I cleared my throat, attempting to distract from the heat that'd hit my cheeks, before continuing. "But I do know she's missing out."

The darkness deprived me of seeing the hazel of his eyes, but they were pinned on me, and even without that mesmerizing color, they transfixed me.

He was all seriousness, none of the joking and smiling from minutes past, and that focus sent a prickling sense of anticipation all through me.

"You seem pretty confident for someone who's only just now getting to know me."

His voice held something dark and alluring in it, and this whole situation was doing things to my insides. "I do know you. Maybe not every little detail, but we know each other. We know enough."

His eyes narrowed ever so slightly, like he might call my bluff. "Do we?"

I nodded. "Yes."

Without looking away, his hand found the side of my face and he slipped his fingers into my hair and palmed my jaw. "There are a few ways we don't know each other at all."

Oh.

My.

Goodness.

So here's one thing I wasn't sure about until recently. Not that I'd spent much time imagining John in romantic scenarios, but because of his *nice guy* vibe with everyone else, I'd wondered if maybe he was *too* nice. I recalled he said his ex had wanted someone who was essentially *mean* to her, and obviously that wouldn't be John. But a quiet little voice in my head had wondered if maybe John was just super vanilla. Like, asked if he could kiss you, waited until there were too many signs type of guy. And don't get me wrong, there were some heroes who *needed* to ask. It depended on the heroine and their story, of course.

But the way my heart pounded in triple-time, the way his hand had just *taken* the touch, sent a thrill through every part of me. And more than anything I'd wanted in a long time, I wanted to know what he'd do next. "Like?"

His gaze grew hooded as it dropped to my lips, then met my eyes again after a lazy perusal of my features. "Like how you feel. How you taste."

A shuddering breath released and my brain said, "Let's go ahead and nail that down, then," but the magnificent man didn't wait for me to say it. Instead, he let his eyes fall to my mouth once more, then speared me with his magma gaze and took what he wanted.

That's right, *took* it. There was need and desire rolled up into the contact between us, a firm, alluring press that had me tilting my head and responding in an instant. His kiss was just the right mix of demanding and permissive. I could stop it at any time, just like I could've leaned away if I hadn't wanted it. He'd given me ample warning without stopping and asking, without ruining this momentum that had been building between us.

The light scrape of his beard on my chin, under my hand sliding against his jaw, the sensation of his rough palm on my knee...

A throat cleared, too nearby to be someone in one of the other seating areas.

I jumped back when the thought fully registered, Rose's stiff, cross-armed pose catching my attention the minute I opened my eyes.

She peered down at us, fury etched across her face. "You are *not* crashing my wedding with this guy."

CHAPTER THIRTY

John

It took a few seconds to orient myself to the new reality. As it was, the axis of my world had tip-tilted to one side when Dahlia had met my kiss with as much enthusiasm and desire as I'd dreamed, and I didn't want anything to nudge it back upright. I never wanted to forget the sweet slip of her lips against mine, the taste of chocolate and champagne and *her*.

But now, here was her sister, interrupting and bringing little storm clouds right along with her frowny face.

Seriously, weren't brides supposed to be happy?

"I have no intention of marrying him this weekend," Dahlia said, rising to her feet.

I joined her, hoping I didn't look as dazed as I felt or as mildly disgusted by Rose's whole thing here. Shouldn't she realize that stupid Devon wouldn't be the person to dictate when Dahlia chose to marry her fiancé? How was no one questioning that element of this whole ridiculous scenario?

"You didn't seem too determined to tell anyone otherwise. It's just so like you to be difficult," Rose said, still pouting and arms crossed like an eight-year-old rather than someone at least twenty years older *and* an oldest child.

Maybe I had the wrong idea, but all the oldests I knew, including my own brother and my partner, were conscientious and hard-working, not spoiled like this one. Also, what was this about Dahlia being difficult?

"I'm pretty sure you ran away in a huff the second he said anything about it, and second, I wasn't about to pitch a fit and make a big show of refusing to do that because, well, why would I? Why would I allow my ex to determine when my own wedding would take place? In what universe would that make sense?"

Rose blinked, then her long lashes fluttered and she looked a little stunned. "Oh. Yeah, I guess that is a little messed up."

Dahlia held out a hand as if to say *thank you*, and I nodded, my hand finding its home on her lower back.

"It is. The fact that he's even here is pretty messed up, honestly..."

Before Dahlia had finished speaking, Rose was already shaking her head like she'd heard enough. "Don't stand there and give me your sob story. You chose to break up with him, and he's Conrad's best friend. I'm not sure what you expected, but he was always going to be a part of our day."

Dahlia's throat worked to swallow, but instead of tears, or anger, or anything else, she simply seemed resigned. "Fine, Rose. Fine. It's your day—your *week*—and you won't have any trouble from me."

"Nor will you—"

"Nor will we get married on the same day, or month, *or year*." I could hear her eyes rolling, and I saw the gesture mimicked on her older sister's face.

"Good. Well, then... carry on. Or go get a room," she said, that parting shot supposed to... who knew. Offend us? We were engaged, and though yes, I felt a little flush at my cheeks, I was pretty sure it lingered thanks to our kiss and not her sister's rude comments.

Dahlia didn't respond. Instead, she turned to me, mischief in her eyes, and pulled on my tie until I lowered my head. She rose on her toes and kissed me.

Just like that.

Clearly aimed at upsetting Rose, and though I had mixed feelings about the motivation, I couldn't help but have one very vivid feeling on the matter of her lips on mine. Something like *yes,* and *more please*, and *never stop.*

I pulled back after a moment, eyes flickering between hers. "Good job."

"Liked that, huh?" One side of her mouth slid up into a satisfied smirk.

"I mostly meant standing up to her, but you can certainly apply that to the kiss as well," I said, brushing my hands down the two sides of my jacket to keep them from reaching for her again.

She sighed, glancing up at the stars, then sank into the seat. She leaned back, resting her head on the top of the cushion and gazing up into the sky, and I wondered whether I should give her more space. It was the last thing I wanted to do, but I also didn't have any idea how to navigate this odd dynamic of wanting her, and her wanting me, but also needing to put on a show for her family. What was real, what was in my head, and what was just because of the circumstances? Had I funneled all the longing for what Aidan and Maddie had found into this situation because I knew ultimately, I was safe from really risking anything in my role of fake fiancé?

Her fingers lightly grasping my hand drew my attention back to her.

"Stay with me? Let's look at the stars."

The slight tug convinced me, though her words would've, too. Didn't she know how much I wanted moments like this with her?

Hard to believe it'd only been a matter of months since we'd been at each other's throat every time we crossed paths. Now here we sat on the same love seat on a rooftop, admiring the stars and feeling something open up in a way it hadn't before. *What* had done that, what part of me, I wasn't sure.

"Sometimes, I think I get so focused on the small things and that's why I get so overwhelmed. The last few months, I think I've forgotten to look out and up and remember there's more to life than just *me, me, me.*"

I pivoted my head to the left to look at her without lifting my head. "It's okay for you to worry about your own life, though."

She glanced at me, then focused back on the show Orion and the Big Dipper were putting on overhead.

"I know. But I think getting out of town has reminded me that all of this... it's going to be fine." She bit her lip as though thinking about saying more, then continued. "I'm not sure I would've gotten to this place of feeling so accepting without you." Her eyes flicked to me. "I can't explain what it means to me that despite the way I've treated you, you've been so supportive."

I nodded, mind scrambling for the appropriate

response. "It wasn't just you... and I'm glad to help," I said, because anything else would've been too much. Admitting I'd helped because I'd felt compelled to in the moment wouldn't have been very heroic, and revealing that I'd been rapidly stumbling into feelings for her the last few weeks wasn't something I planned to do now or ever. She didn't need my mountain of unrequited feelings piling onto everything right now, and soon enough, I'd be able to deal with them when we went our separate ways. I'd take the planned split rather than suffer an unexpected one.

She didn't respond, but her hand fitted itself back into mine and we stayed like that, shoulder to shoulder, heads back and eyes on the magnificence above us. That vastness that reassured her that this, too, would pass, that there was more to life than her problems, had what might've been the opposite effect on me. It made me feel small and unworthy —of her, of this spot next to her. I wasn't someone who suffered particularly low self-esteem, but the risk of opening up to someone again when it'd gone so brutally wrong before gnawed at me.

Because the truth was, I already felt more for Dahlia than I ever had for Tina. Yes, we'd kissed, but could that be trusted? Could any of this?

What I'd always known, even before I'd caught feelings, slapped me across the face with glittering stars and night sky eternity: real or no, the end was coming. This woman who'd once told me she wasn't interested, who'd shoved me back into a place of insecurity and self-doubt with a simple phrase, was quickly becoming the most important person in my life.

And I was a fool to let her.

The sudden harshness of that thought sliced through me and I sat up. "I think I'm going to turn in."

She sat up and stretched, more unbothered than I'd ever seen her. "I'll come, too."

We gathered up our things—her purse, our phones, and she snuck one last chocolate-covered strawberry—and then left the roof. Maybe we'd come out here tomorrow night to avoid the larger gathering. Maybe by then, the stars wouldn't nag me with their beauty, their brightness, their unobscured sparkling.

Somehow, I'd forgotten about the room situation until we stepped back through the door and I saw the bed. That *one* bed. The view of her in that dress and the curious anxiety over what would happen at the cocktail hour with her family, then trying to get her away and those kisses, her sister, the damn in-your-face joyousness of the stars... it'd all distracted me from thinking through how we'd handle this moment.

"You want the bathroom first?" she asked, breaking through my clanging thoughts.

"Uh, no. Go ahead."

She shut herself in and I changed into the threadbare T-shirt and gray sweats I'd thankfully brought. Since I hadn't planned on sleeping in the same room, I'd planned on sleeping in boxers and nothing else, as usual, but that wouldn't fly tonight. Definite no. I focused too hard on my phone when she came out and refused to look at her. No idea what she was wearing nor would I look. *I will not look.*

"Your turn," she said, voice a little rough, maybe from talking so much over the last few hours.

"Thanks," I mumbled, still refusing to look up as I shuffled into the bathroom and went through the motions.

Whether she wore an old sweatshirt or something frilly and stylish, it'd be the death of me. I didn't want to know what Dahlia slept in because I desperately wanted to know what she slept in.

Alas, I emerged from the bathroom and my traitor eyes sought her like I hadn't just spent the last five minutes chanting through all the things I needed to remember—*don't look at her, don't touch her, she's not yours.*

That was the crux of it—she wasn't mine. Certainly not after the next two weeks.

The vision of her sitting on the bed with her e-reader in her lap, hair loose around her, face clean of makeup, sent my pulse skittering and my gut tightening like I'd been punched. Yes, she was that lovely.

She must've been reading something good, because she had a little smile on her mouth, just a hint of a curve and one of so many to admire because she did, in fact, wear something that sent my mind reeling. Just a cropped loose T-shirt and shorts, but there was skin. *So. Much. Skin.*

I shouldn't have thought it or felt it or *anything* about it, but I wanted to touch the expanse between the hem of her shirt and the top of her shorts, the smooth space that looked like a gap I should fill. *Let's not think about filling gaps, eh, Johnny boy?* I shook my head at myself, but I must've made a sound because she glanced up, a question on her face even as she pulled the sheet to cover her up to the chin.

So maybe she hadn't meant for me to see what she was wearing. This made me feel better and worse, but mostly better.

Or worse.

Who could tell?

"Good book?" I asked, working to focus my brain on something other than the woman in a bed I was about to get into.

"So good. It's a comfort reread."

I took my place on the right side, making sure to stay to the edge and not encroach. Granted, it was a king and there was really no way I'd touch her unless I tried. *Maybe you should...*

"You reread books? How often?"

Her wry smile didn't help the twisting inside me, but I forced myself to focus on her words instead of how much I liked her and liked being close to her this way. Getting into a bed with Dahlia next to me would make every future occasion of getting into bed without her there seem markedly worse.

I silently cursed the reality that the simple act of going to bed would now be haunted by this moment.

"I have a few series I reread every year—they just make me happy and I find new things to love about them all the time. But there's nothing like reading a great book for the *first* time. I just wasn't up for the risk this week."

"Risk?" I wondered aloud at her wording.

"You know that feeling—you start a book and have such high hopes and then it just doesn't click with you? Might even be a fabulous book, but you're just not into it for whatever reason?"

I nodded. "The worst." Admittedly, I wasn't as much of a reader as her or even Bruce Almighty or the others in her book club, but I did read. Slow and steady, I got through a decent number of books each year enough to hold my own.

She squinted at me. "You making fun of me?"

I shook my head. "Absolutely not. I love that you're such a book nerd." And then immediately realized the error.

But her eyes lit up. "Yeah?"

I didn't want to explain it, so I just nodded. "Yeah."

And then, she tucked back into her book, reading with that soft smile on her face, turning pages like it was a reflex, and I worked to keep my mind on my own paperback, determined to enjoy the time here and not worry about every little thing I said. I should be worrying about helping her have a good time, convincing her family, and I could worry about the fallout for my own heart and mind when all of this was over.

I'd long since given up holding back due to the risk.

CHAPTER THIRTY-ONE

Dahlia

I woke slowly, only registering the warmth near me after stretching and finding myself pressed up against a body.

An immovable, giant body, which, once I clocked it, sent my heart galloping. I turned my head carefully, hoping not to wake him, and looked at the scene. John lay on his stomach, his head facing away from me but his body taking up the middle of the bed. And there was me.

I lay on my side, my leg kicked over a pillow and somehow under one of his legs, and my hand on his—

I sucked in a breath and snatched my hand back. Because yeah, my hand had been on his ridiculously round butt. Forgive me for saying it, but apparently, sleeping Dahlia couldn't resist? *Oh, good grief, what am I going to tell him?*

I had maybe admired his behind in those sweatpants. *Maybe.* But I hadn't realized that I'd stared long enough to embed the desire to get to know said gray sweat-panted rear *in my unconscious.*

My cheeks flamed and I leaped out of bed before he roused and caught me red-handed, *and I do mean that* literally because my hand was flaming with heat just like the rest of me. I scampered into the bathroom and got cleaned up, searching for something to talk about or do instead of reliving how delectable it had been to wake next to John.

When I emerged, I went straight to my phone and sat gingerly on the edge of the bed. I'd get changed and leave him to sleep in, but I—

I gasped. "What?"

Quickly, I scrolled through my building manager's frantic texts, and then Quinn's calls, stopping at the recorded messages and holding the phone to my ear. Next to me, John roused and rolled over, but I couldn't appreciate the sight of him waking with sleepy eyes and bedhead and ambling into the bathroom because the message was, as had been the pattern lately, bad news.

"Sorry to tell you this, Dahlia, but the pipes broke and we only found it after a puddle of water was seeping out the front door and into the hallway. The whole kitchen and living room were flooded with a few inches, and we're going to need some time to sort this out. Call me back and we'll work on getting it cleaned up better than our temporary job, but you'll definitely need somewhere to stay for the next while. As far as I can tell, nothing got into the shop, but you'll want to check it out today so we can include that in the insurance claims."

My hand dropped away from holding it to my head and I ran through what might be ruined. If just a few inches, maybe only the furniture, and maybe it could dry out? The floors would be warped, but as a renter, that wasn't my problem. Beyond that, it would mean more time until I could get back into my place again.

The flowers would be okay unless the fridges were ruined, and even then, it couldn't have been a full day since we'd only been here since yesterday evening. It would be fine. Everything would be fine and this wouldn't derail the wedding.

"Everything okay?" John came out rubbing a towel through his hair and wearing a pair of jeans and a fresh T-shirt, but he froze when our eyes connected.

"Not really. That pipe they fixed a few days ago flooded and my apartment is a wreck." My voice sounded watery and small even though I didn't realize I'd started to cry.

He moved to me in an instant, dropping the towel and bending down, almost kneeling, and grabbed my hand. "What can I do?"

I blinked, a flare of panic rising in me. "I don't know. I'm not sure what to do."

He squeezed my hands and tucked some of the hair that'd fallen into my face behind my ear. "Let's pack up and get back there so we can clean up. You can grab what you need and stay with me—I've got plenty of room."

"I don't want to impose. I—"

"Hey." He tipped my chin up to look at him. "You aren't an imposition. *You* are never an imposition and I want to help. We'll take care of this."

"Um, okay. Yeah." And even though my words came out uncertain and winded, his certainty, his ability to see a way forward and take me with him to get there, dampened the sense of doom.

Hours later, I dumped my suitcase and backpack in John's spare room and slumped onto the side of the bed. "I don't know how I'll ever thank you for this."

He gave me a small, reassuring smile and sat next to me. "You didn't ask for this. I know that. But please believe me when I say I'm glad I can help."

I couldn't look him in the eyes without getting teary-eyed. It wasn't so much that the flood had ruined anything important as it was one more way I'd had to lean on him. After thinking it through on our drive back to Silverton, I'd realized I should look for other options. I couldn't ask John to go through all of this *and* still attend the wedding. He'd already told off my sister when she accused me of bailing. I hadn't even heard all he'd said, but I'd let him do it.

I'd let him intervene without feeling bad about it... until I realized just what this might mean. It'd only serve to confuse his family more when we didn't get married, when we weren't engaged anymore.

And the dumbest thing? The thought of that, of all of this ending, made my heart downright ache.

But the closer to Silverton we got, the clearer it became. Yes, I could ask Quinn since she lived in a monster mansion or Maddie for the same reason, but both of them were living with their partners and kids. Well, Maddie wasn't, but she'd had so much invaded privacy and she, Aidan, and Luca were just starting to figure out their lives together. They didn't need me squatting there.

Calla would offer, too. So would Sadie or Sarah. Heck, Jane would probably insist I move in immediately. Even

Bruce would likely offer me his spare room, but I couldn't see John liking that, nor would it make sense for me to move into another man's house when I was supposedly engaged to this one.

And there I came back to John. Sweet, handsome, thoughtful, capable John, who hadn't hesitated to defend me, help me, or care for me.

For as many times as I'd regretted how our relationship began and how I'd let it continue in such a nasty way, it was probably for the best. If I'd gotten to know him years ago, I probably would've fallen madly in love with him, and that would've been terrible timing for both of us.

"Thank you. Truly. If you're allowed to help, then I'm allowed to say thank you and be grateful."

He wrapped an arm around me, and I settled my head on his shoulder, savoring his comfort and wishing...

What *was* I wishing? The whole day had been skimmed through this lens I couldn't quite identify, and it had nothing to do with being upset about the pipes. Yes, I hated they burst and I was out of the house, but it was almost like... like the dissatisfaction came from the sense that this time with John, with us as a team and that whole *we'll handle it* thing was fleeting.

A few more days until the rehearsal, then the wedding. A week after that and I'd be faking it one last time for the Wallaces' fortieth, and then...

"You ready for bed?" he asked softly.

"Better get to it. There's more to do at the apartment, but at least this way, I'll get a lot done tomorrow without the drive home."

"That's right. There's that positive spin." He turned his head and pressed a kiss to my hair.

My heart ached. Why was it aching so much? What the

heck was happening to me? I needed sleep. That was it. That was all. It came down to another thing to deal with on top of a stressful week, and here he was being sweet and kind and smelling faintly of his soap and deodorant and *man*.

After another few seconds just breathing him and the peace and safety he cloaked me in, I sat up and pulled him up off the bed, then wrapped my arms around his neck and hugged him. His arms encircled me instantly, and I blinked back tears, his scent and presence, that alluring combination of comforting and thrilling, pressing all around me. "Thank you."

His warm hands smoothed along my back in soothing columns, then he squeezed me to him tightly before stepping away. "I know you'll be up early, so get some sleep."

"Night, John," I said as he walked away, a sense of loss stinging at me as the distance spread between us. I couldn't very well say, "Don't go," because that would mean... a lot. And as much as I wanted to get closer to John, right now, tonight, after exhaustion and upheaval, was not the time.

But when his hand gripped the doorframe and he looked back and said, "Night, Dahlia," and his eyes lingered on mine for a beat too long before he turned away and left, the thought that this wasn't the time didn't hit me so wrong.

Just because *now* wasn't didn't mean there wouldn't be time. Maybe after all of this was over....

CHAPTER THIRTY-TWO

John

Three days. Three days since I'd seen Dahlia.

Technically, I'd seen her, but just in passing. I hadn't had time with her. I hadn't gotten to touch her or really talk to her. I hadn't gotten any of her at all, and I was a man starving for her.

The last time we'd had any meaningful dialogue had been Tuesday night when she'd settled into my guest bedroom I only partly regretted having, which was technically only forty-eight hours ago, but it felt like forever, and since today was Thursday, I was counting it as three.

Don't worry about the math.

Point was, I missed her. A lot. And while I fully recognized the peril that indicated for me and my heart and my general future, I couldn't deny the *need* I felt when thinking about Dahlia. Not physical—or not *just*—I just... needed to know she was okay.

She'd been working her butt off, she and her assistants taking up residence at her shop to deal with incoming orders, a local event they were doing centerpieces for, and of course, Rose's wedding. Add to that having to deal with the water damage, though her building manager had taken the brunt of actual repairs, and she was practically a ship in the night. Azalea had been there whenever she could, so I took heart she had a good team around her.

I sent food and treats and dropped by once a day to check on her. She always seemed happy to see me. I was always way too happy to see her and had to remind myself that once a day was my max except to swing by and make sure they were making progress on her apartment cleanup.

But tonight, I'd asked if I could meet her for dinner and she'd messaged an enthusiastic *yes please*, then followed it up by a request for takeout and sitting on my couch if I was okay with that.

She had no idea how okay with it I was. I loved the idea of having time for just the two of us. I was a social person and loved seeing my friends and family, but lately, all I wanted was time with her to myself. They all seemed to expect that every waking second would be spent on wedding prep, and while it did for her, I mostly spent my days prepping for interviews next week, double-checking details on upcoming events including my parents' anniversary, and thinking about her.

So when she walked in while I was flipping through channels attempting to distract myself from the clock ticking closer to the time when she'd arrive, my heart leapt. Then I chastised that heart and told it to simmer down because I had to get a lock on these feelings.

"Hey, sorry I'm—scratch that. Rewind. Let me just say,

'I'm home!'" She rounded the corner from the entryway and shot me a killer-cute grin.

"Well done avoiding apologizing. I like that." I did like it. I wasn't blowing smoke. She was genuinely trying not to apologize for running a few minutes late, which needed no apology, and I loved that she was working through habits like this one that'd popped up when jerkhole Devon did.

She dumped her purse on the counter but didn't stop until she'd slumped onto the couch next to me, grabbed a pillow, placed it in my lap, and dropped her head down so she lay curled up to sleep right there. It happened so fast, I'd hardly moved. Watching her come straight to me and curl up next to me—on me—made that silly heart of mine swell.

There wasn't anyone here to judge it. Wasn't anyone here to impress with our closeness. This was just... actual closeness.

I brushed her hair back from her face and studied her. She'd shut her eyes and looked relaxed. That quickly, she'd nestled into this spot, and though I was very hungry, I thought I might need to forgo eating indefinitely, if she wanted to stay there.

"You okay?" I asked softly, not wanting to disturb her, but needing to know.

Her eyes blinked open, and she rolled onto her back just a bit so our eyes met. "Yeah. I'm feeling good. Just totally exhausted."

"I bet."

"And... I've missed you."

I tensed, wanting that to be true. "Yeah?"

She bit her lip, nodding and pinning me with those dark eyes that sent my mind spiraling. A crush of longing for this moment between us to be as big as it felt like it could be hit swift and strong, but before that letdown of reality followed, she leaned up and reached for me.

I would never get over the thrill of that action, the unexpected and yet fully welcomed move of her arching up and steadying herself on one arm while her opposite hand reached for the back of my head and pulled me toward her.

Smart lad that I was, I instantly dove into the kiss and reveled in the fact that Dahlia was evidently as hungry for me as I was her. One of my arms found her back, the other sliding into the hair at her neck, and our lips continued their elated exploration of each other. Wanting nothing more than to sink into the kiss and drown in it, I lost any sense of time or anything beyond Dahlia's mouth and hands and the soft sounds she made that only drove me farther into the oblivion of this contact.

Until an unearthly sound shattered the moment and she gasped, pulling back, eyes wide. Her mouth dropped open, then she covered it, and said, "I'm so sorry," behind her palm before her eyes crinkled and shut and she was laughing.

Because that demonic sound from the deep had been her stomach rumbling. We may have been distracted by each other, but her body had decided to make clear it hadn't forgotten about the takeout food warming in the oven or the necessity of eating.

I cupped the back of her head and pulled her close, hugging her to me as I laughed with her. "Guess we can't ignore that, can we?"

She leaned away. "Better not."

I nodded, sorry to see the kiss come to such a firm end but enjoying this light, pure moment of closeness and silliness with her. "Let's get you fed."

We chatted over dinner, and though I wanted to return to where we'd been on the couch and get close again, we both needed sleep. With the rehearsal dinner tomorrow, she'd have a long day and I'd be dealing with her family, both of which required a full night's rest. Plus, I also didn't want us to start anything on the shaky foundations of a fake relationship. We'd talk later, after this weekend, decide where we stood on firm footing, and then I'd know we could move forward. Until then, best stick to keeping up appearances, mostly.

We parted after dinner with friendly goodnights, and my chest did its usual aching routine as I went through the motions of getting ready.

But the knock on my door that came late—long after I'd assumed she'd gone to bed—sent my heart racing.

"So I just need to tell you something real quick," she said, leaning against the doorframe a few feet from where I stood holding the panel open.

"You can tell me anything," I said, enjoying the sight of her wrapped up in a too-large sweatshirt and a pair of small shorts she used for sleeping.

She looked shy, which through all of this, wasn't an expression I'd seen on her often. Quiet, yes. Furious even, yes. But shy? "What is it, Dahlia?"

With a purposeful exhale, she gripped the frame and bit her lip. "I just need you to know how much this means to me. I've been going around in my head about whether I should just show up and tell everyone the truth, but knowing you'll be with me is the only thing that's keeping me from feeling completely upside-down when I think of these next two days. It's been..." she huffed. "It's been stupidly hard and I'm so thankful for you."

"You know I'm glad to help," I said, repeating a line I'd said so many times, it came without thought. It was true, though it hid a lot. It hid all the things I'd tried to hide from myself and couldn't ignore anymore, even knowing how bad the fallout would be.

"I know, and I believe you. What I want to make sure you know is that I feel comfortable with you. I can be myself. And I can't—" She cleared her throat, eyes flicking past me into the room, then back to me. "I can't tell you what a relief that is. Our... friendship... is a safe place for me, and I don't think I'd ever thought I'd feel that way again."

My pulse raced in my veins, satisfaction and a tinge of fear slipping in. "I'm glad. I think you're incredible." That was the least of it. And though some small part of me died at the use of *friendship*, I wouldn't want her to feel otherwise. I'd be her safe place indefinitely, long after the wedding and my parents' reunion. I'd be her friend no matter what. That, at least, didn't have to go back to the way it was before. Those foundations would be solid and stable, even though not the ones I'd choose. But I'd respect her decision. Always.

Her lips parted, those wide, dark eyes vulnerable and open to me. "Likewise, Wallace. You're a pretty special guy."

It almost felt like an apology. My heart clutched at the thought because I recognized the truth of it—she was apologizing. For the whole mess, possibly, but also because all of this would end. Maybe some part of her wished the circumstances were different—that she was in a place to have more with me. There was consolation in that, even if a very poor version of it. "Well, thanks."

"I hope they all behave, but if not, just know I think the world of you." Her eyes glittered at me and something there looked sad.

Why did this all just feel wrong? The center of me hollowed out with these thoughts of how the delicious tension and heat between us would necessarily be traded for purely friendly exchanges, a distance marked by space and time and circumstance that would drive us apart. No, I didn't want that version of our story.

I wanted to take her hand and lead her into my room, into my bed. I wanted to show her how much I felt for her, how much I wanted her, or if nothing else, just hold her and cherish her and love her.

Love her.

Crap.

I couldn't say that. Couldn't *do* any of that. So I nodded, forcing a semblance of a smile out. "You, too, Dahlia. You've got to know you're so... so much more than they have ever let you believe."

She swallowed hard, like hearing those words pained her. "I know."

Before I gave in and reached for her, touched her, I stepped back. "Night, Dahlia."

"Night, John."

CHAPTER THIRTY-THREE

Dahlia

If I didn't murder the bride first, the wedding would likely be the most beautiful I'd ever done. Warrick and Sadie's would surpass it when it happened next month, but still. I could admit it was going to be truly lovely. While the bouquets weren't particularly imaginative, they were classic, and that's what my sister had ordered.

Because her wedding was essentially what I'd planned long before I'd left Devon. And that was just... so weird. But I'd made it to this point, and John would be arriving to the rehearsal dinner soon. Since I'd been scurrying around getting flowers ready at the rehearsal dinner space and also acting as part of the wedding party despite barely being friends with my sister, I'd gotten the debrief but hadn't had much downtime to think through the events.

Until it came my turn to walk down the aisle, trailing behind two of Rose's college sorority sisters and followed by

Azalea, and for some insane reason, it was Devon's arm I hooked mine through.

I'd been paired with Joseph, a nice guy in his mid-thirties and married to one of the sisters, but now here I was, touching Devon. *Touching* him. Close enough to hear his low-spoken, "Just as it should be, Dolly. This could be us any time you say."

Frustration made every muscle in my body tense. He could have anyone he wanted, and yet here he was, pushing this. In his version of a twisted fairytale, he must've imagined that with me, there'd be no work involved. He'd already cowed me to what he wanted in a trophy wife—if we ignored the fact that I left him and was engaged to someone else. And that, apparently, merited repeating.

"I'm engaged to someone else."

His arm flexed and he pulled me closer as he spoke through a false smile. "You can't really mean to disappoint everyone in your family. You're not actually *that* stupid, are you?"

He thought he could talk to me like this and that I'd take it. Because for a time, I had. What he wasn't getting through that thick, arrogant skull of his was I never would again. Not ever.

Fortunately, the short walk down the aisle ended, and I pulled away from him without looking back. John had a meeting for an upcoming event he couldn't reschedule but he'd be at the rehearsal dinner.

I said something to Azalea about heading to the dinner venue so someone would know, but they wouldn't care, with the possible exception of Devon, and I had no interest in hearing more of his nonsense.

Thankfully, the rehearsal dinner itself would be hosted just down the hill at Elk Street Grill, and after that, I wouldn't have to go far to get home to John's. Tomorrow, I'd be loading up the van and hauling everything we hadn't set up yet to the resort where we had the whole reception scene set, and the wedding itself would take place in this beautiful old-fashioned white chapel the resort had recently built for events just like this.

Ten minutes later, I'd hidden in the bathroom until John's text that he'd arrived came through, and I went to find him. The room had filled in with the rest of the wedding party and all our extended family. With it being a destination wedding, this dinner was very large, too—so large that my parents had rented out the entire Elk Street Grill.

Relief hit me when I saw him and before I could stop them, my eyes filled with tears.

He took me by the shoulders and dipped his head. "What's wrong? Who do I kill?"

I huffed a laugh, but he didn't break.

"Seriously, Dahlia. What happened? What can I do?"

I shut my eyes, which only forced two giant tears to track down my cheeks before I wiped my face and sucked in a breath. "They're having me walk out with Devon."

He gritted his teeth. "I'll talk to them."

But I didn't want that. I didn't want the fight. I could handle walking out with the idiot one more time—in the midst of the recessional music and under the eyes of a crowd, he wouldn't hurt me. It really wasn't even *him* hurting me now.

"No, don't bother. Twenty-four hours from now, it'll be done and everything can get back to normal."

His gaze rested heavy on me, inspecting me for hidden injuries, maybe. "We can go. You don't have to stay for this, right? We can just go and get tacos and margaritas and I'll buy you the new Josie Wade book and tuck you into bed early."

He brushed a lock of my hair behind my ear the way he did sometimes and I melted.

But in reality, I stood strong. Because I wanted to see this through—I wanted them to know their games weren't working and I wasn't budging. And when this was all over, we would do that. It sounded like a perfect date to me. I took his hands in mine and squeezed them. "Thank you. That is maybe the sweetest thing you've ever said. But I need to stay. I need to show them I'm strong, and I'm not bending."

After another handful of seconds studying me, he nodded. "Okay. Whatever you want." And then, he took my hand and we moved into the crowd, making our way toward the chart that held our seating assignments.

Unfortunately, my hope that a recessional with Devon would be the worst of the discomfort fell flat when we reached the table. Devon sat with his arm slung around the back of an empty chair. Next to him were my parents, Rose and Conrad, and another set of bridesmaids. My temper spiked, but Azalea quickly took one for the team, earning her yet another round of my eternal devotion, and slipped into the seat Devon had draped himself over.

"I think you guys are over at that table," she said, notching her chin to where she must've been assigned. Two empty seats waited next to a cousin and someone else... I honestly didn't care.

"Oh, perfect, thanks, Azalea."

I tugged John away from the head table, relieved and frankly shocked no one had protested. But it wouldn't look good to be fighting over that, even if they hadn't planned on Azalea at the head table. Which, why not? Why would she not be seated there instead of the other non-family couple? I couldn't pretend they wouldn't seat Devon there, even though he wasn't family.

The rest of the night moved surprisingly quickly. Toasts were made. Devon managed to keep his words on the subject of my sister and her almost husband and avoided all mention of me and John. And I wandered out into the parking lot at the end of Elk Street feeling remarkably relieved. *One more day.*

Devon hadn't even spoken to me the rest of the night, but he'd sent me looks that would've sent heat through me in the past. The sexy, dark-eyed looks he used to seduce a woman, and I wondered how many other people he'd shared those looks with since we'd broken up. Probably too many to count—one more reason I didn't understand why he was bothering at all. Maybe he wanted the Price name by his side, or more likely, he wanted my father's support on whatever future political trail he actually took. The Prices may not've been particularly powerful, but they had scads of money, and if they backed the right guy, that could put them in a place of power like they'd always, *always* wanted.

I fell into bed that night despite wanting to talk with John. He'd been on a call with his mom about something when I'd gone to say goodnight, and if he'd checked on me before he turned in, I must've been asleep already.

Wedding day was a blur. My sister looked beautiful, and whether from relief or exhaustion or actual good feelings, I teared up during the vows. I'd spotted John in the pews but hadn't gotten to talk to him beyond a few texts checking in on each other. Though I hadn't been given any real bridesmaid duties, the flowers and the usual ritual of dressing together in the bridal suite had occupied the entire day.

We did photos before the wedding so that after, once I'd processed down the aisle with Devon and hummed in my head to avoid his words, I released him and escaped dealing with him until we were announced into the reception hall a few minutes later.

My eyes sought John even as Devon stroked his hand over mine where it rested lightly on his—just enough not to be notably uncomfortable.

"You look great, Dolly." He said it low and sweet like he expected it to take root.

I glanced at him with a side-eye set to *kill* and walked away the second we'd entered through the floral archway and the DJ announced us. John found me as soon as I veered away from the crowd, a hand sliding around my waist, welcome and comforting and... *handsome*.

My stomach flipped and I smiled, then wrapped my arms around him. He caught me, nuzzling into my neck. The strangest impulse to stay just like that, surrounded by him—safe, warm, and loved—hit me.

Loved. I couldn't pretend I hadn't felt this care for me, but love? Wouldn't that be, just... romantic? Perfect?

"You're gorgeous, and the flowers are amazing." He pulled back and his eyes did that thing I loved where he flickered back and forth between mine like he couldn't decide where he wanted to look.

"Thank you. They turned out really well. Everything's great." And I felt that. Despite Devon and all of the mess, we'd made it to the end. Finally. And after this, maybe we could see what really lay between us.

"Will you hate me if I kiss you and mess up your lipstick?"

It was the closest he'd ever come to asking, and I didn't bother with a response beyond pressing my lips to his.

A cleared throat pulled me out of the blissful press of his lips, and I turned to see my parents scowling.

"Everything okay?"

"Everyone's taking their seats for toasts. You're at the head table."

My mother's pinched expression was so at odds with her public-facing smile, I nearly winced as though I'd actually done something wrong.

John squeezed my hand in reassurance, and we turned to find our seats, only to find *one* spot next to Devon at the long head table. Every other seat was filled.

My heart rate ticked up, and I gripped John's hand harder. There was no threat here, but I couldn't be the person to make a scene, nor did I want to. But I wasn't about to sit by Devon. *Why would they do this?*

Rose looked right at me. "My day. Take your seat. His is over there." She nodded toward a table of what I'd guess were singles based on the presence of two of our cousins who were always on the prowl.

My stomach lurched at the realization that they were really doing this, but it'd be a matter of a half hour, an hour max during the meal, and then I'd be done. Well and truly done.

Turning to John, I started to say I was sorry, but he shook his head. "Not your fault, but know that you don't have to do this."

The intensity of his expression, his words, it all hit me and made me press my lips together to hold back the tears that instantly threatened at his words. He believed me—he knew it was messed up even if my parents and Rose and anyone else didn't. *He* did.

It felt like everyone in the room was watching me, though they couldn't be. More likely, they were chatting happily, focused on their own group, but I felt the attention crawling over me. "I can do this. I'm just—"

He shook his head again. "You're amazing and they're all idiots." His eyes narrowed on something behind me, probably Devon, and he kissed my temple.

Woodenly, I moved to the empty spot and took a seat. Devon's hand slipped to my thigh and squeezed.

"Right where you should be, Dolly."

I elbowed him, *hard*. "Don't talk to me. Don't look at me. And definitely do not touch me unless you want me calling in reinforcements."

He chuckled. "Oh, yeah? Would that be your beer-brewing fake fiancé?"

I turned to him, seeing him for what he was. Pretty exterior with an absolutely rotten core—the wash of pity for him calmed me in a way I'd never experienced when in his actual presence. "My fiancé, or my friends, or my employees, or my neighbors, or my landlord, or anyone else, Devon. Because people here know me, they believe me, and I feel sorry for you that you're still hung up on me after so long because I'm not yours and I never will be."

His jaw hardened and he glared through a narrowed stare. "We'll see."

I ignored the comment, his presence, and focused on the people to my right, clapping and pasting on a smile as everyone toasted the happy couple and drank to their glorious future. I kept my eyes on John, though he had his eyes on Devon, with occasional glances toward the table with my parents. He looked angry—actively furious—and something about that felt like more consolation.

CHAPTER THIRTY-FOUR

John

Dahlia was helping clean up the decorations because of course she was, and I'd had it. I'd lost the ability to think clearly about things—or, you know what? Maybe I'd discovered clarity for the first time.

The epiphany struck when I saw that empty seat and witnessed Dahlia summon her metric tons of strength to face sitting next to her abusive ex during her sister's wedding reception. The realization was simple: they didn't deserve to breathe the same air.

Rose and Conrad had fluttered out into the late spring evening in stylish travel clothes and slipped into a stretch limo to the cheers and applause of their guests. The party had continued another hour, but now as the bars were closing down in each corner of the room, the guests had thinned, most having found their way to their rooms on the upper floors of the resort.

And me? I'd sat and stewed. When I offered to help Dahlia, she said I could leave and she'd meet me at home. I'd told her that I didn't want to leave until she did, and she'd given me a grateful look.

Why should she be grateful for merely being decent? She shouldn't. And it was these, *excuse my French*, assholes who'd messed up her sense of what was right.

So when I caught her parents chatting and laughing with none other than Devon Schaefer, that temper I'd been leashing all evening finally broke free.

"Ah, John. Sorry about the—"

"Don't pretend like that wasn't purposeful."

Mrs. Price shrugged. "We couldn't be expected to change the seating so close to the event, and as you know, we didn't even know you existed until a few weeks ago."

Months. It'd actually been a little over two months since Devon's first visit, our first encounter, and the news she was engaged had been passed around the Price family. "The bigger issue is that you seated her next to someone who hurt her in the first place."

The Prices both startled like they'd never been so appalled, and Devon narrowed his eyes at me.

"I'm not sure why you'd take his word over hers, but that's insane. She's your daughter and she needed you to believe her. She needed your faith in *her*, not some local wunderkind you want to be associated with."

Mr. Price scoffed and Mrs. Price blinked like she could hardly believe I'd spoken the words aloud. Devon chuckled like this was all a lighthearted joke.

Dahlia's voice caught my attention, and her hand clutched at my wrist. "Everything okay?"

"Your pal here's just telling us how we messed up the seating." Devon glanced around like we were all old friends.

"I honestly don't know why he's upset about something so trivial. It was Rose's night and it turned out perfectly."

"I don't care about where anyone else was sitting. I care that Dahlia was sitting by someone who mistreated her. I care that her parents are complicit in your abuse of her—yes, abuse."

Mr. Price waved a hand like it'd stop me. "I don't know what you think you're doing, but this isn't any of your—"

"Business? My fiancée isn't any of my business?"

Devon chuckled. "Really? Are you still trying to pretend you're together? Give it up, man. She's not yours and never will be. The jig is up and none of us is going to continue pretending. Did you really think you'd play house for a week and she'd be grateful enough to stay with you? You're back to a pumpkin at midnight tonight, buddy."

"Devon, what the hell are you saying?" Dahlia asked, shock in her voice. But then, she continued. "John is a better man than you'll ever be. He's honest, generous, kind, helpful, thoughtful… I could go on and on. Not to mention he's a successful business owner *and* a lawyer, and he's a devoted son, cousin, brother, friend… I literally cannot delineate all the ways he is superior to you."

Well, damn. That was about the nicest thing anyone had ever said about me, and I hated that it'd happened right here, in front of her parents.

Apparently, that little speech wasn't enough to distract them from Devon's accusation.

"Is this true? Are you engaged or not, Dahlia Elaine?" Mrs. Price's words sounded like the answer mattered. Like any of that had anything to do with their treatment of her.

I watched as she swallowed, then firmed her resolve, her chin raising an inch. "We're not engaged."

Damn, but that hurt. It shouldn't make any difference to

me, but somehow, it wedged something sharp between my ribs. Why did I care if she told them it was fake at this point? It wasn't like she was saying everything between us was fake—I knew it wasn't. Even if this all came to an end tonight, it wasn't all fake.

And at the same time, there was a freedom to having it out there, especially for her parents to deal with.

Devon chuckled lightly again, like he'd planned all of this, and her parents both exclaimed with varying degrees of affront.

"How could you do this?"

"Why would you lie to us?"

And I'd had it. I didn't want her fielding their crap anymore, so I broke into the nonsense again. "She lied so you wouldn't keep siccing this abusive jerk on her. You sent him to her, you let him invade her life and peace of mind, and then you're surprised when she felt the need to shield herself from him?"

"Again, why is any of this your business?" Devon's patience must have worn thin, because his tone resounded like the crack of a whip.

"I guess in a lot of ways, it's not. I'm not a part of your family, and I don't live in your precious town." I focused on the Prices, grasping Dahlia's hand in mine. I wanted to shout in their faces, tell them my opinion mattered because I loved her, was in love with her, and wanted the best for her. But these people wouldn't care and that wasn't fair to Dahlia, so I leashed that impulse and continued.

"But I think the world of your daughter and I want what's best for her. That's a hell of a lot more than I can say for any of you. I know she'll stand here and take whatever you dole out, whatever narrative you spin to make your-selves feel justified and good about the way you've treated her time and again, but I'm not going to stand by and watch that. You make it seem like she's this difficult person, someone who's hard to love, but caring for her is the easiest thing I've ever done. I don't know what's broken in you that you've felt anything less than adoration was right for her. This woman is better than you'll ever hope to be. She's the best person I know, and you aren't fit to share the same room as her."

Dahlia's eyes hit mine, wide and amazed and more than a little shocked.

"Ready to go?" I asked, done here.

She nodded. "Yeah. Yes."

We left hand in hand, only diverting from the most direct path to grab her purse and wrap before we exited. We walked fast, but not like someone would follow. I didn't know what propelled me away so quickly other than the urgency to get away from them and to see how she was.

And holy crap, I'd gone all out. I'd said I cared about her, thought she was amazing and deserving of the best— not to *her*, but to her horrible parents. I'd need to rectify that. To make clear that those words were hers, not just for show.

"We'll come back for your car tomorrow," I said, guiding her to where I'd parked.

"Sounds good." She released me and got in, no questions, no commentary.

I had no idea what was going on in her head, but my body had flooded with an odd sort of post-confrontation adrenaline and I had nowhere to go with it. I never sped, ever, not after losing Viv, but I skirted the speed limit and got us to my house quickly. Neither of us spoke.

I didn't know whether that was a good thing or a bad

one, but I couldn't figure out what to say to her in the quiet of the car, in the aftermath.

In minutes, we walked inside, and I tossed my tux jacket on the back of the couch, then worked the bowtie trying to strangle me from my neck, my fingers tangling and jerking. I needed a full breath and just now, I could hardly take one with this material cinched around my neck.

"Can I help?"

Dahlia's voice came just before her hands reached up to help unknot the mess under my chin.

Eyes on her busy hands, I couldn't quite read her. My heart was pounding, chest heaving, and I couldn't hold back anymore. "Dahlia, please. Are you okay? Was that... I'm sorry if I overstepped."

The bowtie snaked around my collar and slipped out into her hands. She held it up and her gaze met mine, a bone-deep weariness in her expression that made everything in me freeze.

The air stilled and everything around us dimmed. The lights, the sounds, the awareness of anything but *her* faded as she prepared to speak. "I'm more than okay, John."

A beat.

A pause.

A few more steps along a trail before the summit, before a precipice.

In another version of this story, I would leap. If she wasn't coming off of what might be a traumatic weekend, if we'd had more time just the two of us, if I was sure my touch would be welcomed and not a burden, I would take her by the hand and ask her to jump with me. I'd wrap her in my arms and claim her like I dreamed of.

But that was not this story. That was not our book.

She cleared her throat, jarring me from the spiraling fantasy of what-ifs.

"I'm okay. You didn't overstep and I—" She exhaled slowly like she needed to steady herself internally. "I'm grateful."

Ah. Of course. Belatedly, I took the tie.

She folded her arms and tucked them close against her body. "I want to talk more. I know we have a lot to discuss. Can we do that tomorrow?"

"Of course. Anything you want. Just get some rest, Dahlia. Anything we need to talk about it can wait."

And though it pained me, I meant it. I didn't know exactly what tomorrow would bring, but our arrangement would officially end in a week, and I wasn't in a hurry to cinch it closed just yet. Tonight felt like a kind of stopping place and I had no desire to let the upset from the evening's events color our reality now.

So... tomorrow would come soon enough.

CHAPTER THIRTY-FIVE

Dahlia

I woke in John's guest bedroom, clarity piled on top of a heap of feelings and emotions and decisions driving me from the warmth to face this new reality.

Everything had changed last night. *Everything.*

In some ways, I was waking to what felt like normal life. I had a little cleanup after the wedding still to do and Sunday orders to check before I came back home because I'd had my assistants do them all while the rest of the team focused on the wedding. I should've planned for someone else to check them, but I'd thought maybe getting into the shop would be a refuge, a necessity after the wedding itself.

Turned out, I didn't need it. I had plenty of distractions here at home.

But that was a change—that *home*. Because home wasn't my apartment anymore. It was here, with John. I'd felt that building, the inevitability of us climbing the walls, and though I'd determined to deal with those feelings and what they'd mean after the wedding, John had forced my hand.

He'd stood up for me. He'd said he cared about me, but more than that, he'd railed at my parents and I couldn't have loved him more in that moment. Not just because he was standing up for me and honoring me so thoroughly, but because it was so far from how he normally functioned, and he'd done it for *me*.

I loved him for that and so many, many more things. It had hit me hard that my family had still balked against John's truth-filled words about Devon and how they'd treated me, and it'd hurt. But the equal if not greater discovery pummeling my mind last night was that I loved John. In fact, I was pretty sure I'd been in love with him for a while now, and I loved him so completely I could hardly breathe from it.

A braver romantic heroine than I would've told him last night, but my reserves were running so low by the end of the day, I didn't have the words. How could I explain myself? How could I make him see that yes, this had all been a lot—too much, frankly—and yet it didn't keep me from recognizing my feelings for him. That it wasn't the overwrought everything pushing me toward him and wanting him to catch me.

Today, we'd talk. We'd get to the heart of things now that the most stressful time together had ended. We needed breathing room, and we could have a little of that this week before his parents' event. Then, we needed to forge a new path. But right now, I had to go see my parents before their plane departed. I had to deal with whatever fallout came from his outburst last night, and then I could move on knowing they were gone.

John was still sleeping when I slipped out of his house

and took his car. Maybe I could even be back by the time he woke, maybe surprise him with pastries and coffee.

I found my parents eating at a small table in the breakfast room. It had beautiful white and gray décor with pops of lemony yellow accents and, of course, flowers by yours truly. Only one other couple occupied a table, but they sat far enough away, I approached without worry we'd disturb them. In fact, it might just keep my parents in check if they were feeling the need to put me in my place.

"Mom. Dad," I said as I approached the table.

They both looked up and the heart I thought had hardened toward them, or the one I'd tried to anyway, squeezed. They looked old and tired as they pecked at spring berries and flaky croissants... not at all like the polished, worldly couple they'd presented last night.

"Dahlia," my father said, a note of relief mingling with the surprise in his tone.

"Can I sit?"

They nodded, so I took my seat. Not wanting to wait for them to begin and cut off my momentum toward saying what I needed to say, I spoke. "I need you to know that I agree with what John said. And until you accept that I will not be with Devon and will not agree to be near him ever again, I cannot continue a relationship with you. That may sound harsh, but I was advised to do this a long time ago and I... I guess I wasn't strong enough."

My mother's face threatened to crumple, her chin wobbling, but she cleared her throat and willed it away. "That won't be necessary."

"We won't plan to include him in anything else. We... well, I won't say we understand because we really didn't know it was that bad between you, and we've always wanted great things for you but... we're sorry."

I swallowed the protest, their refusal to admit ignoring the things I'd told them no longer something I wanted to dig into. I didn't think we'd ever be close, nor did I have any plans to come home for Christmas or do any of those things I might've done if so much over the years had been different.

Instead of explaining that I had great things in my life—too many to count and rising, I simply said, "Thank you for saying you're sorry."

They both nodded, accepting my words with some sense of relief, it seemed.

"I also need you to understand that even though I'm not engaged to John, I hope I will be eventually. And I don't know when he'll be ready to see or talk to you all after the way you've treated him the past week, but you need to understand that I'm going to choose him."

The low-key elation that'd been the bass beat to my morning erupted in my chest then, fluttering excitement pouring through me and leaking out into a smile that split my face. It had to be obnoxious, that grin, but I didn't care. The revelation of my feelings for him was still bursting through me and I didn't bother containing the rush of hope and anticipation.

They both nodded again, and my mom said, "He seems... sure about you."

I didn't try to hide the delight that spilled out of me in a soft laugh, even if I wasn't so sure she was right. They didn't need to know my doubts, the niggling fear that maybe all of what he'd said was for show, just like it had been weeks ago with his family. Deep down, I didn't think it had been, but the soft, vulnerable places in me still feared accepting it as truth. He'd said it all to my parents and in my defense.

But I needed to find out—and I would. I had faith in

him, in us, but I did want confirmation when we'd both had time to process everything that'd happened these last few weeks.

For now, my parents only needed to know what was true for me. "I'm sure about him, too."

Her lips pursed, but not in that judge-y way she had. More like, she got it. She'd seen it, finally, last night.

"I've got some work to do, but I just wanted to clear things up before you go." I stood and tucked in my chair, both of them silent until I was a few steps away.

"Dahlia?" My father's voice stopped me, made me turn.

"Yes?"

"Thank you."

I held his gaze, this man who I wasn't sure had ever said those words to me, and I nodded, accepting the thanks for any number of things. My work on the wedding, my help over the last week, or maybe, just maybe, my showing up here today. My taking their apology and even considering forgiveness.

I left the breakfast room and my parents behind feeling more lighthearted than I had in a long time—maybe as long as I could remember. The weariness that'd settled on me like a shroud last night had cleared with a good night's sleep and tying up this loose end. We weren't fixed, but we were in a much better place. I'd have to tell Azalea, and at some point, I'd need to talk to Rose.

But for now? I had a little work to do, and a man to woo. We belonged together, and I knew just how to prove this point to him irrefutably.

CHAPTER THIRTY-SIX

John

I woke feeling exhausted and more than a little sad. The wedding was over.

My eyes fluttered open as I remembered the incredible swing of events from the nonsense at Rose's wedding to the way the day had ended.

Even if we hadn't acknowledged what I'd said to her parents, how close I'd come to making a real confession that would change things between us, but hadn't said to her. She'd thanked me.

I hadn't expected anything else. In fact, the entire ride home, I'd vacillated between wanting to haul her over my shoulder and toss her onto my bed, and fearing that every step I'd taken since she'd pulled me into her flower shop had been the wrong one. That everything between us had changed irrevocably.

Things *had* changed between us... hadn't they? This

wasn't a casual situation for either of us and I knew that well, but was whatever she needed to say some kind of goodbye? I hated the dread that swirled in my gut at the thought of finalizing the end of this. Of *us*.

Alarm hit when I registered how still the house was outside my door. Normally, I'd hear her bumping around in the kitchen or detect water running in the guest bath. We hadn't talked about her schedule today, but I'd hoped she'd get to sleep in—she needed rest after everything. We needed to talk and I'd hoped she'd be rested, at least on the road to it. I was too full of hopes, though, and I needed to kill that habit.

I was used to feeling foolish over her at this point, and there was no avoiding it now, even if the fear that the last few weeks was all we'd have, that this was the stopping point, wouldn't leave me.

With a reluctant groan, I rolled out of bed and padded into the living room. No Dahlia there, the kitchen, or, after a quick check, her room—I'd already known it, but still. One glance in the garage explained it—my car was gone. She must've had to leave, though I wished she would've woken me.

A spike of alarm hit me. She wouldn't have left like... *left* left, would she? Did she have regrets—maybe she'd decided I had crossed a line by speaking up for her? Would she wish we'd never started all of this in the first place if it'd ended in confrontation with her family anyway?

A bitter mix of heartache and dread swirled in my gut. I didn't want this to be the end. We'd done what we'd set out to—we'd made it through the wedding and she'd left with her head held high despite how her family had conspired to bring her to heel.

My phone buzzed with a text, and I fumbled to swipe

and read it. *"Good morning, Sleeping Beauty. I had to finish wedding cleanup. I did not, in fact, steal your car so please don't report me. Will return soon."*

A laugh burst out of me as relief hit. She wasn't running. She was just doing her job, fulfilling her obligation. I sank into the couch, more than a little embarrassed at how quickly I'd spiraled out. She deserved more than that—more trust, more faith. I didn't know where all of this was going, but I knew better than to think she'd literally run away from me instead of talking through things.

Clearly, I couldn't be left to myself and my needy, insecure thoughts, so I sought distraction. Maybe we could grab lunch when she got home, or see if Aidan, Maddie, and Luca wanted to do something. For now, I'd get cleaned up and... do something.

Three hours later, I still hadn't heard from Dahlia and had started pacing the living room and convincing myself I didn't need to call and check on her. The sounds of the garage door opening stopped me just before I lost the battle and dialed her number.

Not wanting to seem as antsy as I was, I flopped down onto the couch, kicked up my feet, and rabidly clicked the remote so something would come up on the TV and make it seem like I'd just been lounging blissfully, completely mindless of every minute that passed while she was gone.

The door opened and she bustled in, hollering, "Hey! Sorry. That took so much longer than I expected."

No longer interested in maintaining the ruse of my

indifference, I went to her, savoring the sweet ache in my chest at the sight of her. Her cheeks were red and she wore jeans, a T-shirt, and sneakers. She had her hair pulled back into a ponytail with scant makeup, and I forced myself to take the bags from her fingers rather than wrap her in my arms and breathe in her scent.

Okay, you need to calm down, sir.

"Thank you. I brought some groceries, but..." She huffed a little frustrated sound.

"What?"

She set her purse and the other bag she held on the counter. "My building manager called. Apparently, he rushed the contractor to get things cleaned up and it's ready. Today."

"It's ready?" Her words didn't compute, although my body seemed to know something I didn't, because my heart rate had picked up like a threat loomed.

"Yeah. Crazy, right?"

Her brittle smile was the only thing that made me think maybe she wasn't as happy about this as she would've been before... before the last few days, or before this whole thing started.

Words came on autopilot. "So you... we need to get you packed up, I guess?"

"I—yes. Yeah, I guess I better," she said, fidgeting.

"You know you can stay as long as you like, right? There's no rush on my account."

She had to know that—that I didn't want her to go at all, much less right this second when we hadn't even talked about everything. I hadn't realized until this moment how much I'd assumed we'd have more time together—more time where we were forced to see each other every day, even just a few minutes while grabbing coffee in the morning or for a chat before bed. I'd foolishly thought that even if we didn't hash things out today, we'd have time this week to ease our way through whatever we needed to address.

But now...

Instead of immediately refusing, which would've made sense if I looked at it logically, her gaze softened and she paced to me, reaching for my hands, which I gladly surrendered.

"Thank you. I know you mean that and I'm grateful. But I really do need to let myself get back into a routine with normal life. I'm behind on lots of horrible things like accounting and getting into the nitty gritty of my Night in Bloom planning. I know you have a crazy week, too, so I think this makes the most sense."

She smiled again, then released me and rounded the counter into the kitchen to unload the grocery bags.

I didn't want to return to normal. I was no longer lying to myself and pretending we could go back to being not-friends or just-friends. Not after the last few days and certainly not after the last twenty-four hours. Not after nearly confessing everything.

I'd fallen for her hard enough that I'd almost said it in front of her and her toxic family, and that told me something very clearly: I couldn't just walk away. All that mental talk about channeling Aidan's bravery to embrace the moment so I could try again another time... nonsense. I didn't know how I'd convince her I was worth a shot, but I had to. But it didn't make sense for me to push.

I knew that with more clarity than I knew almost anything else—I couldn't push her. Because everyone else in her life and especially her family these last few weeks had pushed. How would I be doing what's right for her, giving her my best, if I became just one more person pushing her to do what I wanted on my time?

Maybe the conversation about our future couldn't happen today, but I did need to know. "I don't want to push you by asking this, but are you... okay?"

She looked up from where she was pulling out ingredients for sandwiches. "I talked to my parents. They... they heard you. And I reinforced what you said, stood up for myself and made clear that if they invite me to something where Devon is present again, I will have to distance myself from them even more than I already have."

I moved to her, leaning against the counter next to where she stood to avoid hauling her into my arms and telling her how proud of her I was. "That sounds like a pretty difficult conversation."

She nodded. "It was. But I don't know that I would've had it if you hadn't called them out last night. So, again, thank you for being so amazing." She leaned up and pressed a quick kiss to my cheek, then my lips.

My chest glowed as my heart squeezed. "I've been hoping I didn't overstep. But I'm really glad you talked to them before they left."

"Yeah, definitely a better conversation for in-person."

I nodded, unable to ignore the conspicuous absence of any mention of the other part of my outburst last night—not just calling them out for their bad behavior, but all the ways I'd danced around and yet practically admitted my feelings for her. Maybe that was bad, or maybe it was just because she had so much to deal with. To be fair, a tectonic shift in the relationship between her and her parents was definitely the larger issue.

Well, unless you're the idiot who told her parents how

much you thought of her, how amazing she is, before you told her...

"Can we eat? I'm so hungry and I want to sit and enjoy a sandwich with you before I face hauling suitcases back to the apartment."

"Of course. We'll swing by and grab your car on the way."

And that was that, I guessed... if I wasn't going to push, then here was a clear chance to move forward without pushing.

Great.

I washed a tomato and sliced it while she toasted fresh bread from Rise and Shine, but my thoughts circled around and around one unbeatable fact. I wanted this woman. I wanted a future with her. But right now, we were standing in my kitchen for what could very well be the last time.

Sensitive as she often was, Dahlia could tell.

"Something on your mind?" she asked, swatting at me with a kitchen towel as we moved around each other.

I exhaled, wishing I had the self-control to keep my dang mouth shut, but the words were already falling out of my face. "I'm glad you're doing well with everything that happened at the wedding and that you talked to your folks. I guess I'm just... I'll miss you. I've enjoyed having you here." That was part of the truth.

She sighed lightly as she placed the top slice of bread on her neatly stacked food. "Yeah. I'll miss you, too. This has been fun." She set down the knife she'd used to cut the sandwich and brushed her hands together as though they had crumbs on them.

Something about that gesture made alarm spike through my mind. It looked like she was searching for the right words. And on the heels of *this has been fun*, it felt like maybe they'd be the final ones. The ones to end things between us, to acknowledge we'd had our time together and now we'd move on or back or whatever direction there was aside from forward together.

"It has. I agree. I'm glad I could do it." To say the very, very least.

She nodded, then pinned me with her dark gaze as she took a deep breath. "John, I know I told you how much it's meant to me, and I don't want to keep repeating myself. I need you to understand it's been overwhelming, but—"

"No, please, Dahlia. You don't have to say anything. I don't..." I cleared my throat, working to find a way to delay whatever neat bow she wanted to tie on things between us. I'd rather have it messy and still happening in one way or another than have it case-closed, no longer up for discussion.

If that meant avoiding the conversation, even if it made me a bit of a coward, then so be it. "I don't want you to worry about me. I'm glad we did this. I'm—you have no idea how glad. But you've been through a lot, so we can save our rehash, or whatever, for a while. You've just had to talk to your parents, and that's already a lot for one day."

Her eyes narrowed and if I wasn't mistaken, she was making a decision. I used to think she was hard to read, but now it felt like I knew her, at least much of her.

When she spoke, her words came out slowly, carefully. Almost like my desperate babbling about how we didn't need to talk had actually worked, though I wasn't sure in what way.

"I appreciate you being so considerate of me." That gaze continued to study me, bouncing around from my face, to my shoulders, to my arms where my hands were tucked into my pockets. "I do think we have things to say, but maybe you're right… maybe it's better if I have some time to get my head on straight after all of this."

That settled over me, a mix of relief and dread. We wouldn't end things now, but we weren't exactly together either, were we? Technically, our agreement would end in a week, but here we were, friendly and enjoying each other by all accounts.

"You look worried," she said softly.

I should stop while I was ahead. Take the win of not having a total handshake ending to this, but I *was* worried. That she saw it so plainly only made my heart twist more. And my stupid mouth betrayed at least one of my biggest concerns before I could stop it. "I'm just hoping you don't regret this."

Her eyes widened and she blinked as she processed my words, then stepped forward and threw her arms around me. I held the mustard out to her side to avoid getting any on her shirt, but those eyes captured mine and my heart instantly slowed to a drum-beat thud.

"You mean not thinking you're a bridge troll anymore?" she asked, her voice low and calming and with a hint of teasing, almost like we might be overheard though we were alone in the house.

I nodded, unable to speak for fear of… I didn't know, but me saying words right now wasn't going to happen, so I nodded again, letting out a small laugh I only partly felt.

She bit her lip, a small smile tugging at the corners of her mouth before she shook her head slowly, never breaking eye contact. "No, John. I don't regret anything that has happened between us."

And if that didn't sound final, I didn't know what would.

CHAPTER THIRTY-SEVEN

Dahlia

It was the dumbest thing to feel sad about leaving John's house and moving back into mine, but I did. As we hauled my suitcases up to my well-and-truly-fixed apartment, I felt this incredible tide of sadness filling me. I wouldn't see him every night and morning. I wouldn't get to share space with him, see him first thing to start the day, or even have a chance to share a bed again, not that we had since last weekend at the spa, but still...

Watching him carry two bags into my bedroom, his forearms giving me feelings I'd never had about such a basic part of the male anatomy, I firmed my resolve. This wasn't goodbye for us. In fact, if I had my way, far from it. But it made sense to move back into my space. We'd been on a whirlwind trajectory from extreme dislike and not getting along to this.

To love.

At least on my end. And I hoped—good grief, how I hoped—on his, too.

All his actions pointed to that. He hadn't said it outright, and I'd turned over his words, or what I remembered of them amidst the crush of frustration and disbelief that conversation had caused in me. Maybe some of it had been for emphasis, for effect, but I didn't think so. After knowing John as long as I had impersonally and as much as I'd learned about him in the last few months, I didn't think he'd say anything just for show.

And as tempted as I'd been to tell him how I felt this morning, I'd sensed that waiting would be better. Well, that, and he'd basically halted all progress with his insistence we not talk. I'd thought about forcing the issue, but there'd been a load of emotions in those gorgeous hazel eyes, and I'd had an inkling. Standing there making sandwiches *after* the wedding, I suspected maybe he was worried I'd tell him how I felt but that it wouldn't be genuine, or it would be, but I wouldn't actually know how I felt in the wake of so much craziness the last few weeks.

So I'd made the call. Risk misunderstandings, maybe, but I wasn't walking away like we were done. I was giving him time, and in truth, I was giving me time. Time to settle into the depth of feeling I had for him, even though looking back at our time knowing each other, it all felt so obvious from this angle.

Time. And then there'd be no way any of the confessions could be blamed on the *moment* or the intensity of the wedding or circumstances. Weeks ago, I would've questioned whether the feelings were, in fact, real, but by now, I knew. I'd known John could get to me from the very beginning. Why else had I shoved him away so forcefully every time we'd interacted?

And now, I needed to set him away gently, just a little, so we could unwind from the wild few weeks we'd had. So we could have the space he seemed to need me to have. It'd give him a chance to know how he really felt, and it'd give me the chance to make clear how I did without him having any room to worry I was mixed up with feelings about Devon and the wedding messing with me.

So when he emerged from the bedroom suitcase-free, I hauled him into a hug and clung to him a little. My heart ached and I had to clear my throat before I spoke.

"Thank you for the help today. And... well, you know."

He nodded, something dire in his expression when he pulled back. "I do. Thanks for, uh, plucking me off the street. I'm glad it was me."

I grinned. "Me, too."

"And we'll see each other, right?" His eyes flickered between mine before jumping around the room like he couldn't stand staying focused on me.

If I didn't know better, I'd think he was wishing we could be done, but I *did* know better. At least, I prayed I was right. He'd said he cared about me and his actions had backed that up, and I wasn't going to let him off the hook. I'd be insane to let John Wallace go.

That said? I had no plans to rush this. We'd already lived an accelerated version of our romance, and right now was the perfect time to slow down, especially since he seemed to need that. But while we were slowing, I didn't want him worried. I wanted to reassure him and I wouldn't mind a little reassurance myself. Nothing in the last few days had told me he'd want to end things, but at no point had we discussed what came after the wedding and anniversary party beyond that we would stop the fake engagement.

"We always said through the wedding and the anniversary party, so yes. Next weekend for sure, and I hope before then. We do live in a pretty small town." Never mind I'd done a great job of avoiding him over the years, at least when I wasn't so tied up with Aidan on projects. What would've happened if we hadn't avoided each other so well?

His big, warm hands gripped my upper arms and those hazel eyes speared me, no longer afraid to hold my gaze. "We did. We will. I don't know what comes next, but we'll figure it out."

We would. Soon, I hoped, but for now, I just agreed with him. "We will."

His gaze flicked down to my lips, and his brow furrowed with decision. We hadn't kissed since the wedding, and I wouldn't have expected it now after the distance between us, but I saw the determination on his face—liked he'd made the call and wanted one last moment of connection before we went our separate ways. We'd talk about what came next, yes, but before then...

One of his hands slipped around my back and up into my hair while the other pulled me close at the curve of my spine, pressing me into him as I tilted my head up and our lips met. His kiss was slow and purposeful, a branding, mesmerizing tasting of me like I was a fine wine or the crowning dish at a chef's table. He kissed me so thoroughly, I almost forgot the reasons I had to not tell him how I really felt, to tell him I wanted everything with him and I wanted it now.

When he inched back, our faces still close enough to feel his warm breath on my swollen lips, he straightened a bit and pressed a kiss to my forehead. The move threatened to break my heart with its tenderness and sweetness, and the contrast between that commanding kiss and this gentleness?

Honestly, it was all I'd ever wanted.

"I'm going to miss you this week," I said, my voice strangely watery.

"I'll stop by, and you know, you can do the same," he said, a little grin on his face that just made me want to kiss him again.

"Fair enough, Wallace."

He chuckled and released me, wandering to the door and leaving with a, "See you soon, Price."

I gazed after him for probably a full minute before shaking myself from the lovestruck haze he'd put me into and got to work. I needed to settle in, unpack, check in with my building manager, and deal with several other things, plus Azalea would be dropping by any time now to say goodbye. After that, I'd likely pass out before I started the week—no days off for me this week since I'd fallen behind with this wedding. It'd demanded way more of my involvement than a normal one would.

After working on my clothes for a few minutes, a knock at my door had me hustling to open it. Azalea stood there with a wry smile on her face.

"You'll never guess who I just saw sneaking out of your building door."

I waved her in. "*Sneaking*? I have no idea. But you may have seen John."

She rolled her eyes. "Fine. He was just walking, and I was coming out of the bookstore so he didn't see me, but still." She waggled her brows.

My stupid grin was a dead giveaway.

She cackled. "*Fake* fiancé, huh?"

"It sure started that way, but turns out our beloved parents have helped me find my person."

Those brows arched high. "Wow. That's... amazing."

She slung an arm around my shoulders and hugged me. We lingered there, savoring the fleeting connection. When we parted, I spoke up. "Thank you. And I should probably tell you that I told the parents off, as did John, and I don't think Devon is going to be hanging around anymore."

She tsked. "You don't want to hitch your wagon to that bright political career? I'm shocked."

We chuckled, and something in me bloomed at the idea that we could laugh about this together. Azalea had her own wounds to deal with, but they were of a different sort than mine.

"On the note of changes, I guess I should mention I'm moving. I'm done with Colorado."

The look in her eye had the usual spark, but I caught a glimpse of something sad that plucked at me before she turned away. "You're always welcome here. There's a lot to love about Silverton."

She chuckled. "Yeah. It's on the shortlist. I'm thinking of trying the East Coast for a while, though. I'll let you know."

I followed her to the door, surprised by how short the farewell would be, but knowing that Azalea and I had never been close. We talked, but she didn't tend to let anyone in from what I could tell, and she'd always done her own thing. But we were closer than Rose and I had ever been, and I loved the idea of her coming here, even if it was via a winding route.

"Thanks for swinging by, and thank you for having my back."

She huffed. "Not a lot of good it did, but I'm glad John had your back, too. He's a good one."

She pulled open the door as I said, "He is. Hey, I love you, Azalea."

She smiled wide. "You, too, sis."

I watched her progress down the stairs and she hit me with one more wave before she disappeared off the landing and descended to the first floor. Even though I always wished we were closer, I felt better about things with my family than I had in years. Maybe Rose and I would clear the air at some point, but since Conrad and Devon were bffs, that was ultimately unlikely.

The best part of all of it was the feeling that I could look forward. I didn't need to worry about Devon showing back up—without my parents' pushing, I bet he'd find someone else to play politician's trophy wife in no time.

And me? I'd be making my own family soon, starting with John if I had any say at all. I just had to get to the other side of this week and make sure he knew it.

CHAPTER THIRTY-EIGHT

John

Sitting still only came naturally to me when I was relaxed and had nothing else to do. I hadn't felt relaxed since before I said goodbye to Dahlia on Sunday—maybe since I'd woken up in bed that morning, but before I'd realized she was gone.

And Aidan? The jerk wouldn't stop heckling me about it. He'd been sending me texts harassing me over the fact that he knew I was restless. I'd spent Sunday afternoon and evening with him and my rotten not-nephew since Maddie had something or other she was busy with.

Now here he came sauntering into the brewery and pinning me with his knowing grin through the glass walls of my office.

"What's your step count up to?" he asked, not a hello in sight.

"Not sure," I said, refusing to look at my watch. I didn't

need it to tell me I'd been pacing around all day, and by all day, I meant the first four hours of the workday that thus far felt like a forty-hour workweek in and of themselves. Liam had already shot me a few concerned looks before he left to help Wells with something for a few hours.

"Don't you have any actual work to do?" he asked, glancing around and eyeing the succulents and plants he'd given me over the years. I'd bought a few, but he'd been my supplier most often.

"I did. I do. But I can't think about anything other than—"

His smile spread slowly, and after a quiet beat, he said, "Dahlia?"

I glared at him.

"Why don't you just go see her at work? Take her lunch or something?"

Pulling at my hair like it might soothe this restlessness in me, I paced a small circle around the office. He'd stopped in the doorway so my path was unimpeded. "I'm giving her space. I don't... I don't know what's happening, but I think it's good? It feels like it's good, and at the same time, I have this sense of dread because technically, we're done after the party this weekend."

"You haven't talked about it?" he asked, his brow furrowing.

I paced another stupidly small circle, then stopped with a huff. "No. *No.* Because she's been in the middle of all this crap with her family, and I don't want to be one more person who pushes her. I can't do that, even as much as I want to know where she is with all of this stuff."

He narrowed his eyes. "But you definitely want there to be more than just the last few weeks, right? And you think she does, too?"

Slumping into one of the chairs set opposite my desk, I scrubbed a hand down my face. "I think so. We've gotten close. And it feels like we both want to get closer."

I eyed him as he sat in the other chair, unwilling to share details, but he could read me well enough to understand it wasn't just circumstantial.

"That's great. I'm really happy for you both."

I shook my head. "You can say that to me after this weekend when I get it figured out, get her to be my *real* date to the party, and she agrees to give me a shot outside of this fake engagement, okay?"

In fact, an idea was beginning to take shape. Because as much as I didn't know with certainty that she loved me, I thought that maybe, just maybe, she did. I hoped and prayed and the thought kept barreling toward me that if I was ever going to take a risk on love again, it was now. It had to be now.

He chuckled lightly. "Come on. Text your girl and ask her if you can bring her lunch, and then let's hit Guac before it gets busy. We'll drop something off to her and you can blame me for making you do it if you need a reason."

For the first time today, I felt lighter, less stressed, at even the prospect of seeing her. We'd texted on and off since our goodbye on Sunday and I'd sent her donuts yesterday, but actually seeing her in person sent a dual response of my pulse hiking and my heart calming through me. All those interactions had been surface-level. Light check-ins that didn't go any deeper than friends would delve. Impossibly, it made me miss her more than I might've if we'd been silent.

No, that wasn't true. I wanted any connection with her I could have. But I was trying to respect that she needed space *and* we were both surprisingly busy. Or maybe not surprising, considering just how in-demand she was and the fact that I'd had a few days off and Liam had been out with a sick baby.

I'd never been like this—certainly not with Tina and maybe not even in high school. I'd never felt so needy and ridiculous, and I couldn't even summon the wherewithal to feel embarrassed about it. Mostly, I just wished I had a reason to be near her but refused to smother her, especially after what we'd just been through. I wanted her to feel safe with me, but I also wanted her to feel like this—this aching, ravishing need to be near me like I did for her.

The hope that she did—at least in some small measure— is what had me texting my dad to see if he was free later for a quick chat.

Aidan's deep chuckle should've annoyed me more, but as we approached Bloom's door, I couldn't pretend I was anything but thrilled to know Dahlia was on the other side of that door and I was about to see her.

"Should I just take it in? I can drop it off for you," he suggested.

"No. I want to see her."

He made a face like he didn't understand and reached for the bag of takeout in my hand. "But I could take it and then you won't be bothering her. She'll get her lunch, and you can maintain this arbitrary need to give her space and continue torturing yourself."

I shoved him and he released the food to me, then held the door open and waved me in with a flourish. My heart rate ticked up as we walked in and Matilda, one of the women who staffed the shop, smiled at us.

"She's in the back."

I nodded, already aware she'd be working away on arrangements and unwilling to spare words for sweet Matilda. I appreciated the woman and her capability—it'd allowed Dahlia to be slightly less stressed, as had the other Bloom employees. But they didn't need my small talk and I didn't have it to give.

The shop door was propped open as usual and the second I walked in, my eyes found her. She had a pencil between her teeth and her head ducked to focus on what looked like a bow she was tying around tightly grouped stems of tulips.

"Need a hand?" I asked, because I was an uncreative dolt and what I really wanted was to have a reason to get close to her in case there was any awkwardness.

Would there be awkwardness now? Would I muck this up because I'd been nothing short of obsessing over when I'd see her again?

No, no awkward. This would be fine.

You're already awkward, just embrace it.

Aidan must've sensed my inner turmoil, especially when she didn't look up or respond.

"She's got headphones in," he said in a low voice.

I had noticed that after I'd spoken, and now I had to decide whether to startle her or... or, what?

Since he'd been tracking my overthinking by some observant cousin magic, he took mercy on me and said, "Dahlia" loud enough to penetrate through her earbuds. Her head snapped up and she saw us, then smiled instantly. She dropped her work, tossed the pencil, and jogged around the large worktable with her arms out.

Before she reached me, I shoved the takeout into an empty space on the table next to me and wrapped my arms around her as soon as she reached me. Relief, excitement, joy, and a nagging sense of having missed her too much stole my breath as much as the contact itself. I hugged her as tightly as she did me, but then she was pulling back.

Her hands came to my face, and she pulled me down into a searing kiss. Her lips moved over mine like she'd missed me as much as I had her, and my heart grew a few sizes at the evidence. One of her hands slipped around and her nails scratched against the short hair at the back of my neck. I wanted to groan, wanted to delve into the kiss deeper, and right when I would've, she leaned back.

Her brown eyes sparkled, a pleased smile pulling at her perfect lips for a second before something shifted in a flash and she eased back and looked away. "Sorry, Aidan."

Aidan? Aidan *who?* The second she'd touched me, awareness of anyone else's existence had dissolved into nothingness. And why was she putting space between us now? Why were we not still kissing?

"No apologies, though I can step out if you two need a moment alone."

I turned and shot him a hopeful look right as she said, "Not necessary, but thank you. Sadly, I need to get a few things done before I can enjoy this lunch, and I'm sure you guys have things to do."

Ah. Right. Super busy week for her, and technically for me even though I'd felt unproductive and distracted since waking Monday morning. Also a disappointing dismissal and I hated the trill of concern that rang in my head. It was almost like she was embarrassed at having kissed me like that. If only she knew...

"We'll get out of your hair. I just... I wanted to see you."

I stopped short of saying I *needed* to see her, even though that wouldn't have been an exaggeration.

Aidan cleared his throat and I got the message, though nerves crawled up my spine. "So, I'll see you at the anniversary party?"

She pressed her lips together but couldn't completely hide her smile. Relief rushed in at that expression of pleasure and maybe even relief. It placated the part of me that was running in circles, losing its mind over her embarrassment and fearing that this, *this* would be the last time we were together.

But no. I'd made a choice earlier and I wasn't going back. I was going to believe in us, believe in myself and her and the two of us together and what we could have. Which meant I had to shut down my inner Chicken Little and let things play out.

"Absolutely. I'll be there early with flowers and then run home, but I know you've got a lot to do that day so I'll meet you there." She bit her lip and a look flashed across her eyes, but she held up a hand in a little goodbye way and added, "I'm so glad you came by, and thank you for lunch. I can't wait for the party."

A vision of rounding the table and cupping her face took over. I'd pull her close and press another slow kiss to her mouth, then her cheek, then her forehead. Instead, I reluctantly waved back as though we weren't standing eight feet apart and said goodbye. "All right. We're off. Let me know if I can help at all."

And in a different version of the story, I would've told her I loved her then, too, like couples did when they parted, even for short durations.

But I wasn't about to throw that out here, while she was working, or in front of my cousin, though he wouldn't be bothered by it. He'd already made it clear he thought we'd be great together. His concerns all those weeks ago that we didn't get along were irrelevant and he knew that based on the updates I'd given him on and off over the last few weeks, and especially after seeing me Sunday night.

"I will. See you Friday," she said, taking the food in her hand and holding it to her like it gave her comfort in some way.

"See you then."

I turned and followed Aidan out, only looking back once to find her watching us leave. I winked and she grinned, and my stupid heart did a backflip at the reward even if I couldn't ignore the reality that we'd always planned to go to the anniversary dinner together. This wasn't even a real date. But the hope that'd taken over so much of my usual doubt pressed at me, urged me to keep moving forward. It begged me not to inspect every second of our interaction and worry over her embarrassment or the way she put space between us.

It told me to keep hoping.

Out on Silver Street, Aidan laughed and shook his head. "I knew you were a goner, but I didn't realize just how far gone."

A good old-fashioned shove didn't shut him up, because he continued. "Good news is I don't think you need to worry about her wanting something after this weekend."

My pulse spiked, that newly persistent hope warring hard with that tendency to doubt. "No?"

He confirmed it. "Nope. I think she's a goner, too."

CHAPTER THIRTY-NINE

Dahlia

We sipped coffee and I polished off my slice of the day, enjoying the cheery yellow walls and bright blue coffee mugs that were the hallmarks of Rise and Shine.

"Hey, have any of you guys heard about a new coffee shop coming in over on Snow Street?" Quinn asked, holding her little espresso mug like she was at a tea party.

"Yes! It's coming in right next to a donut shop, I heard. Is this real?" Sarah asked, more than a little anticipation in her voice.

I raised a hand. "I've had the donuts. John has been sending me them by the half dozen and you guys, they are..." I paused for effect and because those donuts deserved a moment of respect. "Glorious."

Everyone clapped and laughed.

Calla chimed in. "I couldn't care less about donuts, but I'm glad for another coffee shop. You guys do a great job, but it gets so crowded in here. I saw the line out the door and down the block to the corner of Main and Elk Street during Christmas."

Sadie sighed. "It was a nightmare. I thought poor Garrett was going to lose his mind from lack of sleep and we even had seasonal help. But I'm on the more the merrier train for sure and I can't wait to try out their coffee. I heard they're going to roast their own beans and everything. This town is growing and between us, Diner, and the resort, we're still hurting for breakfast and caffeine options."

Quinn smirked. "I love you."

Sadie's brow furrowed and the rest of us chuckled at her declaration. "Um, I love you, too?"

The rest of us downright cackled while Quinn scowled. "That should *not* be a question, but I hear the confusion. I love that you are so welcoming and aren't viewing another shop as competition. If another music store opened, I'd probably have to set something on fire."

"Quinn! You can't talk like that," Calla reprimanded even as she laughed.

I giggled at their ridiculousness. "I don't think she means her competition."

Quinn glared at Calla. "Of course I wouldn't burn down a building. I just mean like... a bunch of Amazon boxes or something in the fire pit or some strongly worded messages scrawled onto notebook paper and burned so the smoke lifts them into the ether and carries the message into the person's dreams."

We all stilled. Maddie found her words first. "That sounds like a very specific course of action."

Quinn shrugged one shoulder. "Julian may or may not have introduced me to the idea a while back, and now he fondly calls me his little pyro."

We all burst out laughing again, the silliness and happy glow around this group reminding me how much I had. I'd debated making time for this, still feeling the post-wedding and post-familial visit crunch, but I'd learned that putting them off often ended up creating more work for me in the form of texts and calls and unannounced visits. I loved them for that—for never leaving me alone too long.

"Dahlia, I can't help but notice you've been grinning ear to ear all morning. It's quite the contrast to the last few months." Sarah's softly spoken observation did the work of turning the subject from Quinn's Firestarter tendencies.

"It certainly feels better than the last few months. I'm just so happy to be sitting here with you all and to know you. It might sound cheesy, but I am so deeply grateful for your friendship and support through all the craziness." They'd been there for me in big and small ways lately, but mostly through the steady stream of texts and messages reminding me they love me and were here for me and believe me. Literally those words, scrawled on handwritten notes tucked into my mailbox or under my door, texts into the group chat and even e-mails. They'd inundated me with love and support even when they weren't physically standing at my side.

In seconds, they all burst from their chairs and reached for me, Sarah and Sadie wrapping me in their arms first, then Quinn, Calla, and finally Maddie joining. Quinn was also the first to break.

"Okay, that's enough of that and now tell us everything about the wedding and your fake fiancé and why you look like maybe it isn't all that fake anymore."

So I did. All the details, top to bottom, complete with John's confrontation after the wedding and my moving back to my apartment, then the sweet meeting yesterday and the upcoming anniversary dinner, and finally, a hint about my plans for tomorrow.

When I got to that part, who I had a meeting with in fifteen minutes, and what it meant to me, more than one of my friends gasped. Sweet Sarah's eyes immediately shone with tears and she pulled me into another hug. Quinn grinned like a maniac and Maddie looked like she'd just closed a billion-dollar deal funding grant for her foundation.

"I love this. I love it. Tell us how we can help," Maddie said, bursting with energy to do something. The woman could scale a mountain with that determination and I wasn't one to turn her down.

"Well, the biggest job right now is to keep your mouths shut. Even you, because your adorable husband-to-be is best friends with John, and I won't have him accidentally ruining the surprise. I have a feeling Aidan is a terrible liar."

Maddie beamed. "Oh, he's awful at it."

I tipped my head like, *obviously*. "Other than that, just be there, and hopefully you'll be joining me to celebrate my new, actual engagement in a little over a day."

Nerves hit, but that was nothing new. I'd been up and down about my plan, nervous and unsure of how it'd all come together. Then he'd stopped by the shop yesterday, and the final plan struck like a stroke of genius.

Or this would be one of those moments where I not only fail, I fail *spectacularly*. John's regular texts and thoughtful gestures of donut deliveries and lunch drive-bys kept me hopeful, and that kiss yesterday reassured me he hadn't lost interest. I'd jumped at him the second I'd seen him because my head had been so full of John Wallace that seeing him in person had been nothing short of sweet relief. But then I'd realized just how wild I might've seemed, and I wanted him to know this wasn't fleeting or all passion fueled by Rose's wedding.

So I'd backed away and reined in all the anticipation and glee at seeing him in order to save the moment for later... to let things play out how I felt they needed to so he could be sure about us.

I could only pray he'd be as receptive to my plan as I hoped.

My friends all cheered like my own personal bandstand, and then we said our goodbyes since I had a meeting to get to.

The second I stepped out of Rise and Shine's door, the little bell jingling behind me as it shut, anxious energy swooped around in my belly. Walking quickly around the corner to Elk Street, I stopped under the sign. Wallace and Sons Law Office. And with one last intrepid breath, I stepped inside.

In a total anticlimax, I found the tiny waiting room empty. After craning my neck to see down the hallway, I heard laughs. Nancy Wallace bustled around the corner and gave me a delighted smile. "Dahlia, honey, come on back."

My pulse skyrocketed. I hadn't actually invited Mrs. Wallace, though maybe this was better. Actually, no. It *was* better. It was. Now I could do it all at once and get it over with.

I entered Mr. Wallace's office, admiring the bookshelves lining his walls and the beautiful dark polished wood of his desk and the fancy leather desk chair. *Huh.* I'd always thought he'd work at something more... humble, I guessed, since nothing about the man was ostentatious.

"Fancy, right?" Mrs. Wallace asked with a wink as she gestured to a chair next to her and across from her husband.

"It's beautiful," I said, still standing, feeling like I should wait for him to sit first.

John Sr. extended a hand and I shook it, an odd sense of surrealism setting into the moment. "All about the first impression. It only took a few interactions with the new crowd to tell me I needed to revamp things around here and make sure they recognized my experience and authority. If a bunch of old fancy books, a nice desk, and this comfy leather chair helps that, all the better."

I smiled, then took my seat, appreciating his frankness and deciding I'd meet it with my own rather than tiptoeing around the reason I'd come. I'd been building up to this all week anyway.

"John and I were never actually engaged." It burst out of me before I even said thank you for meeting with me or anything like a greeting.

Nancy gasped and John Sr.'s brow furrowed.

"Can you explain what you mean?" he asked.

With a deep breath, I dove in, explaining how John was being so kind as to do me a favor and leaving out his desire to make his parents happy in favor of the fact that we'd wanted the whole town to buy in so the relationship would be airtight.

Nancy cleared her throat like she was resisting yelling or crying and my stomach sank. I didn't want this to hurt them, so I hurried up with the rest of it. "I'm sorry we lied to you, and I'm even more sorry that it's me telling you this instead of John."

It made sense he never wanted them to know—never wanted to cause them any pain. But for my plan to work, I needed their help.

"Honey, don't apologize for having to do what you did. I'm sorry you were in that position in the first place. I wish—

I just thought you two were so good together. I know we only saw what we wanted to see, I suppose, but he's been so happy..." Her eyes shone but she fluttered her lashes to banish any threatening tears.

"I have been, too. I—that's why I'm here. This whole experience has made it clear to me that your son is an amazing person."

They both smiled, though their faces still wore those faint lines of worry and pain. I pressed on, just hoping they'd truly forgive me and go with this next part. "In fact, I love him."

"Oh, thank the good Lord!" Nancy threw her hands up, then leaped at me and gave me the second attack-hug of the day.

We laughed together and John Sr. smiled on as we did. When she released me, only a modicum of her enthusiasm spent, I filled in the gaps. "He stood up for me with my parents, and what he said led me to believe he may feel the same way."

Standing up to my parents, going along with my plan to be my fake fiancé, taking care of me in big and small ways at every turn, even before we were friends... yes. John had left clues, and I had to believe I was reading them right.

"Oh, I think he does. I really do. Of course we've hardly seen him the last few weeks, but I just know it."

Nancy's boundless faith in us had emotion clogging my throat yet again, but I cleared it and made my final plea.

"I think you're right. And if you're okay with it, I'd like your help to get him to see that I feel the same way and it's not due to the circumstances or gratitude."

"Go ahead and tell us what you need, Dahlia. You have our full support." John Sr. gave me a small nod to urge me on.

I'd thought about this—what gesture would make it crystal clear to John what my intentions were, and how much he meant to me and that his opinion counted. It had to be irrefutable, irrevocable, impossible to misunderstand. Circling back through our conversations had shown me the perfect means to that end. No way wouldn't he get my meaning with this plan. Though I'd sensed a hint of worry on and off when we interacted since the wedding, I also knew he was in this with me. He didn't want this to end tomorrow any more than I did. So all of this... this long week leaning into work and into the time apart, would be worth it. I had to believe that.

"I want your help with a prenup. I want it legal and official and everything it needs to be. And then, if you're up for it, I'll need your help tomorrow night to make it happen."

CHAPTER FORTY

John

I'd been pacing again. Apparently, my life was a big track I set on and couldn't stop walking until I was with Dahlia.

We'd rented one of the smaller ballrooms at Silver Ridge Resort because my mom loved it and Mike and Jenny had agreed we should go all out. The handful of tables were draped with cloths and set with coordinating crisp white napkins and fancy place settings that included shining silverware and delicate bone china.

In the middle of the tables sat the unbelievably beautiful centerpieces Dahlia had created for the evening. I'd known that Jenny had ordered them months ago, but it hadn't ever occurred to me to ask her what they were going to look like. They were all calla lilies—my mother's favorite flower—with other tiny white blooms like stephanotis and lush peonies woven together with strings of glittering jewels that looked like rubies. Even thinking the names of these flowers I never would've known before these last few months with Dahlia reminded me of how much I'd changed and grown in that time. I didn't know flower names until I started paying attention, and I'd only done that because the person who'd captivated me was mildly obsessed with them.

I chuckled to myself and admired the arrangement. It was beautiful and a little over the top just like my mom would love.

Their ruby wedding. Was it dumb that this bejeweled detail, which was obviously part of Dahlia's job, made me love her more? I loved her creativity, her ability to see and create beauty, and that attention to detail that consistently stunned me.

I'd wondered if, as the day went on, I'd be able to breathe, or if nerves would take me in a chokehold and snuff me out before I ever got to the night. But no, because here we were. Putting finishing touches on things and slipping speech notes onto the small podium. The time had come, and when all of this came to an end, I hoped with everything in me that Dahlia and I would be just beginning.

I patted my pocket, reassuring myself that I still had what I needed. *Yep. All good. Just keep it together for another few hours.*

"John, guests are arriving and they'll start passing hors d'oeuvres in just a minute." Jenny patted my shoulder as she bustled past in her black dress, my two nieces repeating the action in their red ones, though Laney couldn't quite reach my shoulder, so she jumped and kind of smacked my back instead. I straightened my suit jacket, having opted to include all three of the suggested colors as indicated on the invitation—black suit, white shirt, red tie.

"Coming. Mike's out there, right?" I asked, trailing

behind after one last glance to make sure everything was in place.

"Yes, he is. And Dahlia's right there—ah, there she is!"

My heart flipped and leapt and scrambled around in my chest like an excited puppy when I saw her in a stunning deep red dress that had another off-the-shoulder neckline with a little dip right at the center. A tiny tease in an altogether demure and stunning dress that looked classic and gorgeous and forgive me, but I wanted to admire her in it for a while before getting her out of it.

Not helpful right now!

"You look gorgeous," I said, leaning down to kiss her cheek, then watching as her red lips curved into a pleased smile.

"I know I've seen you dressed up a bunch of times lately, but I do have to say, for a mangy beer brewer, you sure do clean up nicely." She patted my smooth jaw—I'd even shaved for the occasion.

"I'm glad you think so," I said, and would've stayed there admiring her and forbidding myself to touch more than her waist when Mike snapped right in front of my face.

"Focus, man."

Irritated, but aware he was right, I spoke to the woman next to me. "Dahlia, this is my overly schedule-obsessed brother Mike. Mike, this is my—this is Dahlia."

It seemed wrong to introduce her as my fiancée at this point when I knew very well we had things to discuss—that I had plans. I wasn't about to explain to him the whole thing, and he already knew we were technically engaged. We'd talked weeks ago and I'd mostly dodged him, but he was busy enough, as was Jenny, I hadn't faced their interrogation. Jenny had only given me raised brows and said I owed her lunch when she saw me earlier during setup.

"I'm so glad to meet you, Mike. Your girls are adorable." She winked at me, obviously noting the surprise that she'd met my nieces. But of course she had—Jenny had likely hauled them into her shop months ago to make the order for tonight, plus Silverton was small. Dahlia had been here three years and my brother worked just down the street from her store, so she would've seen him often.

"Nice to meet you, Dahlia. Forgive my brusqueness, but would you mind if I steal this one away while we discuss our toasts?" And then my older, serious, frankly a little boring but awesome big brother winked at my fake fiancée.

Uh, okay. Weird. But, whatever. Maybe he was trying to be charming and not seem so uptight.

"Of course. I'm going to grab a drink and chat with people. Toasts are in a little while, right?" She licked her lips, and her shoulders rose on an inhale.

"Yep. So I'll see you in just a few."

Her throat worked and something about that swallow almost struck me as nervous, but Mike patted my shoulder in a move that jumpstarted me toward him, leaving Dahlia behind.

Twenty minutes later, my brother wrapped up the first toast to my parents and everyone applauded. I was next, and though I didn't normally get too nervous, everything about tonight had my palms a little sweaty and my heart pumping faster than I'd expected.

I took my place by the mic and found my notes. "Tough act to follow, but I suppose he has the birthright to go first."

Stupid joke, but people gave me a courtesy laugh. "It's incredible to be here tonight with you all, celebrating these two." I nodded at my parents, who sat at a little sweetheart table just to the left of where I stood. "As their son, I've gotten to see a lot of their relationship over time, but it isn't until the last decade or so, and especially the last few years, that I've truly understood what an incredible thing it is you two have built."

My mom, in a show of incredible restraint, pressed her palm to her bejeweled chest in response, and my father nodded ever so slightly. With their acknowledgment, I continued before the nerves got to me too much.

"You've stuck together, and like Mike said, you've shown us what's possible—what it's like to weather storms and come out together. You've modeled generosity to each other, your children, and your community. You've given me support as I've wound my way around, searching, waiting for my own imperfect match." My voice quavered a little there, the knowledge that I believed I'd found that match plucking at my composure.

Before I opened my mouth to continue, out of the corner of my eye, I saw Dahlia take the stage—or, really, a small, raised platform so the guests could see both the speaker and my parents, but still. My attention shifted fully to her, and she was walking up to me, that fiery, determined look in her eye.

"Hi," she said, eyes sparkling and demeanor oddly calm considering she'd wandered up during my speech.

What on earth was she doing? "Uh, hi. What's up?"

"Have a minute?"

The crowd, all twenty or so guests in attendance, were whispering and shifting, everyone clearly as confused as I was. What could be wrong? But then, I glanced at my folks and saw the wry smile on my father's face and the way my mom had her arms wrapped around herself like she was physically restraining her own body.

Those nerves exploded in my chest, and my heart sprinted. "Uh, sure."

Dahlia gave me a long look—though it probably only lasted a second or two—then stepped closer. "Mind if I use this for a sec?"

I backed away from the mic a step, but she caught my hand and held it tight. Hers was a little cold, but that grip wasn't about to let me go, so I halted in place.

"I'm sorry to interrupt, but don't worry. Nancy and John know what's going on and they're on board, right, guys?" She turned to smile at them, and I whipped around to see their reactions—my dad clapped and my mom shot double thumbs-up into the air like rockets.

Dahlia's eye caught mine and she winked. This might've served to calm me, but right now, all it did was make my mind reel. She had talked to my parents? They knew what she was doing?

Anticipation and hope and that stupid fight or flight sent my pulse to the moon as she started speaking again.

"You may have heard that John and I were engaged recently." She stopped for a beat while the crowd nodded along and a few people clapped. "Without getting into details, I'm here to admit that we weren't actually engaged."

The room fell into silence, and that pulse that I'd thought couldn't go any higher suddenly doubled. Tripled. Shot past the moon and out to Saturn. What was she doing? Why would she tell everyone this, and why the crap was she doing it now?

Confusion and anxiety twisted up in the knot of my clamoring heart as she continued.

"You probably all know that John is a good man. He's a helper by nature, and in this case, John did me the biggest favor ever by pretending to be my fiancé to protect me." Her words wobbled at the end, and she cleared her throat while I stood there, dumbstruck, mind too numb to even begin parsing out what she meant in doing this.

She squeezed my hand and forced my eyes to hers. "I'm sure he's wondering why I'd tell you this and you're all wondering what I'm doing right now. I'm not just admitting to you that we faked an engagement, I promise."

The crowd gamely chuckled and my mom hollered, "Bring it home, honey."

Dahlia's grin flashed before she reached down onto the shelf of the podium and handed me a plain manilla folder. "I need you to review this document for me, if you would."

Too far into whatever was happening to stop or question it now, I took it with my shaking free hand. "Okay."

She released my other hand and I set the folder on the podium and opened it. Thanks to the adrenaline and nerves, I could hardly read at first, so I blinked hard a few times and focused.

Prenuptial Agreement.

This Prenuptial Agreement ("Agreement") is made and entered into this day...

My head snapped up and that sprinting herd slowed to a thud so rapidly, my vision nearly grayed. Dahlia was biting her lip.

"What is this?" I asked, my voice a rasp.

"It's for you. And me."

"Why?"

She'd been so composed so far, but in an instant, all that came crashing down as her face crumpled for a flash before she shook herself and sucked in a breath. "Because I love you. I love your petals and your roots, your leaves and your thorns. I love it all—*want* it all. And I'm pretty sure you love me. And you told me you'd never marry someone without a prenup, so I made your dad help me with one."

Her words emerged strained, the emotion in her voice weighing on her and clawing at my chest.

I'd heard the best thing of my entire life, and I couldn't find the words. She'd used my phrasing I'd thrown out at our dinner with my parents, and I never imagined them coming back to me, not from her or anyone, but hearing them now, that embrace of my whole person, sent my heart flying.

Not wanting her to doubt that I wanted forever with her, I pulled her to me and kissed her, framing her face with my hands when I pulled back. "You're such a romantic. I told you."

She grinned, swiped at her tears, and grabbed the papers, getting down on one knee, even in her fancy dress. She held the small packet out, grinning and a few tears still slipping and said, "John Marcus Wallace, will you be my real fiancé?"

I heard and saw nothing but this amazing, thoughtful, beautiful woman on her knees asking me the best question I'd ever imagined her asking, and I grabbed the papers from her hands, ripped them in half, and then hauled her into my arms all while saying, "Yes, I'll be your real fiancé."

We hugged, then kissed again, and the crowd that had faded away slowly came back into my awareness, their raucous applause sounding far too substantial until I glanced out to see even more people surrounding the guests now standing at their tables, evidently having seen this whole show.

"But why'd you tear up the prenup?" she asked as she hugged me again, quiet enough only I could hear.

I turned my head so I spoke into her ear. "Because I don't need it with you."

She pulled back to look at me, elation covering every inch of her, then launched herself back into my arms.

Soon, hands on my shoulders were tugging at me, pulling at us from both directions, and people were hugging us—my parents, her friends, my brother and Jenny. After a few more minutes of the celebration, I kissed Dahlia's cheek as she skittered off the stage with Maddie and Aidan and returned to the mic.

"Well, that was a surprise." A huge laugh went up, everyone's congenial mood having multiplied tenfold at witnessing Dahlia's little stunt.

"I never saw that coming, but I admit, it was a good one. And what it does is free me up to be a little more honest." I flashed a grin and everyone clapped. "Because what I've always wanted, what my parents have, is the way they love each other, imperfect though they may be. I know it hasn't been perfect for you guys or anyone else, and I'm smart enough to know that there have been times it's probably felt hard and painful, but you kept at it to get here."

I smiled over at them, warming up to the mic and the moment, more hope, love, and elation racing in my veins than I'd ever felt.

"Not long ago, we had a conversation about this, and we joked about never telling a woman she's imperfect." A few whoops and claps sounded, but I continued after a glance toward my folks. "When I explained the thought, though, they heartily agreed. What each of us deserves is someone who loves us, imperfect as we are. It doesn't mean my mom didn't work on my dad's diet and try to get a little more salad than steak in him, or that he doesn't help her when her desire to help people gets too intense and she wears herself out."

My dad slung an arm around my mom's chair, and she nestled into him, attention still on me.

"What it means is, there's no ultimatum. There's no 'I'll love you if you change x' or 'When you've fixed this or that other thing about yourself, you'll be worthy of me.' There's only ever been, 'I'll love you,' full stop. No conditions. No contingencies."

Clearing my throat of the emotion there, I brought it home. "Thank you for modeling that kind of love for us, Mom and Dad, because seeing you have it is the only way I can let myself say yes to that flower girl over there." I notched my chin in Dahlia's direction and I heard my mom's, "Ohhhh," like she could hardly stand to stay in her seat.

"So now, let's toast. To Nancy and John, may we be so hardheaded, enthusiastic, and determined to love as well and last as long." Everyone raised their glasses and toasted the air, cheers breaking out and filling the whole room.

I took my obligatory sip, then left the stage as Mom's best friend took her spot at the mic, chuckling about *that* being a tough act to follow and everyone agreeing. I went straight to Dahlia, snagged her hand, and pulled her behind me out of the room.

CHAPTER FORTY-ONE

Dahlia

He towed me along behind him without stopping, on a mission so focused I worried maybe he was upset. But no, this was just John. This stealthy show of intensity sent a thrill through me as I hustled along after him in my heels.

"Slow down, you maniac, I'm in three-and-a-half-inch heels," I said through a laugh, elated at how everything had gone.

He squeezed my hand and did drop his rushed pace to a directed walk but didn't look back, even when he pushed open the ballroom door and pulled me out after him. I hoped he wasn't upset at the way I'd gone about it.

It'd been a risk. A huge one. We still had a lot to talk about, but I needed John to see that I chose him. Overtly, no mistaking it, out in front of everyone we knew.

He kept walking, down the hall and around the corner

into a small alcove lit with lights from above. The hallway seemed darker but tucked into this little nook with no foot traffic passing made it seem intimate. As he turned me to him, I prepared to explain myself—the reasons I'd made the grand gesture instead of just pulling him aside beforehand and having a private moment.

But I didn't get a word out. His gaze locked on mine and stole my breath with the severity there, an intense expression that had me complying as he backed me into the wall. Each of his hands found a home, one at my hip and the other at the back of my neck, and then he took my mouth in one of those delicious, possessive kisses that made my toes curl.

I kissed him back for all I was worth, pouring every bit of love, surety, and desire into the contact. This was crazy, and definitely making out in a hallway thirty feet from everyone we cared about was a little nuts, but I couldn't have pulled away for all money in the world.

This connection between us was real—there'd always been chemistry. I'd felt it the instant he'd looked at me that first day years ago. It was why I'd pushed him away so immediately, and why I'd had to work to keep him away every interaction after.

Falling for John had felt like an inevitability, and looking back, it was amazing I'd held out so long. Then again, once we let our guards down even a little, it'd happened fast.

Apparently, John wasn't quite as caught up in the swirl of emotion and passion since he pulled away long before I was ready for him to and pressed his forehead into mine.

"I love you so damn much, Dahlia. I can't believe you just did that."

I pecked his lips quickly and rested my hands on his

shoulders. "I hope you don't mind that I did it tonight. I just wanted to make it... special."

He loosed a breathy laugh. "I'll never forget it."

"I would hope not."

His brows dipped. "You should know I had my own grand gesture, though not quite as grand. I had this whole thing I was going to say, and then there you went, ruining all my plans."

I wondered what he had in mind, but he clearly liked how I'd ruined them well enough. We grinned like idiots at each other until I remembered I needed to say some things. "I need you to know that this has nothing to do with my family or Devon or any of that mess. Well, other than the whole reason we ended up getting together was due to those circumstances, but not because I'm mixed up or confused or worn out from an emotional roller coaster with all that and not making good choices."

His soft smile skewered my fluttering heart, and his words came out low. "So you mean you really do love me?"

"Yes. I love you so freaking much it's insane. I was just thinking how inevitable this feels now that we're here."

He nodded, then took a step back and lowered to one knee. Despite everything I'd just done, my heart thundered as he took my hand and reached in his pocket. Out came a velvety black box.

"Dahlia Elaine Price, I've been falling for you since the day I met you. We've resisted and pushed against it, but I think we've always belonged together. I love you, and I know there's so much more to discover, but I trust you. I believe you. I think you are the most incredible woman I've ever met, and I would be honored if you would marry me." He chuckled, his eyes a little glassy. "And I hope you'll forgive me for letting you beat me to the ask."

I yanked him up from the floor and pulled him to me, kissing him with everything I had before breaking away to give him my answer. "Yes. Even though you already knew the answer, I am very happy to say yes."

He grinned, smile beaming so beautifully it made my heart glow in my chest.

I shook my head, marveling that we'd both come to this conclusion. "Are we crazy? Stupid? Setting ourselves up for failure? It's only been a few months."

"We're not crazy or stupid. I think maybe we were before, letting our first meeting color everything after." We shared a regretful grin before he steadied me with his warm, large hands on my hips. "But I'm not worried it was too fast unless you are. If you're not worried about all the family stuff, I'm not. Our friends know us, and at least from what I glimpsed out there, they're all very supportive. In the end, I'm choosing you. And you know your own mind and I trust you."

His love was such a beautiful thing, but I recognized that his trust was paramount. That had been the symbolism in his tearing up the prenup, though we still needed to chat about that. It was what he'd kept sheltered and tucked away right along with his sweet heart for so many years, and I was honored he'd given me both, and I loved so much that he'd been planning to do it all along as evidenced by the beautiful ring on my finger. "I trust you, too, John. Even before I loved you, I trusted you to be there for me. You showed up and that was all it took to push me over the edge."

"So you're saying whoever you grabbed off the street was bound to be standing here with you?" His eyes glittered at me though he hid a smile.

I shoved him a little. "No, not at all. I pulled you into the shop, but then you showed up over and over again. And not just physically—you supported me, backed me up. You reminded me who I was and everything I had here, and you never once made it about yourself. This situation let me see even more of *you*, and John, I hate to tell you this, but you are amazing."

He dipped his head and pressed another searing kiss to my mouth before releasing me again. "You're amazing, and I can't believe we're actually engaged." His grin could've lit the entire resort.

"We are." We did the smiling stupidly thing for another minute before I said, "But what about the prenup? I respect that it's something you want, and you don't have to tear it up for me to believe that you want to marry me."

His thumbs arced over the skin of my neck, and he shook his head slowly, almost like standing here practically gluing me against the wall a few doors down from his parents' anniversary dinner was his favorite place to be.

"I don't need it. That was never the main issue. I didn't know how I'd ever trust someone enough to want to commit to them, but you burrowed your way into my heart with your willingness to trust me and show me what that looks like and I get it now. There's no proof, no guarantee... only the choice to trust and love. And I love and trust you."

"You know for a beer nerd, you are really good with words," I said, harkening back to all the perfect things he'd said to me.

He grinned. "Glad to see I'm good at something."

I rolled my eyes. "Are we fishing for compliments now? You know you're good at a lot of things. And thank goodness chatting with people is one of them, because I invited all our friends to witness our engagement."

"I thought I saw a few unexpected faces after your big

move. I'm sure my parents are glad for the additional revelers," he said, a crease in his cheek from that smile I loved.

"They're not staying for dinner, but we probably do need to go say hi before they go. I just..." I held onto the lapels of his jacket for a moment. "I just want to say that I'm so glad you gave me another chance, and then another. That you didn't let my pushing you away keep you from being my friend and... well, ultimately, this, I guess."

Instead of responding with more pretty words, he hugged me to him, holding me in his warm, solid embrace before pulling back enough to tilt my chin right and lean in to capture my lips with his in a soft, warm, slow kiss that had the usual effect on me. We were just getting started with so many things—we still had a lot to learn about each other. And this kiss?

It was only the beginning.

He ended the kiss with a peck to my cheek, then my forehead, then took my hand in his. "All right then, fiancée. Let's go see our friends and let them celebrate our epic romance."

"Oh, we have an epic romance, do we?"

He winked. "Heck yeah, we do. Fake engagement turned public declaration of love real engagement? Followed by a ring passed down through my family now on your finger? One for the ages."

My eyes flew to the ring I'd barely had a chance to inspect and then my breath caught. A flower. This perfect little ring held a diamond surrounded by sapphire petals. "How..." How could it be so completely perfect?

He beamed. "It was Dad's grandmother's. It's antique but shines up well. It wasn't her wedding ring, I don't think, but I thought it might be just right. If you want something else—"

"I want this one." I clutched my own hand to my chest like Gollum cradling his precious.

"Good." That smile flashed. "There's this too, so you can wear it around your neck in case you don't want it on your finger during work." He pulled out a simple, elegant gold chain and slipped it over my head.

He'd considered that, not knowing I'd never want to take off his ring. But that I could, that he'd done what he always did and thought of a way to care for me, was too perfect. I touched it lightly, pressing the metal into the skin at my collar bone and laughing out a watery, "You thought of everything, huh?"

He grinned, so broad and joyous. "Glad you think so. See? Epic. The only thing that would make it better is if you were wearing a corset and stockings and I had a kilt or... whatever the dudes wear in your historicals."

I burst out laughing and hugged him to me as we walked back toward the ballroom. "You're ridiculous, but I love you. And yes, please, let's do discuss kilts. Wallace is Scottish, right?"

He grinned. "Love you, flower girl."

CHAPTER FORTY-TWO

John

Warrick Saint and Sadie Miller's wedding had to be one of the most beautiful things I'd ever seen. I could admit it without shame—I loved a good wedding. Seeing people I cared about join their lives and commit to a future together was a truly blessed occasion.

Okay, so maybe I felt that way more now that I had a woman with my ring on her finger dabbing at her eyes in the bridal party and we had a date on the calendar for our own wedding. But I liked to think I was a big enough man to celebrate my friends even before I found out Dahlia was my person.

That's what it felt like here in the aftermath of the last few months—a discovery. Something that maybe my heart had known, but I'd been too scared to even acknowledge. Maybe it explained her initial reaction to me, or mine to her. Maybe it explained why it took unusual circumstances and a bit of force to get us to see each other for the imperfect matches we were for each other.

"I now pronounce you husband and wife. You may kiss the bride."

The pastor said the words and Warrick dove in, hauling his tiny bride into his arms and kissing her—*oh, wow*—yeah that was not exactly a fit-for-public-consumption kiss, but I had to laugh and clap like everyone around me. Warrick and Sadie had been through a lot to find each other and after a long wait to get engaged and nearly a year-long engagement, their time to celebrate had finally come.

The recessional played and both of Warrick's brothers recessed out with the bridesmaids. Though I'd always thought of Sadie as quiet and introverted, and she certainly still was, she had six bridesmaids, one of whom was her new sister-in-law Sarah Saint, who looked like she might need to stop and pop out a baby any second. But her adoring husband Wilder ushered her down the aisle with hearts for eyes right behind the oldest Saint brother Wyatt and his wife Calla. Sadie's sister, Marguerite, walked with one of Warrick's cousins from out of town, Quinn took her exit stroll with her own husband Julian who'd shockingly become one of Warrick's best friends in the last year and then came my gorgeous Dahlia with Warrick's friend Pete, and finally, Maddie and Bruce. Apparently, Bruce and Warrick had bonded in the last year and Warrick was nothing if not a man who liked to include people and have them join the party.

I waited patiently—well, maybe not so patiently—as the families recessed, and then finally got to leave. Aidan was laughing at me the whole time. "You realize you're totally obvious, right?"

"Obvious how?" I asked, not really caring unless it was that I also felt some pretty serious hunger pangs.

"That you are desperately in love with your fiancée and want to be able to call her wife as soon as possible?" He said this with zero criticism—only humor and a definite note of understanding.

"Takes one to know one."

He laughed. "Well, yeah. Exactly. But I get to marry mine in like two months, and you're stuck waiting until the fall."

Shaking my head, I made a show of sighing and rolling my eyes. "Always trying to one-up me with your older cousin superiority. Really, Aidan. It's unbecoming of a land-scaper and the future Mr. Reynolds."

He glared. "Pretty sure I'll stick with Wallace and she'll stick with Reynolds, but if she wants me to be Mr. Reynolds, I would be."

I chuckled at that. "Fair enough. I'm not all that inter-ested in being a Price after meeting that family, but I guess we better talk about it."

We got caught in the crowd of people and slowly moved into the cocktail hour area. Dahlia's arrangements here were stunning as usual. She'd mentioned someone from a big bridal magazine had come to photograph the wedding and I could see why. The little white chapel was even more beau-tiful than for Rose's wedding and as we moved into the lodge, it was downright magical.

Of all the things Dahlia and I had discussed in the last month since our official engagement, we hadn't nailed down what kind of wedding she wanted. She'd said something like "no tulips in November" when we'd been combing the upcoming months. I'd need to get her to tell me what she really wanted soon. In the meantime, I craned my neck to see where Dahlia was, but then Aidan interrupted.

"They're getting announced into the room in a few minutes after they take some photos. You want to go watch?" he asked, swiping at his phone after tapping out a message, likely to Luca, who was hanging with my folks.

"Nah. I can wait. Let's grab a beer—I hear there's this great local place on tap at the main event bar."

He chuckled and we moved to grab a drink only to be halted by a slate gray suit and steely eyes.

"Julian. Good to see you. No photos for you?" I asked, always interested in what the man had to say and knowing by now he didn't want a handshake as part of the greeting. He had lifetimes of business acumen and intelligence locked away in that giant brain of his and I hoped now that Dahlia and I were friends, I'd have a chance to get to know him better.

"They got through the whole wedding party quickly, and now it's just the bride and groom. I believe Dahlia and the other women are just... watching."

He seemed genuinely perplexed by this, but I was more interested in why he was talking to me. Not that I didn't want him to—he just didn't typically initiate conversation.

"What can I help you with?" I asked, only slightly embarrassed that I'd reverted to that line in this social situation. Aidan made no sound next to me, but I could just feel his amused smile directed at me.

"It's actually what I can do for you." He handed me a white security envelope. "Use it or don't—your choice. Dahlia's a good woman and though my wife tells me all the time that I shouldn't use my powers for... anything other than good, to me this seems very clearly good." He gave a small nod and took a step back, leaving me to stare at the envelope.

"Well? Open it," Aidan urged.

I tore it open and unfolded the paper inside and began reading. "*Whoa.*"

Aidan stood next to me, his head ducked so he could see it, too. "Well, he's done if you let that get out."

But instead of responding, Julian actually spoke up. "I should've mentioned, I've already sent this information to the proper authorities. I didn't think it was fair to ask Dahlia or you to choose, and I have no qualms with ruining someone like him. So... happy engagement."

Aidan and I looked at each other, then both watched the abrupt but rather delightful man walk away. What he'd done was ruin Devon Schaefer thoroughly enough that he'd likely be in jail and would never have a political career. The paper he'd given me had a whole laundry list of crimes including embezzling from the very city he claimed to love *and* sleeping with the mayor's wife. *Yikes.*

"Well, I can't top that," Aidan said, patting me on the back. "Let's go tell the girls."

Something about that caused a cup of happiness to spill out into my chest. Our girls were friends and he was my best friend. We'd shared a lot over the years, but knowing Maddie and Dahlia were friends gave me an additional layer of joy in the midst of all the newness and anticipation of our real engagement.

They announced the party in and Warrick and Sadie led the way into the ballroom where they had their first dance. They would've been sickening to watch if I hadn't been holding Dahlia's hand, caressing the soft skin and knowing she was mine, that we'd have this soon, that we'd be next.

Well, technically, Maddie and Aidan were next, but still.

While the mother-son dance went on and Warrick danced with a very spirited Jane Saint, Dahlia leaned over and whispered in my ear. "I think I want an outdoor wedding."

"Yeah? Where are you thinking?" I asked, ready to say yes to anything she had in mind.

"I think up near the spa. Maybe just in one of Wyatt's fields if he'll let us use part of one, or maybe Genevieve has a good outdoor space, and then we can have the spa do the food." Her eyes searched mine.

Yes, the spa had accommodations but not for hundreds of people like this wedding. Certainly not for a large wedding at all, though of course people could easily just drive up the canyon for it.

"It's certainly beautiful up there."

She nodded. "It is. My soul feels full out there. But I also think that's where I really started to fall for you. When you let me alone in that room to stew and I realized I wasn't hurt anymore, just ready to move on... that was when it really started happening."

I nuzzled her neck, wishing we could slip out of here, but knowing neither of us wanted to miss the reception. "That's a good reason."

"I also don't want a lot of people. I thought about just eloping—"

"Sounds good. Let's go next weekend." I pressed a kiss behind her ear.

A breathy chuckle escaped. "Can we wait until after Night in Bloom?"

Those words hit and I paused, their meaning taking a few seconds to fully register before I pulled back and found her beautiful dark eyes. "Wait, really? You don't want to wait until the fall? I thought this was a crazy busy time—you have weddings lined up the entire summer. I want you to be able to enjoy yourself."

"I had someone cancel—they're eloping, actually. And it got me thinking. But I don't want to be on some island in the Caribbean—though I do propose we consider that for a belated honeymoon in the winter sometime before Valentine's Day. I want to be here, with our family and friends, and I want to do it as soon as we can."

My smile was an instantaneous, almost grotesquely big thing. She grinned back and we kissed. "I'll marry you any day of the week, Dahlia Price."

She dropped a kiss to my lips and then beamed back at me. "Good, cause Genevieve said the best days are Tuesdays and Wednesdays."

I laughed at the news that she'd already done her research. "Sign me up. As long as I get to become your husband, I'm in."

EPILOGUE

Dahlia

I twirled in the dress and Maddie, Sadie, Sarah, Quinn, Calla, and Azalea all clapped. Nancy Wallace rushed me and pulled me into her arms.

"You're a princess, Dahlia! You're perfection! John isn't going to be able to say his vows, he'll be too busy feasting on this vision in front of him!" She held out my arms, getting another look.

And as over the top as she was, so very Nancy of her, I couldn't totally disagree. Plus, her enthusiasm always made my heart glow, her clear affection and honestly, love for me, already so special to me. She wasn't a replacement for my own family—I hadn't disowned them or even lost them. In fact, my relationship with them felt better than it maybe ever had these days, distant though it was. Rose seemed to have forgiven me for breaking my promise that I wouldn't marry John this year—*whoopsie daisy.*

But the Wallaces had embraced me in much the same way John himself had—imperfectly and completely. I had never imagined gaining more than just the man I loved and yet here she was, reminding me yet again I was joining their family.

And that grin she was giving me, gazing fondly at me like I simply dazzled her, made me beam right back at her. The dress was truly perfection. The same woman who'd made the gorgeous one I'd worn to Night in Bloom last year had done me the incredible honor of making this one. A lacy off-the-shoulder neckline and a bodice with tiny hand-sewn flowers and leaves winding up the front. It dipped in to make my waist look amazingly small and then little white vines of the flowers spread into the skirt, slowly turning to gnarly, artsy roots that laced seamlessly into the gauzy skirt and flowing out. Not super puffy or anything, but enough that I did feel like a fairy princess. It was porcelain thread on top of the same color of material, but the effect was subtle, stunning, and simply my favorite garment I'd ever seen.

My hair was pulled back and worn in curls that Jayla from Cut made look freaking amazing, and I'd made my own little flower headband piece that sat at the crown of my head to frame it before it cascaded down my back.

"I'm not going to pretend I don't feel amazing, because I totally do, thanks to my fairy godmother," I said, winking at Maddie. It'd been all her—in fact, she'd commissioned the dress before I could say no and only told me ahead of time because she was worried I'd try to buy something else. The fact that the artist of a designer had something already in the works and could adjust it to my size was another miracle.

Don't mind me, but I also took it as more confirmation

that all of this was meant to be. I wasn't someone who believed that in a facile way or liked to toss out the saying in all circumstances. I'd lived enough life to know very well not everything is meant to be. I wasn't *meant to be* with Devon, an abusive, horrible person. I wasn't *meant to be* pressured by my parents, nor was Azalea meant to be treated as a cast off.

But the beauty of life is what can grow from the ashes, isn't it? And this day felt so much like a lone flower triumphing, bursting through a scorched earth landscape.

Nancy kissed my cheek and excused herself to go check in on her family and see if Jenny needed help with the girls, and I held up my champagne glass. "To the very best friends a girl could have—thank you for being here, for supporting me no matter what, and for being along for this wild ride. And, sorry not sorry, thank you for my amazing dress, fairy godmother."

Everyone laughed and Maddie demurred, as always, but they touched glasses with me and each other, the light *ting* of their toasts little exclamation marks on the moment. My heart felt so incredibly full it could burst, except then I'd ruin this gorgeous dress, so I held it together. "I love you guys so much!"

"Don't start crying or everyone will, and then the makeup we just spent hours getting perfected will run!" Azalea's warning was a good one and irritable enough, I had to laugh.

"Fair point, fair point. Keep it together, ladies."

Sarah swiped at her eyes, her post-baby hormones still fully at work. "Sorry. *Sorry*. Don't look." We all grinned as she dabbed under her eyes with a tissue.

"Wait. *Wait*. What's in your glass, Calla?" Quinn's voice cut through everything.

Calla shrugged. "Some orange juice."

Quinn's eyes narrowed. "Like a mimosa?"

Calla tucked her lips between her teeth and her eyes shot to me. I knew in an instant and screamed. "Ahhhh! Already? Oh my gosh! How far along? Seriously?"

Everyone realized what this meant—Calla was pregnant again. Her first baby wasn't even a year old, and that orange juice was a perfect tell.

"I was waiting until after today to tell you guys, but I'm super early, like eight weeks. I'm..." She laughed until sound stuck in her throat, and she cleared it. "I'm so happy and overwhelmed, I basically just walk around alternating crying and laughing."

"Well, Wyatt always did want a big family. Glad you're up for it, woman. I'll be happy to pick up my various copies of *People* and *Entertainment* with you and your perfect pregnant belly gracing the covers when they come." Quinn raised her glass and then took a long slug as everyone agreed. Calla's first pregnancy had been covered ad nauseum, and finally, she and Wyatt had started making the most of it to control when they were photographed, and more power to them.

We took turns hugging her and I made up the rear. She set down her orange juice on a nearby countertop and hugged me close. Before she could say any nonsense about being sorry, I said, "I'm so happy this gets to be another memory of today."

When I pulled back, she had her lips pressed firmly together, eyes brimming.

"No more of this! Congratulations, Calla, but seriously. You guys are going to be a bedraggled mess if we keep this up." Azalea nudged my side and I backed away.

"Fine, fine. That's fair enough. The first look is in..." I

checked my watch and my stomach flipped. "Oh my gosh, ten minutes."

Everyone erupted into action then, bustling around like little chickens without heads, and I loved the energy, enthusiasm, and mild panic of the moment. Ten minutes and my future husband would see me in this dress and the day would sweep us away.

John

Aidan patted my shoulder when I crossed in front of him on my fifteenth lap around the small space where we were waiting before I'd move into position for the first look.

"You'll be fine."

"Will I, though? Will I? Because I feel like I might throw up. What if she changes her mind?"

I didn't really think she would. We'd only grown closer in the last few months and here we were, a little over six months after that fateful day her ex had busted into Bloom, and this was it.

This was when I'd know. And even though I knew she wouldn't bail on me, there was that small, dark place in my heart just waiting for this to turn out to be too good to be true. My love for Dahlia had only expanded. My life had grown sweeter, brighter, and certainly more flower-filled in the months since our lives had converged and I didn't want it any different.

Aidan's low chuckle drew my attention to him right as he wrapped an arm around Luca, who was grinning at me like I was a loon. "She's not going to change her mind. *She's* the one who chose the date. She's the one who proposed to you. Twice!"

"He's right. She's totally head-over-flower-loving-feet for you and there's no chance she's a runaway bride. Not for you, anyway."

Mike's agreement with Aidan did me no good. Nor did Luca's snickering, though I couldn't say that I blamed him. What could they possibly know about this mildly terrifying and undesired feeling? Mike had been married for like fifteen years. He'd gotten married before there was any risk to it.

"Son."

My dad's words stopped me, and I faced him, itching to pull at my hair but refusing to mess it up in the two minutes before I walked out there.

John Marcus Wallace, Sr. looked at me with his kind, wise eyes, and just that fatherly steadiness gave me a hit of calm. He took my shoulders in his hands and speared me with his blue gaze.

"That woman loves you. You've chosen to trust her, and she's trustworthy. I know it's new but that doesn't mean it isn't right. Like you once said, it won't be perfect and neither is she, but you're going to love those thorns and gnarled roots and such. You've chosen well—now let yourself enjoy it."

I swallowed past the tightness in my throat. "Thanks." Looking up at my brother, father, Luca, and Aidan, something bubbled up in me. "Thank you all for being here. Standing with me."

They all murmured their responses, quietly acknowledging my desire for them to be here in this moment. Later, Jenny would join us and so would the girls. My mom would pop in any moment now to kiss my cheek before I took my place at the end of the aisle, and the adventure would truly begin.

"Photographer says it's time," my mom said as she bustled inside, instantly teary at the sight of me despite having seen me on and off all day. She kissed near my cheek—we'd already learned her lipstick would come off and even through her enthusiasm she knew we didn't want to have to scrub it off before photos.

With one last glance at them, I took a breath. "Here we go."

I exited the small outbuilding and walked the path that wound around to a private garden. We'd talked through how this worked, and knowing she was walking toward me from the other side had my pulse climbing higher.

We'd been moving toward this moment for weeks, but in some ways, it felt like months, and if you got real woo woo, maybe even years, but at this minute, I could hardly hold back from running toward her.

Rounding the corner, my breath caught right before it burst out in a laugh. Because I was walking as fast as I could and there, at the opposite end of what felt like an inter-minable walkway, Dahlia was holding her dress in each hand and moving at a clip just shy of a jog.

The closer she got, the tighter my chest felt, but not from anxiety or tension nor worry—from love. My god, could I hold this much love and adoration for a person without breaking open?

We met in the middle in a less than delicate crash, her reaching for my face and guiding me to her. I held her at the waist, having been warned by both the photographer and my mother not to touch her hair or face before pictures. Didn't matter—this kiss wouldn't leave that pretty rosy lipstick in place for long.

Pulling back, I marveled at her. "Dahlia, you're... I'm..."

She beamed and giggled without irony. I felt that—that brimming happiness spilling out and over these wildflowers surrounding us. We hugged, holding each other for a minute while I composed myself. The emotion assaulting me wouldn't stop, and it was clear that all that elation had to leak out somewhere.

I swiped at my eyes and pulled back, finally finding words. "You look incredible. Are you sure you want to do this? I'm pretty sure I'm batting way out of my league here."

She was already shaking her head. "I wouldn't want anyone else even if Jack McKean himself waltzed in here and proposed."

I widened my eyes comically huge. "Please don't say that name—you know he and Julian are friends, right?"

We grinned at each other, happy to be mentioning Julian Grenier, Patron Saint of stealthy, karmic justice. Devon had already lost any good name he'd once had, and the fact that Rose, Conrad, and Dahlia's parents had personally apologized to her long before they'd showed up here for the wedding spoke to just how swift it'd been.

She caught my gaze with those dark eyes that'd captivated me from day one whether I'd liked it or not and shook me by the tux. "No one could tear me away from you, John, because I chose you just like you're choosing me. Flowers, leaves, stems, roots, and all."

If possible, I fell a little bit more for her, and ducked my head for another kiss. "My goodness, you are imperfect."

"You, too, love."

Thank you so much for reading John and Dahlia's book! Their relationship makes me want to curl up and eat a cinnamon roll, and I hope you found some joy in reading about it. If you're curious about the other characters in this story, be sure to find them in the other books in the Back to Silver Ridge Series. If you've already met the whole crew, consider getting back to the roots of Silverton with the Morrison family (Liam!) in Unexpected Love at Silver Ridge. And finally, if you're like *many* readers and are ready for Bruce's story, find it in his book, Made for You.

Veterans of Silver Ridges Series

Back to Silver Ridge Series

Almost Perfect, Book 1

Almost Real, Book 2

Almost Sure, Book 3

Almost Home, Book 4

Almost True, Book 5

Almost Ready, Book 6

The Silver Ridge Resort Series

Unexpected Love at Silver Ridge, Book 1

Second Chance at Silver Ridge, Book 2

Patrolling for Love at Silver Ridge, Book 3

Fire and Ice at Silver Ridge, Book 4

Soldiers Overseas Romances

Sweet Military Romance

The Rambler Battalion Series

Sweet Military Romance

AUTHOR'S NOTE / ACKNOWLEDGMENTS

Wow, the end of the Back to Silver Ridge Series! It's wonderful to round things out with John Wallace, who popped up in the first book set in Silverton. Don't worry, this won't be the last, but I love seeing him find his happily ever after.

These two took me on a RIDE. They had ideas about how things would go. I had them tagged as enemies to lovers but those two sweeties just wouldn't do it—particularly John. Their story unfolded one way and then got revamped to go another, and by the end, it just made so much sense that they did what they did. I really love the way it turned out, and I hope you do too.

Thank you to Zee Monodee, my unendingly patient editor, who was instrumental in wading through the many possibilities and helping me shape this into what it needed to be.

Thank you to Amanda Cuff, my proofreader, for fixing my eight million comma errors and laughing at the "bud" line.

Thanks, as always, to Amanda, Ashley, and Genny, my awesome Beta team. Thanks especially to Genny who gave it to me straight and helped me make this book SO much better (if you didn't hate Dahlia, it's thanks to her suggestions, haha!). And to Amanda for just loving these two so much— what a delightful response and encouragement :)

Special thanks to Judith G for naming Escape and Caroline B for naming Glazed.

Thanks to all the readers and bookstagrammers and booktokers who've been supportive of the series and have helped make it so much fun to write in Silverton. THANK YOU.

Claire Cain lives to eat and drink her way around the globe with her traveling soldier and three kids, but is perhaps even happier hunkered down at home in a pair of sweatpants and slippers using any free moment she has to read and cook. Or talk—she really likes to talk. She has become an expert at packing too many dishes in too few cabinets and making houses into homes from Utah to Germany and many places in between. She's a proud Army wife and is frankly just really happy to be here.

You can also join Claire's facebook reader group for exclusive content and fun: https://www.facebook.com/groups/clairecain/

Website: http://www.clairecainwriter.com

E-mail: Claire@ClaireCainWriter.com

Newsletter sign-up for new releases, exclusives, and freebies, including a free book:

http://www.clairecainwriter.com/newsletter

amazon.com/author/clairecain

bookbub.com/authors/claire-cain

instagram.com/clairecainwriter

facebook.com/clairecainwriter

goodreads.com/clairecainwriter

pinterest.com/clairecainwriter